I would like to thank all of you who have read this series. In particular, those who encouraged me to "finish the last damn book!"

Most notably, Bill D.

I0548317

Books, eBooks, and audiobooks by Tony Marvin

The Templar Chronicles Series
Betrayal – Darkness Engulfs the Knight
Fugitives – Stripped of the Cross
Dispersion – Dawn of a New Knight

Science Fiction
The House on Crescent Street

Action-Adventure
The Making of a MERCYnary

Cover Art and Website development by
LDerrickson Digital
www.Derricksondesign.com

Published by Pen and Steel

Introduction

Little is known about Jacques De Moley before becoming the last Grand Master of the Knights Templar. It is believed he had little formal education since he described himself as an "unlettered soldier." He was born around 1244, became a Templar in 1265, and was elected Grand Master in 1298.

When Jacques De Moley was arrested in 1307, he was 63 years old. He had spent the last two years before the arrest devising a new crusade and attempting to stop a plan to combine the Knight Templar and the Knights Hospitaler into a single Order. It appears that Jacques was in Poitiers trying to convince Pope Clement V of his new crusade when the Pope informed him of the allegations against the Order. Upon hearing these accusations, the Grand Master asked the Pope to ensure justice was done, and then he quickly returned to Paris. On October 13, 1307, he and the majority of Templars in France were arrested under the orders of King Philip IV.

Just a few days later, Jacques confessed to the alleged practice of having new Templars spit on a crucifix and deny Christ. Both of those charges were common accusations of Guillaume de Norgaret against anyone he tried to convict on the stage of public opinion. There is a lot of conjecture about these two accusations since these are the most common confessions given by captured, imprisoned, and often tortured Templars. Some believe this was a real practice of the Templars that originated after many years of fighting in the Holy Land. When a Templar was captured by the Islamic forces, they could not be ransomed back like many other Latin soldiers of high rank. Unless they converted, the Templars could expect to be summarily executed upon being captured. Some historians believed the Templars decided it would be better to pretend to deny Christ and spit on or near a cross if that would allow them to survive and escape. Others argue that given what we know of those men's honor, bravery, and devout nature, they would never deny Christ.

In 1308, another commission of inquiry was convened by eight cardinals. This time, torture was excluded as part of the proceedings. It is believed that the Grand Master and most of the other Templars who were questioned recanted their earlier confessions. But, in the Bull "Faciens

Misericordiam" by Pope Clement V, it says that Jacques reaffirmed his earlier confession. When the Bull was read to the Grand Master in 1309, he said that the cardinals lied and that he had denied the charges. Some believe that the cardinals lied to save the Grand Master's life, since if he had recanted his original confession, he would have been labeled a "relapsed heretic" and burned at the stake. Others believe the cardinals were coerced by King Philip IV and his minions. Still, others think that Grand Master Jacques de Moley may have cracked under the strain of his imprisonment and was confused.

Whatever the truth is regarding the 1308 commission, from 1309 until his death, Grand Master Jacques de Moley never wavered in his renunciation of the crimes the Templars were accused of. He remained in prison for the rest of his life and was questioned under torture at least two more times. The only crime he would confess to was lying in his original confession back in 1307. A crime that he stated was not against God but against his beloved Order, the Knights Templar.

CHAPTER ONE

It took nearly a month for Father Lull, Mary, and Derrick to reach Bergen, Norway. It took them a couple of weeks to secure passage on a ship that was returning to Norway from a trading journey to Amsterdam. Although it took longer than expected, there were still not many Templars in Bergen. A few Templar ships had arrived, and the men were actively engaged in establishing a base of operations some miles south of the city along one of the many fjords. Father Lull, Mary, and Derrick were happy to learn that the other two ships from their small flotilla had arrived safely in Germany and were on their way to Norway with the rest of Admiral Gregory's fleet.

One morning, the three woke to see ship after ship sailing up the fjord toward their little settlement. Mary was happy to be reunited with Sir William. She was surprised to hear that the young squire, Louis, had been knighted and was on a solo mission to the Holy Land for the King of Scotland. Mary found it difficult to picture the talkative young man remaining focused long enough to do anything of that nature. However, she had to admit she barely knew him.

Mary asked if they had heard anything about Sir Henry or Odo, but it appeared she was the last to see them. The last thing she witnessed was their arrest in front of the Paris commandery, after which she fled on her horse. After that, no one knew anything about them or Father Thomas. Sir William was not surprised that Sir Henry and Odo had been arrested. He was stunned to hear that Father Thomas had betrayed them. He had not truly trusted the priest, but he had not thought of him as a traitor.

Admiral Gregory and Cinead were both introduced. Cinead hugged Mary and said, "I have heard you are a fearless woman and not afraid to tell these foolhardy and prickly Templars what bampot's they are." Then he released Mary and slapped Derrick on the back, adding, "I hear you are a good hunter. I think we will have need of that talent soon with all these mouths to feed." Neither Mary nor Derrick knew how to respond to Cinead, and Mary was uncertain what a "bampot" was.

Before their inability to reply became obvious, Father Lull asked the Admiral, "What are the plans now? How long do you think we'll be here? What will we do about the rest of the members of the Order still held by the King of France? Is there anything that we can do to help Grand Master Jacques de Molay? Surely the rumors could not be true that he confessed to the crimes the King has accused the Order of."

Admiral Gregory said, "Give me a moment, good Father; I've only just arrived. You ask questions faster than a cabin boy on his first voyage out to sea. We have men in France now gathering what information they can, and as soon as that intelligence arrives, we will decide what needs to be done. For now, we have established a base of operations here. I will head north to the city of Bergen and discuss our situation with the leadership there. They have been forewarned of our arrival and have agreed to help, or at least not hinder us, if we do not create any problems. I recommend we begin making ourselves an asset to the local communities. We have several ships and experienced seamen whom we can utilize to enhance the fishing economy. Also, we have many men who are experienced carpenters, masons, tanners, blacksmiths, farmers, and other tradespeople. First, we need to get to work on building permanent shelters."

The Templars did not take long to establish themselves in the area. Within a month of Admiral Gregory's arrival, they had built several buildings and developed a productive fishing trade. They were in the process of obtaining some farmland with plans to plant rye, oats, and barley. They had also begun the construction of a mill and purchased a few sheep and pigs. It appeared that they would be relying on fish as the major protein staple for the time being.

They found they were the object of curiosity among many nearby villages. Almost from the first day, locals showed up to speak to the Templars. The locals helped provide them with important information about the area. They learned that although Bergen was the closest large community, there were three small settlements that were much closer to them. These settlements seemed to have between eighty and a hundred and fifty people in each of them.

Derrick was out hunting one early morning when he noticed what he first took for a very large deer. The deer still had velvet on its large antlers. As he observed the animal, he saw some differences between it and the deer he was used to. This animal's fur was much thicker and lighter than the deer of France and Scotland. Even from a distance, Derrick could see that its hooves were much larger. As he watched the

5

animal, more of them began moving into the clearing. Derrick was surprised to notice that they all had antlers. He had never known so many males to group together in a herd.

Derrick was about to shoot an arrow when he heard a twang and saw an arrow strike one of the large deer. The other deer in the small herd charged off at the sound. The animal that was struck took a few steps in the direction the rest of the deer had scattered in, but then fell forward on its front legs and then over onto its side. Derrick kept still, trying to see the other hunter; he knew the general area where the hunter was, from where the arrow had originated, but he saw no one. As he watched, Derrick saw a part of a bush move, and a man stood up straight. He was covered in branches and leaves to match the bush he was hiding in. The man looked to where Derrick was crouched and waved him forward; then the camouflaged man moved to where the deer had fallen.

Derrick rose from his crouch and slowly followed the man to the deer. As the two met at the dead deer, the other man smiled and said in broken French, "My name is David. I would have let you take your shot, but as I had staked out this location first, I felt it was my right. If you help me pack the animal back, I will go back out with you near dusk and show you another place where you can find a small herd of reindeer."

Derrick replied, "I am Derrick, and I would be happy to help you."

Derrick removed a long knife from his belt and began field-dressing the reindeer. David watched for a moment and said nothing, then walked a short distance to some trees and cut a long pole. By the time David returned with the pole, Derrick had finished field dressing the reindeer and had put the heart, liver, and kidneys back in the now-empty abdominal cavity.

David looked at the pile of offal next to the deer and said, "You've wasted a lot of useful parts here." David cut the intestine off near the stomach and began to squeeze out the intestine's contents in a pile. He then tossed the now-empty intestine into the deer carcass. David then cut the esophagus off at the top of the stomach, squeezed out the contents of the stomach, and placed the emptied stomach in the body cavity. Next, he took the bladder, and noting that there was still urine in it, he tied off both ends with a couple of pieces of sinew to preserve its contents. He then placed the bladder carefully in a bag he carried over one shoulder.

David looked at the remaining pile of entrails and said, "We will leave the rest for the wolves, although I hate to leave them anything."

David tied the deer's front legs together while Derrick tied the rear legs, then Derrick slid the pole through the legs. David tied a strap around the antlers and attached it to the pole to keep them from dragging on the ground as they carried the reindeer back to his village.

Neither man spoke as they hefted the pole to their shoulders and began the trek to David's village. The village was about thirty minutes away. Derrick thought there appeared to be about a hundred people living there. They deposited the reindeer near a sizeable central lodge house. Two women took charge of it, and within a few minutes, the animal was skinned, and they had started butchering it. David slapped Derrick on the shoulders and said, "Come along. We'll get some food and talk a bit before heading back out."

The two men entered the lodge-house. There were about twenty people inside, men, women, and children. They were engaged in various tasks like fletching arrows, sewing clothes, and making bread. David introduced Derrick to a few people, although David appeared to be the only one who spoke French. The others he met greeted him with a nod or words Derrick could not understand.

There was a large kettle in the center of the room, which produced a mouthwatering aroma. David took a couple of wooden bowls, filled them from the kettle, and handed them to Derrick. Then David got a loaf of still-warm bread from the women who were baking. David guided Derrick to a long trestle table and gestured that they should sit.

David broke the bread in half and handed half to Derrick, saying, "The bread is made from dried and ground birch bark and soured milk. We had a poor grain harvest this year, so we made do with what we had. Honestly, I prefer it to rye or wheat bread. The food in the bowl we call skause. It's made from meat, white carrots, and cabbage, in a thick broth, with cumin, mustard, wild horseradish, and whatever else the cooks of the day decide to throw in the pot."

Derrick said, "Thank you. It smells very good."

When the two men finished, Derrick asked, "How would I say thank you to the cooks in your language?"

7

David replied, "Takk."

Derrick approached the cooks and bakers and said, "Takk." To them, they nodded politely and went back to their work. Derrick returned to where David sat and asked, "How did you learn French?"

David responded, "My mother taught me. When I was young, she told me that if I was going to speak for the village, I should know the languages of those we trade with so I wouldn't get cheated. My mother has a saying regarding business transactions: "Everyone lies." So, I learned French, English, and German."

Derrick asked, "Are you the leader of this village?"

David said, "In a manner of speaking, I am, but the old ways of village leaders and various tribes are dying out. Most decisions are made in Bergen. I handle local disputes, ensure everyone helps when needed, and attempt to keep everyone fed and clothed. Our village was further from Bergen and more independent. Bergen gets bigger every year, and our village becomes more politically connected to it. In a few years, I will have little to do as a leader."

Derrick nodded and asked, "The deer here are very different from the deer I am used to. They are larger and move in larger herds than back in France. I've also never seen so many males gathered together."

David responded, "The herd was made up of both males and females. Unlike other deer, both male and female reindeer grow antlers. That was no large herd; we consider that a small group of reindeer. You want to avoid the large herds of reindeer; they can gather in groups numbering in the hundreds. When spooked, the herds start to run in a circle. It makes it very difficult to select and shoot an individual deer. More than one hunter has been killed by the rampaging mass of deer stampeding right over him. We try to hunt groups of less than twenty. It is safer and more effective."

David then showed Derrick around the village and introduced him to several people. Derrick noticed they did not speak much, even by his normally quiet standards.

As the sun passed its zenith, he and David left the village for the location David had told Derrick about. True to his word, they located a group of about ten reindeer. Derrick soon harvested one, and David helped Derrick take it back to the Templar's camp. Derrick introduced David to the camp's leadership, along with Mary, Father Lull, and Cinead.

David soon became a regular visitor to the Templar's settlement. David aided them greatly in learning the local language and customs. Admiral Gregory considered David to be his local advisor whenever he had dealings with the Norwegians. Soon, members from the Templar camp also began visiting David's village. Derrick, Mary, and Father Lull often spent an entire day among the Norwegians and learned much about the local flora, fauna, and customs.

Mary grew very fond of David's mother, Julie. Julie's husband had gone fishing with five other men about twenty years ago, and none of the party had returned. Julie never remarried. She had devoted her life to her son and collecting things. As far as Mary could tell, Julie was the only person who lived alone in the community. Her dwelling seemed to have become the repository for every cast-off item in the village. Julie had things organized into piles all throughout her home. If anyone required something they didn't readily have, they would go to Julie, who usually came up with the needed item after some rummaging through her piles.

One day, while trapping ptarmigan, David asked Derrick, "Is Mary your wife or a relative?"

Derrick, somewhat surprised, said, "Neither. We are not married or related in any way."

David looked at Derrick as if he were about to say something, but instead remained quiet and returned to setting up the basket trap. When they had finished setting the traps and began walking back to the village, Derrick asked, "Why did you ask about Mary and me?"

David replied, "I was curious; she is always with you. Whenever she walks by, your eyes follow her. You both appear to like one another. I don't understand why you aren't wed."

Derrick didn't have a reply for some time, but after mulling it over in his head, he finally said, "I guess I don't know if she would have me."

David laughed and said, "Derrick, my friend, you often see things more clearly than most. How can you miss how Mary feels about you? You need to marry her before one of the men in my village decides to carry her off."

Derrick spent the rest of the day mulling over what David had said. When they returned to the village, Derrick saw Mary helping Julie carry what appeared to be a weatherworn and broken bench to Julie's dwelling. Mary smiled at Derrick when she noticed him, and Derrick felt a warmth in his chest and a lightness of being as he found himself smiling back. Smiles did not come easily to Derrick, but he couldn't seem to help himself this time.

CHAPTER TWO

Sir Louis de Champagne stood at the prow of the ship he had been on for over a month. Unlike Admiral Gregory, Captain Juan refused to allow Louis to get involved with any of the ship's operations as they traveled from Scotland to Constantinople. The voyage should have taken less than half the time it had. Bad weather and the conservative actions of Captain Juan delayed their arrival. When the vessel finally dropped anchor, Louis was anxious to get off the ship and get on with his mission.

Louis knew this was only the first step in what would be an extended mission, but he felt a strong sense of relief as he and his trunk of possessions departed the ship. Louis had rarely been as frustrated with an individual as he was with Captain Juan. The man seemed to do everything in slow motion. In some, this might have indicated that they carefully considered all options. With Captain Juan, it became apparent to Louis that he was slow because he could not decide what to do and was just lazy. To make matters worse, Captain Juan was an arrogant ass who quickly became offended by anyone who offered any advice, guidance, or opinion.

Much depended on what Sir Louis hoped to accomplish, not only for his Lord, King Robert the Bruce, but for the Knights Templar and potentially for all of Christianity. Louis was on his way to the Holy Land and then into the Far East searching for the elusive Prester John. Louis and King Robert believed Prester John was not an individual, but a title taken on by a man who held the office of the commander of a massive Christian army in the East. There have been many stories about this leader and his army in the West for many years. So far, no one has ever contacted this elusive commander or his army and then returned with solid information. Louis and Robert the Bruce believed that with so many rumors, there must be something to it. Louis was determined to locate the great Christian host of the East and convince them to join the Latin armies. Together, they would cleanse the Holy Land of the infidel.

Louis was surprised to discover that King Robert was an ardent supporter of returning to Outremer and reclaiming the Holy Land. Louis had thought King Robert would be so committed to achieving the independence of Scotland that he wouldn't have time to think of the Holy Land. Yet, Robert the Bruce told Louis he was prepared to commit

Scottish forces to a new crusade as soon as he completed the Scottish War of Independence against the English. Louis also hoped that retaking the Holy Land would allow the Templars to have a home far from the kingdoms of Europe. A home where they would be free to clear themselves of the evils they were being charged with.

Louis left the dock area and rented a room at a local Inn. He was a little nervous about leaving his possessions in the room. Still, he had always dreamed of coming to the Holy Land and felt compelled to explore this city, which stood as a gateway between east and west. As Louis walked the cobbled streets, his senses were assaulted by the multitude of colors and strange smells. Constantinople was exotic, colorful, and clean compared to Paris.

As Louis strolled through an outdoor market, he encountered more people from other countries than he had even known existed. Many people wore robes, but others wore garments of varied descriptions in a myriad of colors. Louis noted that many of the neighborhoods were separated by orchards or fields with gardens and crops. Most of these agricultural areas were bordered by low stone walls.

After wandering the streets for a couple hours, Louis saw four small tables in front of a shop. He sat at one of the tables to watch the people as they passed. A young man stepped up and asked Louis something in a language Louis could not understand. He tried to indicate to the young man that he didn't comprehend what he was saying. The young man became somewhat agitated with Louis's failed attempt to grasp his meaning. Louis tried to speak to him in French, which only caused more confusion and frustration. Louis was just rising to leave when another man dressed in a long robe stepped up and said something to the young man who was upset with Louis; this seemed to calm him. As the young man walked away, Louis thanked the robed man, hoping this new stranger would understand what Louis said.

To Louis's relief, the robed man spoke to him in perfect French. The man touched his chest and forehead, bowed slightly, and said, "Peace be upon you. Please let us sit and talk. I am Asim ben Aninn.

Louis said, "Thank you. What was that man saying to me?"

Asim replied, "The young man was telling you that these seats are reserved for establishment patrons. I informed him that you were my guest and that we would like some figs, olives, cheese, and Qamar aldeen. I hope you do not mind, but I always enjoy meeting new people from distant lands. Although there used to be many French people in this great city, there are few now. Most that are still here have long been residents of Constantinople and know less of their native country than I do. I am assuming you must have newly arrived in our city. If you don't mind the intrusion, where exactly are you from?"

Louis replied, "I am Louis de Champagne, and as you surmised, I am from France. If you don't mind me saying, your French is excellent. Where did you learn?"

Asim smiled and said, "I am a trader of spices and rare items. My business involves traveling to both the east and west. That is why I have my primary home here, right in the middle. Ah, here is our refreshment."

The young man returned and placed a platter with olives, cheese, and what Louis thought looked like an oddly shaped purple fruit or tuber. The young man also put a glass filled with a thick orange liquid in front of each of them.

Asim said, "Please join me. The cheese is not the best, but you will find no sweeter figs anywhere, and the olives are wonderful."

Louis watched as Asim selected one of the figs. Asim then sliced it in half, revealing the inside, which looked full of seeds. Asim scooped out the insides, seeds and all, and ate it. Louis then took a fig and copied what he saw Asim do.

After eating part of the fig and taking a small drink of the apricot nectar, Louis found the fig and the juice too sweet for his taste. So, he ate some of the cheese and a couple of olives. Louis said to Asim, "Thank you for the food. I don't think I have eaten anything as sweet as these figs. This city is quite different from Paris, the only other large city I have visited. I find Constantinople more colorful, open, and appealing."

Asim said, "Yes, this is a wonderful city. Even if I were not a trader, I would choose to live here. You can meet people from all over the world here. Latin folk, like yourself, used to be common, but now there are very few of you in Constantinople. Are you here as a pilgrim or on business?"

Although Louis had considered how he would answer this question, he was unsure exactly what to say to this man. He took a bite of cheese to stall for a moment. Sir Louis did not wish to lie to this man, but he had only just met him. After he swallowed, he said, "I guess you could call it a pilgrimage. I have a token from a friend who has died that I wish to take to Jerusalem and bury there."

"That is a long and difficult journey, my friend. I assume you are a Christian?" replied Asim.

Louis said, "Yes, I am. I know it is a long way, but I feel it is something I must do to honor my friend."

Asim was silent momentarily, then said, "Honoring a fallen companion is very important, I grant you, but the roads are not easily traveled by the inexperienced. A Latin Christian will not be happily greeted by some."

Louis said, "You are not a Christian?"

Asim laughed and said, "No, my young friend, I am a follower of Allah. I have many dealings with Christians and Jews and can claim many friends among the infidels. Yet, I am a Muslim from the soles of my feet to the top of my brow."

Louis was speechless. He knew he would meet Muslims, but did not expect them to be like this man. His thoughts must have shown on his face, for suddenly, Asim laughed out loud and said, "I am sorry. I do not mean to offend, but you look like you just ate something distasteful. I assume you had thought we Muslims were wild men wielding a scimitar, intent on killing all Christians. I am sorry to disappoint you, but you will discover that most Muslims are very tolerant of other religions. We may disagree with you, but most believe a man can worship as he wishes. Some Muslims are less tolerant and will not be friendly or may try to cause you harm, but they are the minority. Yet, you are likely to encounter some of them in the desert. So, again I warn you to be careful."

Louis was trying to untie his tongue when Asim stood. Asim took a few coins from a pouch within his robes and laid them on the table. He touched his chest and forehead and said, "I must be going. I wish you a good and safe pilgrimage." And left Louis sitting alone. He remained seated, lost in thought, as the young waiter returned and took the coins and the remains of their meal.

CHAPTER THREE

Sir William de Sevrey was having trouble acclimatizing to the life he found himself in. When he first arrived in Norway, he was busy helping Admiral Gregory organize the Templar base. Admiral Gregory had not been officially placed in overall command of the Templars in Norway. Still, most of the men looked to him when they had questions or needed direction. Sir Jules attempted to take control on a few occasions, claiming that because of his higher birth status and "greater knowledge," he should be in command. Jules gathered several men to his cause, primarily those who came from the higher nobility and felt that someone lower born, like Admiral Gregory, should not give them orders.

It all came to a head during one of the regular Templar meetings. The meeting was held in what would become the Templar church once it was completed and sanctified. Shortly after arriving in Norway, the Templars decide to continue their practice of regular meetings of all the knights and sergeants-at-arms. These meetings initially focused on where and what to build, what to plant, how to establish trade, and other items of immediate consequence. Admiral Gregory was deferred to as the man in charge during these meetings. As often as not, Sir Jules would interject the opposite viewpoint of whatever Admiral Gregory recommended. Admiral Gregory's opinion usually won out, and his ideas were implemented. Sir Jules' support grew more vocal as time passed, even though their numbers remained few. Sir Jules' group had recently decided to attempt to block Admiral Gregory or anyone who supported him from speaking.

At the meeting, William stood and attempted to speak when several of Sir Jules' men began talking over the top of him. They even pounded their fists on the tables so Sir William could not be heard. Sir Jules was surrounded by his supporters, where he sat silently with a satisfied grin as William struggled to be heard.

Admiral Gregory stood and left the building. William hadn't noticed the Admiral go, nor did the men making all the racket to drown Sir William's words. The Admiral reappeared in the doorway carrying a large bucket. He made his way to the table where the men yelled and pounded their fists to create the disturbance. Without a word, he threw the bucket of ice-cold water on them. There was stunned silence until the soaked men rose to their feet as if they were about to attack the Admiral, who merely stood his ground, frowning at them. After a few tense moments, Jules' followers quieted as they realized they were not armed. The Templars never went into their meetings with weapons. They also knew they were outnumbered, and Admiral Gregory would not be easily subdued.

Sir Jules broke the silence. He stood, shook some water from his gloves, and said, "Brothers, could we have expected any better from a low-born man. I will grant that Gregory is a fair sailor and has a reputation as a fighter, but as I have been asking, does he have what it takes to be a leader? We have all just witnessed his open disrespect for fellow brothers and true Knights of the Temple. What more evidence do you need? I propose we make Gregory the captain of our fishing vessels, and we select men of true lineage to take overall command of the Templars."

Manney de Trio, a knight known for his pride, deceit, and laziness, stood as water dripped from him and said in his loudest voice, "I propose we elect Sir Jules as our new Grand Master!"

There were shouts and thumps of approval from those who supported Sir Jules.

Admiral Gregory merely stood there until the uproar died down. Then, as he started to talk, Jules' supporters began to yell again, stamp their feet, and pound on the table so that he could not be heard. Sir Jules, still standing, raised his hands over his head, and the men quieted. Jules said, "Let Gregory speak. He has already shown us what he thinks of his brothers by dumping water on them to quiet their opinions. Let us be more respectful than he has been and listen to the wisdom of Sergeant-at-Arms Gregory."

Admiral Gregory said in an even but powerful voice so that all could hear, "Fellow Templars, Sir Jules has brought a valid point. We do need to elect a leader for our community here in Norway, but we still have a Grand Master. As far as we know, Grand Master Jacques de Molay is still alive. Until we receive word to the contrary, that position is taken. I propose that instead, we elect a governor of our colony."

Jules interrupted and said, "I suppose you want to be considered for the position?"

Admiral Gregory replied, "It is not right for a man to nominate himself, and I, for one, think that Sir William de Sevrey would make a fine governor."

There was a pause as every man in the room turned to look at Sir William.

William was probably more surprised than anyone else in the room except Jules. Everyone was waiting for William to reply to the nomination, but he didn't know what to say. Much to his surprise, he had discovered that he liked the responsibility of leadership. William found he was good at establishing a respectful relationship with the men, and they instinctively followed his leadership. Yet, as he considered the notion of being in overall command of this fledgling community, he did not feel it was the correct choice. He decided at that moment that any leadership he accepted here in Norway would be temporary and that he should be subordinate to another. He would see that the community of Templars here was firmly established, but then he would move on. Somehow, he knew he needed to secure a different location to aid the Templars. He even believed he knew where that should be. William felt he must do more than hide from the persecution being waged against the Templars. He needed to establish a base to strike back at those who accused them of the false crimes.

In his heart, William felt that Norway was just another stopping point. Norway appeared safe to them for now, but they couldn't fight back against those who wished to destroy the Templars. They needed a place where the Kings of Europe and the Church could not reach them. He and Admiral Gregory had spoken of this many times, but had not yet reached a conclusion.

William knew what he must say, "I appreciate Admiral Gregory's confidence in me, but I do not feel that Governor is the right position for me. I will gladly serve in any other position that Admiral Gregory would have me do if he were elected governor. I believe the Admiral has shown great leadership in his years of service to the Templars prior to the unjust arrests that have driven us to where we find ourselves today. Since then, he has been the central figure we have rallied around in Scotland and here in Norway. Although I respect the knowledge Sir Jules has to offer, I believe our Governor needs to be a man of action while we get this community on its feet and plan our next step to clearing the honorable name of the Knights Templar."

There was an outburst of agreement from the great majority of the men. The volume was loud enough that Jules' men could not be heard over the others calling for Admiral Gregory to become Governor. Knowing he had lost and could do nothing about it, Jules rose and left the meeting hall with his supporters.

Derrick, Mary, and Cinead were seated at a table outside a short distance from where the Templars met that evening. Not being Templars, they had not been allowed in, and truth be told, none of them would have wanted to be present. They witnessed Admiral Gregory exit the hall, fill the bucket with water, and then return to the meeting. Next, they heard voices raised in anger, causing the three of them to halt their conversation while they watched the door to the meeting hall expectantly. After a few minutes, they saw Jules and his lackeys leave the meeting and gather near the stables, just out of earshot from where Derrick, Mary, and Cinead sat. After a few minutes of Jules and his men speaking, someone in Jules' party must have noticed the three of them watching because they suddenly turned and glared at Mary, Derrick, and Cinead. Then Jules' group walked away and moved out of sight.

Mary looked at Cinead and Derrick and said, "Now, what do you suppose that was about?"

Cinead replied, "That I don't know, but I don't trust Jules. We would all have been better off if someone had pitched that tadger over the whale when we sailed from Scotland."

Mary laughed and said, "Cinead, someday you must teach me what all these Scottish insults mean."

Cinead said, "You are too much a lady for me to sully your ears with such explanations. Just assume it's not a compliment if I use phrases you don't know to describe Jules or his dobbers."

CHAPTER FOUR

Father Thomas knelt alone in his room, praying. It was still about an hour before he was to meet with Cardinal Soprano. It was dark outside; the sun wouldn't break the horizon for a couple of hours. Shortly after the Templars arrived in Lucerne, Switzerland, he started rising early for prayer.

The Templars' numbers had increased significantly when another group of Templars joined them during their journey to the Swiss Confederacy. The two groups of Templars had quickly melded into one company.

Sir Henry de Creon had been made the leader of the combined companies of Templars. Cardinal Soprano, who accompanied the group at the request of Pope Clement V, was helping the Templars get established. In recent years, the Papacy had become nearly a prisoner of King Philip IV of France. The pressure from the French Crown caused the Pope's actions to vacillate between supporting and attacking the Knights Templar. Recently, the Pope felt the only way to protect some of the Templars was to secretly send small bands into hiding outside of France. As other Monarchs in Europe joined in the apprehensions of the Templars, the options of where to send them grew smaller. Although most of the European Monarchs only half-heartedly confronted the Templars, it was still not safe to send them to those countries. The King and Queen of Portugal had taken a protective stance regarding the Templars in their country, but the Pope did not feel he should send any more Templars that way.

Cardinal Soprano and Pope Clement had decided that they could establish a haven in the Swiss Confederacy. The government in the Swiss Confederacy was less centralized, and parts of the country behaved very independently from the rest of Europe. Therefore, Sir Henry was put in command of about a hundred other Templars and sent east. Cardinal Soprano accompanied the group to give them more authority to establish a monastery. Almost all the men under Sir Henry's command had spent some time in the prisons of Paris, and several had been mercilessly tortured. Many of these men were not soldiers but were craftsmen and priests who had been part of the Templar organization. They had been arrested because they had attracted the attention of King Philip's men for what they may know about the location of Templar assets.

Along the way to the Swiss Confederacy, they encountered another group of about forty-five Templars under the command of Sir Gilbert de Lyon. These Templars had been stranded on the Island of Crete just after the arrests had taken place in France. After finally getting ferried across to Italy, they made their way on foot to France. They had heard many rumors but hoped they could discover what had truly happened once they reached France. After the two groups met, Sir Gilbert decided to join Sir Henry's Templars in their travels into the Swiss countryside.

Originally, the band of Templars had intended to stay in Bern, but the city was larger than they had expected. It was also more heavily traveled by tradesmen outside the Confederacy, so they decided to move on. They searched for a city with few direct lines of contact with the monarchs in the rest of Europe. After some discussion, they chose to settle in Lucerne. At first, the knights attempted to appear to be a regular monastic order, establishing a monastery. Soon, the locals noticed differences among this group of brothers compared to other monks and priests. The Templars were more inclined to have friendly, mundane conversations with the locals. The Templars also appeared to be very industrious and progressive in building and establishing businesses.

The Templars quickly purchased land, built a grain mill just out of town, and then began work on living quarters with a large central gathering hall. What really made the locals wonder about the new monastic brothers was their obvious military bearing. Before long, the villagers of Lucerne witnessed monks and brothers practicing with swords and maces or riding off into the countryside with spears and lances tied to their horses.

Father Thomas was initially vexed by the actions of the Templars. They were supposed to be lying low, so the King of France did not hear word of them hiding in the Swiss Confederacy. When Cardinal Soprano noticed Father Thomas berating a couple of knights carrying halberds, he pulled him aside. He said, "Father Thomas, there are a few things you need to understand. Firstly, although these men took holy orders and are clergy members, they also took knightly vows and spent many more hours with a sword in their hands than they have with a cross in them.

Secondly, the people of Lucerne are unlikely to object to having a few men trained in martial arts around, provided they do not cause problems. This confederation is still relatively new, and the German barons to our north are already attempting to claim parts of the Swiss Confederacy as their own. The locals will welcome disciplined soldiers in their community who don't rape their wives and daughters or get too drunk or steal their goats. They are likely to overlook what might seem odd behavior from a monk. Lastly, Father, you must learn that if you want these men to believe you have changed and are on their side, you must stop constantly expressing your disapproval."

Father Thomas had wanted to disagree, but he knew Cardinal Soprano was right. Thomas was still not certain he was the man Cardinal Soprano thought he was. In the time he had known the Cardinal, he had come to trust the man's judgment and insights into human nature. Thomas still had not told anyone how Odo had really died. He was uncertain if Cardinal Soprano would absolve him of murdering the young squire just to protect the lies he had spread about the Templars. To some degree, Father Thomas still did not trust the warrior monks. He still felt they behaved too haughtily and indulged in eating and drinking too much. He also did not like the familiar air they used with one another.

Above all else, Father Thomas was afraid. He feared he was too weak to maintain the façade of being a good man. Cardinal Soprano was the first person Thomas believed wished to help him. For some reason, the Cardinal had taken a special interest in him. The Cardinal had gone out of his way to attempt to restore a faith in God and the Church that Thomas wasn't sure he ever truly had. Father Thomas also feared Sir Henry de Creon. Henry had witnessed Thomas' betrayal firsthand, and it appeared Henry would never trust or respect Thomas. Sir Henry always seemed to be watching Thomas as though he were just waiting for Father Thomas to show his true colors.

CHAPTER FIVE

Sir William and Admiral Gregory had gone to the mill to watch the first batch of grain ground into flour. The mill had been the most expensive building to construct. It also required the most planning since most other structures don't contain several heavy moving parts that all need to line up exactly. Nor do they require two massive stones, one rolling across the surface of the other. They were able to harvest the logs for most of the construction, but they had to purchase the millstones. Luckily, the Templars had some of the best masons and carpenters in Europe, and they had previously built many mills. The mill was a major step in making the Templars in Norway self-sufficient. The farmers would pay the Templars two bushels for every ten bushels of grain ground into flour. In a climate like Norway, grains were difficult to grow. Having the mill meant the Templars could focus on other crops that were easier to produce.

Gregory and William stood with several other men, mostly craftsmen who had helped build the mill. The group watched the smaller stone roll across the larger one, pulverizing the grain into a powder that could more easily be used to make bread. As they watched, a Templar knight approached them with another man in tow. The knight said, "Governor-Admiral, we have an issue requiring your immediate attention."

Admiral Gregory hated the "Governor-Admiral" or "Governor-General" titles the men insisted on calling him. He sighed and said, "What is it now?"

The Knight said quietly so that only William and Gregory could hear him, "It appears that we have been robbed."

The Admiral looked at Sir William, then back to the knight, and said, "Show us."

The four men were soon standing in the building they had constructed to store the two shiploads of gold, silver, and other valuable items they had brought from Rennes-le-Chateau. Father Lull was inside the building, accompanied by two other priests. The three priests were talking in hushed, anxious voices. When Father Lull noticed the admiral, he approached him and Sir William and said, "As near as we can tell, about forty bags of gold coins are missing. Each bag weighed about twenty pounds, but we have not completed the inventory."

Admiral Gregory, face flushed with anger, said, "How could this have happened? The room has only one entrance and is always guarded by two knights outside and two inside."

Father Lull replied, "We do not yet know for sure, but it appears that Sir Jules arranged it so that four men loyal to him were guarding the chamber last night. When the relief guards arrived in the morning, they found no one on watch. They immediately secured the entrance and got me. I sent for the two other priests who oversee the inventory of our assets. When we first entered, we thought nothing was taken. As you know, we have a large amount of wealth here. As we continued our investigation, we discovered the missing bags of gold."

Admiral Gregory said, "Where is Sir Jules?"

The knight who had originally informed Admiral Gregory of the issue said, "He is gone, with about twenty other knights and a handful of auxiliary personnel. We are also missing about thirty of the Fjord horses we recently purchased."

Admiral Gregory sighed loudly, took a breath, and said, "I want the treasury secured, a complete inventory done, and double the guard. I also want four groups assembled. Each group will comprise five knights, five archers, and at least one of the hunters who knows how to track in this country. They are to leave as soon as possible to look for the thieves. They should avoid engaging with them if possible. Find them and report back." As men scattered, Admiral Gregory said, "Sir William and Father Lull, I want you to accompany me."

The three men walked back in the direction of the mill. Admiral Gregory said, "Father Lull, it appears you were correct when you told me you thought the treasure was not secure. We need a more protected location. Since you have hidden this treasure successfully in the past, I am putting you in charge."

Father Lull said, "I believe we should go to the stone masons. The master masons are a skilled group of men experienced at working in secrecy. Master Acel is very good at contriving secret passages and traps for those who might attempt to enter unbidden."

Admiral Gregory replied, "I am aware of Master Acel's skill; if he can be pulled from his other duties at the Church site, by all means, use him. Do whatever you deem necessary to get it done." After a moment, Gregory's voice lost all its anger, and he said, "I cannot believe Sir Jules would steal from us or that he could get knights to assist him. Knights who had sworn oaths that clearly condemn an act such as this. Jules is a pompous ass, but he is one of us."

Sir William said, "We might need to look more closely at what we have become as an Order. We all took vows for a very different purpose than what we seem to be facing now. Most of our leadership is rumored to have turned against the Order by confessing to crimes that make us all suspect. Maybe it is time to reestablish our oaths of brotherhood and make our purpose clear. Lately, it seems our only goal is to build this community, but is that really all we are about? I, for one, do not believe that a base in Norway should be our ultimate goal. This is only a stopping point while we find a more permanent home. A home where we would be free from the persecution of the Church and the European monarchies. I know Sir Louis is off looking for allies in Outremer. Even if he were to find any, I don't see how we could establish a base of operation there that would not be controlled by the Church and the European monarchs."

The Admiral looked at William and deflated even further as he said, "You are right. I have focused too much on building a few structures, purchasing land for crops, and establishing a fishing trade. Too little focus has been placed on who we are as an Order.   I will call a meeting of some of our leaders, and we will begin discussions regarding our ultimate future."

CHAPTER SIX

About a week after leaving Constantinople, Louis was riding a horse alone in a vast desert. He led two other horses and a donkey, which carried most of his possessions. Louis had bought the animals and supplies with some of the money King Robert the Bruce had given him. Louis had heard stories of the deserts of Outremer, but even in his wildest dreams, he had not thought it would be like this.

He thought he had brought plenty of water, but now he had none left. He had been told there were wells along the route, but he had found none. He had hired a guide to take him as far as Adana, but had foolishly paid the man half the money in advance. On the second night of the trip, the man disappeared along with two horses Louis had purchased for the guide to ride.

The sun beat down on Louis mercilessly. It seemed that as soon as the sun appeared on the horizon, it was blazing hot, and the air was so dry that Louis noticed that even in this heat, he wasn't sweating. It seemed like the sun was drawing and evaporating the moisture straight out of his body before it could settle on his skin. The horses were having a harder time than the donkey was. Perhaps he should have listened to the man selling him the animals. He had told Louis that to cross the desert, he would have more luck if he purchased the smaller, leaner horses. Louis, being a knight, chose large, heavily muscled animals.

Four days after his guide had left him, Louis ran out of feed for the animals. He could still only see endless sand in every direction. The next day, Louis gave the animals the last of the water. On the morning of the eighth day, Louis had lost one horse that lay down and refused to rise. Louis was no longer riding but was walking in an attempt to save the last two horses. He had tried to walk only at nighttime and rest during the day, but he just couldn't make it work. It was extremely hot during the day, with no shade available. The unrelenting heat beat down on him so brutally that he could not rest under the blazing sun. He eventually resumed walking after a few hours of unrestful sleep during the hottest part of the day.

The next day, the other two horses refused to rise, and Louis had no strength to fight with them. In a daze, he grasped the lead rope tied to the donkey and continued in what he hoped was the correct direction. At some point, as Louis hypnotically stumbled forward, he suddenly realized he no longer had the donkey with him. His mind, as if in a fuzzy half-remembered dream, reminded him that his supplies were with the donkey, but he was beyond caring. It took all his focus just to keep putting one foot in front of the other. Sir Louis' brain could not hold onto a thought for any length of time. The areas of his skin exposed to the sun were red and blistered, and his tongue was swollen and so dry it felt like a thick hunk of leather in his mouth. Louis was nearly sunblind; everything appeared to be just wavy shapes drifting in and out before him.

At some point, he had the brief realization that he was lying on his back, and as Louis tried to rise, he discovered he could not even move his legs or arms; all his strength had failed him. He had the brief presence of mind to think, "I am dying." I'm sorry, Sergeant Bertrand. I failed to take your surcoat to the Holy City.   And then Sir Louis de Champagne closed his eyes.

CHAPTER SEVEN

Admiral Gregory met with fourteen other members of the Templar leadership; seven were knights, three sergeants-at-arms, and four were masters of their trade. All were men who had been committed to the Templars for several years. Admiral Gregory started by asking, "I do not want to insult any of you, but it has been brought to my attention that some of our party may not be as committed to the Templar organization as we had once been. I would like to hear from each of the soldiers if you still hold to the vows you took years ago when you became Poor Fellow-Soldiers of Christ and of the Temple of Solomon. And from you, master craftsmen, if you still hold to the vows you took when you committed yourselves to the Order."

Sir William knelt to one knee and said, "Admiral Gregory, I am still a Knight of the Temple of Solomon and still hold to the vows I swore to God, the Church, and the Order." The other knights and sergeants followed his example and knelt to reaffirm their vows.

Admiral Gregory looked to the masters, two master masons, one master carpenter, and one master shipwright. Master Acel was a man in his fifties; he was a burly, hard man used to commanding masons and other craftsmen who worked under his leadership. His arms were as rippled with muscle as any Templar soldier. He was bald with an unruly beard. His look was nearly as hard as the stone he worked with daily. His bright blue eyes twinkled with amusement as he said, "Well, Commander of the Vault of Acre, or Admiral, or Governor, or whatever title you are going by today. My knees won't allow me to kneel and then stand back up as quickly as these young bucks, but I'll tell you the same thing I told your Grand Master Jacques de Molay some twenty years ago. I am foremost a man of God, although I don't understand most of what the Church teaches, so I will follow what my simple mind tells me is right and just. Next, as a master mason, I will follow that code, provided it doesn't compromise my commitments to God. Lastly, I am loyal to doing the jobs that the Templars ask of me as long as they don't force me to break faith with my first two commitments. In short, I will accept and follow your commands if you do not attempt to force me to break my oaths to my brother masons or go against what I know in my soul to be right. Luckily, I have no wife to confuse things and can place my priorities in the order I see fit. As a master mason, much of my art is secret, just like you Templars have your secrets. Bound up in the secrets of my craft are many teachings and stories that we believe are gifts from God to us."

The other masters all nodded in agreement with Master Acel. Admiral Gregory glared at Acel momentarily and then said, "Coming from you, Master Acel, that is as good as any oath I have ever been given. Although I take issue with a couple of your statements. Your reference to yourself as simple-minded is a bald-faced lie, and we all know that. The only one whose wisdom I may seek before yours is Father Lull. Also, I do not understand why you would have trouble deciding what title to give me. As I recall, only yesterday, when I asked if that foundation for the new stables would be finished anytime in the next week, you called me a 'loggerheaded, hedge-born, barnacle'."

Acel smiled and replied, "If the capstone fits...."

Admiral Gregory smiled back and said to everyone, "Now that we've got that out of the way, let's get started on why we are meeting. I assume you all know about Sir Jules and the men who went with him yesterday. I have teams who are tracking them as we speak. The bigger issue is the commitment level of the men here and our long-term plans. We have been concentrating so much on building our community here that we have not discussed our next step. While I have been focused on establishing our community, Sir William has been occupied with what we should do next."

All eyes turned to look at Sir William. Taking that as his cue, he said, "I have been thinking long about what we should do and what the intent of the Grand Master was when he sent me to take the map to Admiral Gregory. I believe the Grand Master wants us to take the remnants of the Templars and find a new home where we can establish ourselves without fear of the influence of a few evil men bent on destroying us."

One of the knights, Sir Humphries, said, "What map?"

Admiral Gregory said, "The map in question was smuggled out of the Holy Land many years ago. The map shows more of the world than any map I have seen. Most interestingly, the map shows a large land mass west of Greenland. I have spoken with some of the local Norwegians, and their sagas tell stories of men sailing west from

Greenland. Those men who returned have also claimed to have found land in that direction."

Sir William jumped back in, "This new land would be a perfect location to build a base of operation. It is all but unknown to the leaders of France, England, Spain, and Germany. Not to mention the Church."

Another knight, Sir Reynolds, said, "Are you proposing we remove ourselves from the protection of the Holy Roman Church? What of our oaths to the Church? Besides, the Church is worldwide; we cannot go anywhere the Church does not rule."

Master Acel said, "I don't mean to speak ill of the Church, but I wonder; the oaths you gentlemen swore, were they to the Church, the Pope, or God who is overall? I know the Pope is the mouthpiece for God here on Earth, but what if the Pope is not correct in something he says? Is he a flawed man like the rest of us and mistaken, or is God wrong? I am not a priest, but I have learned Latin in my studies. I have access to the Scripture and have studied it to the best of my ability. I have found no mention of a flawless Pope or any other religious leader in the Scripture, except Jesus. The Bible tells us of numerous holy men who lead God's people. Still, in every instance, these Godly men showed great failings and corruption, often leading the people astray. Personally, I think the Church of today may be a little off-center, and any good builder will tell you that being just a little off-center at the heart of a project will be devastating later.

Sir William replied, "I do not know what to say regarding our oaths to the Church. It still bothers me greatly; I still hold my oaths to the Church as sacred. But the Church also swore to guide and direct us, to protect us from earthly kings. Yet, the Church seems to be complicit, or at the very least bystanders, in the lies King Philip is spreading about us. I would hope that once we have established a safe base where King Philip has no influence and the Pope cannot call for our arrest, we will be able to establish our innocence. After that, we can re-establish our relationship with the Church."

Admiral Gregory said, "Gentlemen, Sir William and I have discussed this previously, and I am inclined to agree with him. I will not ask you to decide right now. I want you to go to the men under your command and receive an oath of recommitment to the Templars from each one. If a man is hesitant to commit to us, then have him come speak with me. I will allow him the opportunity to withdraw from us if it can be arranged. I also want each of you to consider the option of us leaving for this new land to the west. I have here a copy of the map the Grand Master had Sir William bring to me, if you care to see it. You are not to mention the map or us considering leaving Norway to anyone outside of this room. We will meet again in one week. At that time, I wish to know which of our men are still committed to us. I also want your thoughts on this idea of traveling to the lands in the west."

CHAPTER EIGHT

Sir Henry de Creon met with his advisors, who included Cardinal Soprano, Sir Gilbert de Lyon, and Garrard de La Languedoc. Sir Henry had been very arrogant in his youth, and as a young knight, he would not have listened to advice from anyone under his command. Over the last many months, some of it spent as a prisoner and victim of the Holy Inquisition, he had changed his mind about his invulnerability and superiority.

Sir Henry told those assembled, "We have the grain-mill up and running and have already established contracts with local farmers. Our quarters' building is nearly complete. The church has been laid out and is awaiting Cardinal Soprano's final okay so the masons can start laying the foundation."

Cardinal Soprano said, "I will not authorize the building of the church as you have designed it. I know you Templars like your round churches, but it is too big a risk. I believe we are quite safe here from any intervention from King Philip, but a round church is an unnecessary risk. We do not know how the locals will behave if we confirm that you men are Templars. I, again, request that we redesign the church in a more standard form. The people here already know that many of you are trained soldiers, but we don't need to build a permanent structure that screams out that you are Templars."

Sir Henry said, "Cardinal Soprano, we have already hidden everything about who we are. We no longer wear any distinctive insignias that mark us as Templars. We fly no flags, and there are no red and white or black and white crosses on our surcoats, shields, or draped across our horses' flanks. Now you ask…."

Sir Garrard cut off Sir Henry and said, "Sir Henry, the Cardinal makes a good point. I also took the vows of a Templar, and it galls me to hide, but that is precisely why the Holy Father sent us here. We are to lie low and wait for the proper time to reestablish the Order of the Knights Templar. For now, we need to be more discreet. I believe the Cardinal is correct. We continue to tell anyone who asks that the Pope has sent us here to establish a monastery. When asked about our obvious military activities, we explain that our brothers include many soldiers displaced by the loss of the Holy Land. All of this is the truth. Building a round church will defeat our purpose for coming here in the first place."

Sir Henry took a deep breath and sighed, "Fine, Cardinal, you can change the design. Have the master mason make the necessary alterations. Let us move on to ideas to generate income.

"Even with the mill working, we still need additional sources of revenue. There are about a hundred and fifty of us, and that is a lot of mouths to feed. The Holy Father has given us a fair sum of money to establish ourselves, but I do not want to be like the foolish man who buried the money his master gave him. What can we do to use the funds we have been entrusted with to become self-sufficient?"

Sir Gilbert said, "As I mentioned last time, we have a couple of men in our command who were an integral part of the banking and loaning operation of the Templars. I have spoken with them, and they said that we will need to be careful with our limited funds, but they have come up with several options. They believe we should offer the local merchants a safe location to store their money. For an additional fee, we can transport funds under guard to other locations as they require. This would be a slow-growing but ever-expanding part of the business.

"After evaluating ways of generating funds more quickly, we feel the safest option is for us to advance money to some of the more experienced farmers here. We will provide them with the funds to purchase land and hire laborers. They will have seven years to repay the advance. They will compensate us with fifty percent of their harvest until they repay the money in full. If they fail to repay the loan within seven years, we will reclaim ownership of the land. They said that this system provides a steady influx of income. The money from selling our portion of the crops usually amounts to the land's price in five years of good harvests. They also indicated that the farmers do not repay the loan about half the time, so often we still own the land at the end of the seven years. We can then lease the land to the same farmer or resell the land with the same arrangement. They claimed this system is more likely to provide a steady influx of money than if we buy the land and attempt to farm it ourselves. Additionally, it protects us during years of bad harvests."

Sir Henry said, "Sir Gilbert, I am not knowledgeable on matters like these. How much of our funds will you need to start this banking operation?"

Sir Gilbert said, "I believe that if you allow us to have half of our available funds to get things started, we will be able to cover all our start-up expenses by the end of the first year. Within three years, we feel we can refund the initial investment fourfold. They believe the profits will multiply year after year if handled carefully."

Sir Henry said, "If no one has any objection, I think we should do as Sir Gilbert suggests."

Cardinal Soprano said, "As long as no interest is charged, I am fine with it."

Sir Garrard said, "I had a visit from the local Seneschal. He inquired if any of our men would be interested in accompanying him and a few of his men into the mountains north of us. There have been reports of Austrian incursions into the area, and they would like to investigate the matter further. Our men would not be paid anything, but I believe aiding them would be a good idea. It would help our image with the local officials and potentially the leaders of the Swiss Confederacy. It would also be good as a training opportunity for our men."

Sir Henry asked, "How many men are you talking about?"

Sir Garrard said, "I was thinking ten knights and sergeants."

Sir Henry said, "Do we have any squires that could be sent along with them?"

Sir Garrard replied, "We could take our six trained squires, but I think it would be better to leave them here. Those six are the only well-trained squires we have, and I am using them to train the local boys who are interested in becoming squires. The families of these boys have agreed that they may train with us after they have completed their daily chores at home. This means we only have them for a few hours each day, so I'd rather leave our trained squires here to instruct the recruits. Besides, I think this will mostly turn into just a few days of riding and camping in the mountains."

Sir Henry replied, "Fine, sounds like a good idea. Select the men to go. Who will you put in command?"

Garrard said, "I would like to be in command if you could spare me for a few days."

Sir Henry thought about how things had changed for him since they had come to the Swiss Confederacy. At the beginning of the trip, he and Garrard were co-commanding the group. Then they included Sir

Gilbert in the command structure when they encountered him and his men. The shared command had worked adequately, but by the time they had reached Bern, they all agreed they needed one overall commander. To Sir Henry's surprise, the other two men selected him to be in charge. Both Gilbert and Garrard were more experienced than him. Yet, they both felt they were better suited to being his immediate subordinates. They believed he would make a better overall commander. Sir Henry was honored and reluctantly accepted. It wasn't until later that he realized it meant he had to deal with all the minor details while Garrard and Gilbert could focus on just their limited commands. It also meant Henry ended up spending far more time inside than outside. To his surprise, Sir Henry found he enjoyed being responsible for growing this community of men into a productive and self-sufficient organization.

CHAPTER NINE

One day, Derrick was exploring the Norwegian woods near the village. He noticed smoke coming from a very small hut that could not hold more than one or two people. Initially, he thought the place was on fire, but there were no flames, and the hut was made of dried thatch. It would be consumed in a few moments if it were on fire. Derrick wondered if it could be a smoker for drying meat, but just then, a completely naked, tall man suddenly burst out of the hut. He began to roll around in the snow and yelled words Derrick could not understand. Derrick thought perhaps his original assessment was correct, and the man was on fire. Then mysteriously, the man stood and calmly returned to the smoking hut. After maybe ten minutes, he burst out again to roll in the snow, yell, and then return to the smoking shelter once more.

Derrick watched this odd behavior for about thirty minutes. Then to his surprise, the man leaped out of the hut and, instead of rolling in the snow, he began to run. He raced across the frozen landscape with long strides, yelling like a madman, still completely naked. Derrick noticed that the path the man ran on was well-worn. It followed a large circular course with various obstacles which the man leaped over, crawled under, or scaled as needed. The man ran two complete circuits, never slowing, and then returned to the smoking hut to restart the craziness. Derrick decided the man must be insane and continued with his exploration.

Later that evening, Admiral Gregory asked William, Cinead, Derrick, Mary, and Father Lull to accompany him to the Norse village where David ruled. As the group from the Templars camp entered the lodge house in the Norse village, they were asked to sit on benches around the large, elongated fire pit. David sat on a stool at the far end of the fire pit on a slightly raised platform. Many of the Norse villagers were also in attendance at the lodge house.

Derrick noticed the insane man he had seen running naked through the woods was standing among the other Norwegian men. He was now dressed and was not acting strange or crazy. He was behaving just like the others, talking and drinking. When Derrick had an opportunity, he quietly asked David about the man. David replied, "That is Leif. Why do you ask about him?"

Derrick told David what he had witnessed in the woods earlier that day. David laughed and said, "That does not surprise me. Leif looks at things much differently than most of us, and you would not be the first to think him touched by the gods, but no, Leif is as rational as you or I. He is a skilled craftsman and artist, one of our best trackers, and in practice, he is one of our best fighters, highly skilled at grappling. Leif often follows old and nearly forgotten methods to improve his skills and strength. He, along with a few others, believes that sitting in a sweat hut until it becomes unbearable and then rolling in the snow will toughen their skin like leather, making it harder for a knife to cut them. There is one more thing I will tell you about Leif. He would be one of my best warriors, but he has the heart of a poet and not a killer. He prefers to craft objects of wood, sing, tell stories, and play music. Some might think he is meek, but that would be a mistake. I believe Leif feels the spirit of life more than the rest of us and sees value in a life well-lived rather than in the glories of war or the possession of wealth."

Admiral Gregory approached David and Derrick while they were speaking of Leif. Gregory said, "David, I have heard tales that in the past, some of your people have traveled to a distant land in the west, beyond Iceland and Greenland. What can you tell me about this?"

David replied, "Ah, you want to hear the story of Leif Erikson. That is a long tale, and we really should start with the story of his father, Erik the Red."

Admiral Gregory sighed and said, "I don't need the entire saga, and I think we can skip the father's adventures. Tell me about Leif."

David said, "I am a reasonably adept Jarl for this village and can hold my own in discussions of policy and trade negotiations, but I am no storyteller. There is one among us who is unmatched in telling of the Saga of Erik the Red and Leif Erikson."

David then called out, "Leif the Poet, come tell us of your namesake Leif Erikson and his adventure to Vinland."

At the mention of his name, Leif stepped forward and stood on the platform beside where David sat. Leif faced the fire pit, and the people in the room quieted expectantly. As the fire cast a flickering reddish glow across his face, Leif waited for the assemblage to quiet completely. Then he paused a second longer for dramatic effect. Only then did Leif, the poet, begin, "Leif Erikson was called by God to bring the

Christian faith to the inhabitants of Greenland. So, he set out on a voyage from Norway with a crew of hardy men and his well-made ship. As they plied the waters westward, the Devil gathered all his might and made war against Leif and his crew to stop them from doing God's holy work. The swells of the sea grew massive, and the winds pushed the ship off her course. The waves crashed over the ship's sides, and the men panicked and began to lose heart, fearing they would all perish at the hands of the Devil.

"Leif stood up in the center of the ship and said, 'Do not fear this storm; it is the handiwork of the great deceiver. God is greater. God will not allow us to perish. I promise you, not one of us shall die. Be of good heart, and you will see the great and mighty hand of God.' The crew all heeded the words of Leif Erikson and composed themselves and weathered the storm with the conviction and courage of the Vikings of old.

"After several days, the storm slackened and then abated altogether. Yet, when the sun finally showed, the crew realized they were far off course in waters they did not know. They were also fearfully short of provisions. Again, they began to lose faith in their God, and Leif said, 'Do not fear. God holds us in His hands. He will not let us succumb to the wiles of the evil one.' Just then, land was sighted to the west. The men rowed hard toward the shore. They found a good sandy beach on which to land. As they stepped out of the ship onto the shore of this new and strange land, they were greeted by two men from Greenland. These men had been shipwrecked there for many months.

"The men told Leif and his crew that this new land had grains and grapes that grew wild, and they said to Leif and the others that there was an abundance of game. Leif and his men were very famished and immediately went inland. After traveling only a small distance, they found grapes and grains, just as the two shipwrecked men had claimed. They gathered fruit and grain and made a rough bread. Other men from the crew caught several rabbits and birds and cooked a feast to rival a Yule celebration. Before they ate, Leif thanked God for bringing them safely to a place of plenty.

"After the feast, the crew gathered provisions and prepared the boat to make their way back to Greenland to complete the work God had called Leif to do. Their journey this time was easy. After a short time, they made landfall in Greenland and converted the inhabitants to Christianity.

"While there, Leif Erikson heard about another man who had also seen the land to the west after his ship had been blown off course. His name was Bjarni Herjolfsson, and he lived in Greenland. So, Leif sought Bjarni out, and after getting details of Bjarni's voyage, Leif began to make plans to return to the land in the west and spend some time exploring. Leif's father, the great explorer Erik the Red, planned to go with Leif on this voyage. The day before Leif and his crew departed, Erik fell from his horse and decided that the fall was an omen of God, indicating that he should not make the voyage with his son.

"Leif Erikson, with his crew of thirty-five brave men, set sail in his ship for his second voyage to the lands in the west. Leif and his men first made landfall on this new land in an area that was rocky and devoid of any life. Leif named this Helluland. After a brief exploration, they set off again, hoping to find more hospitable areas. After going around a cape, the explorers discovered a site that showed great promise for fishing and had a large, forested land that went on for as far as they could see. The climate in this area was mild, and the fish and woods promised good hunting and building materials for a camp. Leif Erikson decided to make a camp and spend the winter there, as winter was fast approaching. As the men caught salmon and hunted around where they established their base, they discovered this area was thick with wild grapes, so Leif named the place Vinland.

"One day, as the men gathered timbers to bring back to Greenland with them, they met the inhabitants of Vinland. These men had red skin and appeared fierce and wild. When these Vinlanders came upon the crew, Leif's men reached for any weapon within their grasp to defend themselves. Believing God would protect them, Leif stepped out from among his men with no weapon and greeted the fearsome band. To the surprise of the Greenlanders, these native men were friendly. As they began to communicate as best they could without a common language, the Greenlanders discovered these Vinlanders had come to trade with them. The red men brought food, animal skins, and other items to trade with Leif and his men. These Vinlanders wore pants and shirts made of leather or fur. Some had beads, stones, and bones ingeniously woven into the garments. A few among them had great head coverings made with feathers that surrounded their head and even flowed down their back.

"Leif and his men spent the Winter in Vinland and then returned to Greenland with a supply of timbers and grapes. As Leif and his men sailed back, they encountered a group of castaways and rescued them, bringing them to Greenland. After this second rescue of stranded sailors, he earned his nickname, Leif the Lucky."

After the evening spent in Jarl David's village, Admiral Gregory and the others rode back to the Templar camp. Sir William asked, "Do you think we can believe these stories about Leif Erikson finding lands to the west filled with grapes, great forests, and friendly, red-skinned people?"

Father Lull answered somewhat absentmindedly, "Well, the sagas of the Norsemen have always had mystical and fantastical aspects in them, but they often contain seeds of the truth. If you noted during the telling of Leif's two voyages to Vinland, some points were repeated. He found lands west of Greenland, rescued castaways during both trips, and discovered lands with many grape vines growing wild. I would assume that there was likely only one voyage and that those repeated aspects of the story are probably at least partly true."

Admiral Gregory added, "Since we have a map that comes from a completely separate source, the Chinese, I am inclined to agree with the good father. I think it is highly likely that there is at least some truth to the sagas of Leif the Lucky."

CHAPTER TEN

Louis' mind slowly drew out of a fog. He couldn't see or move. He was still lying on his back, but strangely, his skin felt cool and damp. He tried to open his eyes, but he didn't seem to be able to move his eyelids. He was aware that something was lying across his face. He tried to raise his hand to brush across his eyes, but he didn't have enough energy. It felt like his hand weighed too much for his arm muscles to lift. As if the exertion of trying to raise his hand was too much for him, he drifted back to sleep.

When Louis awoke the second time, he still couldn't see, but he was aware that someone was attempting to get him to drink some broth. He suddenly became aware of his hunger. When Louis tried to swallow a mouthful of the broth, it made him cough and vomit. The individual who had tried to feed him turned him on his side and said something in a language he couldn't understand, but the voice sounded feminine. He got the cough under control but soon drifted out of consciousness again.

Louis was still on his back when he awoke the third time, but his head and upper torso were propped up slightly on something soft. He was still blind but felt a little stronger and more aware of himself. He slowly raised his hand to his face, but before he reached it, the same female voice that had spoken to him earlier said something he didn't understand. She grabbed his hand and firmly moved it back to his side. Then she called out in a louder voice. After a few minutes, Louis heard a rustling and felt a warm blast of air. Then a man's voice said in passable French. "Ahh, I see Adonai has seen fit to keep you alive a little longer, my friend."

Louis tried to speak, but he could only make a grating sound, which caused him to cough again. The cough hurt like someone scraping his throat with a dull blade.

"Don't try to speak, my friend. My wife has been taking care of you, but you still need rest, and your body requires more water and food. Your eyes have been swollen shut, and the skin you left exposed to the sun has been burned. My wife has applied a poultice that will help, and wrapped a bandage around your eyes. We must leave the bandages in place if you hope to regain your sight. My wife does not speak your tongue, so if I am not present, you will need to be guided by more tactile instructions from her. My name is Dudel, and my wife is Adi.

"Let me tell you of the miracle of how Adonai saved you with a little help from Dudel and Adi Askenazic. A donkey wandered into our camp three days ago while we were preparing our evening meal. The poor creature was half-crazed from thirst. Adi is very good with animals, and she was able to calm the animal and get it to slowly drink water while I removed its pack. I beg your pardon, but I looked through the items out of curiosity. When I discovered a surcoat from a Templar among them, I surmised these items must belong to a Latin. It was good that Adonai guided me to do this search of your belongings because, after finding the surcoat, I determined to follow the trail of your beast of burden. Retracing the animal's path was easy since there was no wind, and the donkey's trail was still visible in the sand.

"I found you just after sunset. You were no more than 2000 paces from our camp. I am not strong enough to carry a man of your size, even with the help of my honorable wife. You were in no shape to help, so I prayed and received no answer. I was not surprised by this; we often need to work out many puzzles for ourselves, and although we must seek guidance in all things, sometimes we must use our brains. I thought I could build a sled and have my pack animals drag you to our camp, but I am not a craftsman, and it would likely take me most of the night to build a sled, even if I had the required materials. Suddenly, I slapped myself on the head and said aloud, "Dudel, you idiot. If you cannot bring the big man to your camp, move your camp to the man." This may sound like a lot of work, but my estimable wife and I are very practiced. Breaking down and setting up the camp is a routine chore we do almost daily when traveling. So, I prayed Adonai would keep you safe as I went and got my wife. I sent her to you while I moved our camp.

"I thought we would have great difficulty getting your donkey to accompany us, but the creature had already grown attached to my wife. He followed her willingly as she slowly coaxed him with water and food. So, we have re-established our camp here. Now we will wait until you can travel. I think that is enough talk for today, my friend. You should rest now. Perhaps when you awaken next, we can remove the bandages over your eyes, and we will be able to speak some more."

They did not remove the bandages the next time Louis woke or the time after that, but they did speak some more. To be more accurate, Dudel talked; Louis mostly listened, although his throat was getting better, it still hurt to speak. On the third time Louis woke, he told Dudel he wished to remove the bandages from his eyes. Dudel communicated this to his wife, and from the sounds of things, Adi was not in agreement. After some heated words, she must have agreed because Dudel told Louis, "Adi said she will remove them if you insist."

Louis nodded in the affirmative and lifted his hands to the bandages to remove them, only to have Adi strike his hand with what felt like a stick. Dudel said, "Adi will remove the bandages."

After the bandages were removed, he cautiously opened his eyes. As his eyes adjusted to the light, he could only see indistinct blobs. At first, Louis thought his sight must be permanently damaged, but soon objects came slowly into focus. He could see that he was in a tent, and there appeared to be two children with him. There was a woven floor covering and a few clay vessels, but he saw no other people except the two children.

Louis asked in a cracked, hoarse voice, "Where is Dudel?"

One of the children responded in a concerned voice, "Can you not see me? I am standing right here?"

Louis' eyes began to focus better, and as he looked closer, he could now see that the children were not children at all. The boy was a man, and he had a long beard. The woman was clearly no young girl. Yet, there was something out of place; Louis couldn't grasp it at first. As the truth dawned on him, Louis said in his rough voice, "I'm sorry. I just thought..." and trailed off.

Dudel laughed and said, "I know what is troubling you. I guess you haven't seen many dwarfs previously. Adi and I come from a long line of little people. My father, Rabbi Askenazic, is even shorter than I am."

CHAPTER ELEVEN

When the group arrived back at the camp, they were greeted with the news that Sir Jules and his men had been found. Admiral Gregory, Sir William, Cinead, Mary, Derrick, and Father Lull immediately went to the meeting hall. In the hall, three men were waiting for them: Sir Justin de Lile and Sir Gabriel du Capet, both knights Templar, and Claude, a local who acted as the group's guide and tracker. Sir Justin had been put in command of one of the parties searching for Sir Jules.

Sir Justin was fast becoming one of Admiral Gregory's most dependable men. He was quiet and unassuming but easily took command when put in charge of other men. The men under his leadership always followed his lead instinctively, without complaining. The Admiral found that if he assigned Sir Justin a task, it was completed correctly, on time, and with no complaints from him or the men under his authority. Sir Justin had also shown himself to be an accomplished hunter, rivaling Derrick's skills at tracking and stalking. The Admiral had decided some time ago that he liked the young knight's self-effacing manner and planned to advance him into more commanding situations. Admiral Gregory asked as soon as he entered the hall, "What did you men discover?"

Sir Justin said, "Governor-General, we discovered Sir Jules and the renegades about thirty miles East. They appear to have taken up residence in a village. The village has about 150 to 200 locals living in it. Sir Jules and a few of the other knights appear to have homes that they are living in, but most of the group is sleeping in the meeting hall. They are building more dwellings that I assume are for the men sleeping in the meeting hall. So, from what we observed, they plan to stay there for some time."

Sir William said, "Are you sure they are not just passing through the village? I find it hard to believe that those men could so easily become part of a community in such a short time. They only left here nine days ago. Sir Jules may be very knowledgeable, but he is not easy to get along with. Most of the men Sir Jules took with him are not much better, and some are far worse. He has made little effort to get to know the locals around here and often referred to them as backward and country bumpkins. I'm not sure how he would ingratiate himself with these Norwegians so that they would allow him to move into their village."

Mary said, "Perhaps they had pre-arranged things with the villagers."

William said, "Even so, I can't see that particular group of men making themselves welcome."

Cinead said, "You forget they have quite a bit of gold. Gold is the quickest way to make friends anywhere in the world. A man will let a scoundrel marry his daughter for enough gold."

Admiral Gregory asked Sir Justin, "How certain are you that Sir Jules and his men will remain in the village?"

Sir Justin replied, "We watched them for two days, and I sent Claude into the village for a closer look. By all indications, they are planning on staying for a while. More telling is that in addition to building homes, Sir Jules has his men improving the village's defenses. However, they don't have much in the way of fixed fortifications, even with the improvements. From what I observed, I don't believe they will be going anywhere soon. I left three knights and all five archers to keep an eye on things, then we rode back to report what we found."

Admiral Gregory nodded to himself as if he were mulling things over, then he said, "Alright. Sir Justin, I want you to select thirty knights and well-trained squires. Sir William, I want you to see that each man has enough provisions for two weeks. Derrick, I want you to select twenty archers. Ensure they have extra strings and that their arrows are covered to remain dry if it rains. I want everyone on horseback and ready to depart by first light the day after tomorrow."

Sir William asked, "Are you planning on attacking the village? What about all the villagers? There are women and children there."

Admiral Gregory said, "I hope that won't be necessary. Once we arrive, I will ask for Sir Jules and his men to surrender to us."

Cinead snorted and said, "Little chance of that glaikit surrendering. He's a wee toady and not man enough to do the right thing."

Admiral Gregory looked at Cinead and said, "I don't know what a 'glaikit' is, but I assume from how you used it that I would accept your assessment of the man. I agree he is very unlikely to surrender; he knows he has little chance in a trial, but I must make the offer. I will ask the villagers to turn the men over if they refuse to surrender. If the villagers cannot or will not surrender the renegade Templars, I will request that the villagers be allowed to leave the village. I hope we can bring Sir Jules and his men to justice without harming the villagers. I will do whatever I can to keep the locals out of it, but my hands may be tied if they choose to harbor and defend these men."

Mary asked, "Maybe David would agree to go with you. As Jarl of his village, maybe he could speak to the Jarl there and help."

Admiral Gregory said, "That's not a bad idea. I'll ride to his village in the morning and ask him to accompany us. Now, Sir Justin, tell me about these insignificant defenses."

As Admiral Gregory, Sir William, and Sir Justin discussed the village's layout and defenses, the rest of them left the meeting hall. Mary was walking close to Derrick, a bit apart from the rest of the group. She said, "It sounds as though you will be going off with Admiral Gregory and the others to confront Sir Jules."

Derrick said, "Yes."

Mary said, "You will be safe, won't you? I wouldn't want anything to happen to you."

Derrick said, "I'm sure I will be fine. Uhm, I also wish you to be careful while I'm gone."

Mary said, "I doubt I'll be in much danger. I'll probably spend most of my time with Julie at David's village."

Derrick reached his hand out and took hold of Mary's. Then he stopped walking and pulled her to a halt. She turned to face him as he said, "Do you think we should get married?"

Mary's face turned a little red as she said with a touch of heat in her voice, "Should we get married?! Like it's some duty we need to attend to?"

Derrick, who was already close to panicking, tried to give a response, but nothing seemed to come to mind. His thoughts seemed like they were swimming in a sea of thick mud.

Mary looked at him, waiting for a reply, but she could tell his brain had disconnected from his mouth. She was still angry as she said, "Was that supposed to be an expression of what you want to do, or are you just thinking you should marry me, so you'll know I won't run off with some other guy while you are away?"

45

Again, Derrick didn't know how to reply. He knew he loved Mary and wanted to be with her, but he didn't know how to say it. So, as his mind spun with thoughts, he could only look at Mary. Mary's eyes filled with tears as she gazed back at Derrick, frustrated by his lack of response. She started to turn and walk away from him, but he still held her hand and refused to release it.

He pulled her closer, then embraced her closely and kissed her passionately. Mary's tears fell as she resisted his arms and lips at first, but then she melted against him and returned the kiss. As the kiss ended, Derrick finally found some words. He said, "Mary, I love you and wish to be your husband if you will have me."

Mary looked into Derrick's eyes and said, "Yes, I will marry you."

CHAPTER TWELVE

Father Thomas met with Cardinal Soprano in the Templar church, which was finally under construction. Father Thomas was becoming increasingly concerned about the attention the displaced Templars were attracting. He had discussed this with the Cardinal on several occasions, and the Cardinal always downplayed his concern by pointing out how far Lucerne was from any direct contact with Paris. The last time had been when Sir Garrard had taken a group of knights and sergeants to help the local Seneschal scout out the mountains to the north.

The scouting party encountered a band of approximately forty Austrian soldiers. The Austrians attacked the scouting party from Lucerne without warning. The squad of Austrian soldiers was in line abreast when they ambushed the Templars and the seneschal's men. The Austrians fired arrows at them, which did little damage. Garrard quickly reacted to the attack and led the Templar contingent directly at the Austrians, killing and wounding several and routing the remainder. This increased the popularity of the Templars in the town of Lucerne, much to the consternation of Father Thomas.

Father Thomas was terribly annoyed when the villagers started warmly greeting not only the soldiers among their group but also the priests and monks. He felt certain that many, if not all, of the locals would soon discover they were Templars. Thomas wanted to scream at Sir Henry regarding this situation. He knew that Sir Henry would not listen and would perhaps strike him, as he did once not long ago. Instead, Father Thomas went to Cardinal Soprano.

They chatted as they walked to the Cardinal's chambers. Once there, Thomas said, "Your Eminence, I fear these Templars will get us all arrested or killed. They don't seem to understand the precariousness of the situation. If one merchant mentions to another that Templars are hiding out in Lucerne, and King Philip's men hear this, we are lost. The whole reason we came to this out-of-the-way backwater was to be anonymous. After Garrard's stunt, every villager is aware of our presence. Soon, someone will discover that we are not just a bunch of monks sent here to establish a monastery."

Cardinal Soprano sat silently and let Father Thomas finish. Then he said, "My dear Father, most of the villagers were aware of our presence within days of our arrival. Although I agree that Sir Garrard's actions, and those of his companions, have shed a little brighter light on us, that is not all bad. Having the locals accept us as part of their community is a good thing. I agree that it would be a bad idea for us to announce ourselves to King Philip publicly. Yet, I do not think the King's men would find it beneficial to come to Lucerne and arrest us.

"The King has already achieved what he was after in accusing the Knights Templar of those atrocious crimes. King Philip has taken all the properties and assets of the Templars that he found in France. He refuses to hand those properties and other possessions over to the Holy See. Pope Clement V is attempting to force King Philip to relinquish all that was confiscated from the Templars. Yet, I seriously doubt King Philip will obey. He seems to believe he is above the Pope, even in matters of the Church. So, as it stands, the King now owns all the Templar assets that his men have been able to discover. At this point, the Templars themselves are just an annoyance that the Crown must deal with.

"If King Philip should hear there is a group of Templars hiding in the mountains of the Swiss Confederacy, why would he care? The Crown would have to expend a great deal of effort and expense in an attempt to arrest them, and what would he gain? No, my dear Father, I think we are safe from King Philip here, especially if the locals support our presence."

Father Thomas could not believe what he was hearing. Did the Cardinal not know how petty and devious King Philip IV was? Thomas was certain the King would do anything to capture any Templars he heard about, particularly if the King were to hear that some of those Templars had been a part of the ten knights that publicly humiliated the King when they confronted him at his own fortress. Those knights had momentarily roused the citizens of Paris in support of the Templars against the Crown. Thomas also believed the king would not be happy to hear that Father Thomas, whom the Crown had sent to the Pope, was with these outlaws.

Father Thomas was feeling afraid. He feared that he would end up a prisoner of King Philip IV. He feared that everyone would discover that he had murdered Odo. He feared Cardinal Soprano would realize Father Thomas was not the man he supposed. The fear burned inside him, being fed by the feeling that no one seemed to be listening to him. He believed he was the only one who saw the situation clearly. All this worry and frustration boiled inside him and turned into anger. Father

Thomas knew that if he showed his anger or fear, it would be counterproductive to protecting himself. Therefore, Father Thomas said to Cardinal Soprano, "I am sure you are right, your Eminence. I worry too much, but I would hate to see all we have established here destroyed."

Cardinal Soprano said, "You are right that we do not need to announce the fact that these men are Templars. I will talk to Sir Henry about your concerns, but I still wouldn't be too worried. I am sure we are quite safe here from any of the maneuverings of King Philip IV."

Thomas said, "Thank you for listening to me, Your Eminence." Then he left Cardinal Soprano. As Sir Thomas returned to his room, his anger and fears grew. The swirling mass of vial juices in his gut and mind festered and rotted. As he walked, he became more convinced that he was the only one who recognized their danger. He had to do something to protect himself from the foolishness of these men. They clearly didn't understand King Philip the way Thomas did. Thomas was certain the King would want these Templars arrested at any cost.

Thomas decided that since the others were blind to his concerns, he must do whatever was needed to protect himself. Thomas began to plot. He wondered what the King would do if Thomas could show that Pope Clement V was actively assisting these outlaw Templars? Wouldn't the King reward a man who helped him bring a Pope and several Cardinals to justice? If one only cared to look, it was obvious that the Pope and the College of Cardinals were in league with these evil Templars. Templars who had sold their souls to the devil and cost Christendom the Holy Land. Would Thomas be rewarded with a Bishopric or possibly more?

A slow smile moved across Thomas's face. A smile that would have appeared as a grimace if anyone had been around to see it. Thomas felt a comforting resolve rise within him as he determined what must be done to protect himself. No more trying unsuccessfully to follow the false ideals of Cardinal Soprano. He would do what needed to be done, and just maybe, he would receive a reward from the King. He had to figure out how to get word to King Philip IV without anyone knowing.

CHAPTER THIRTEEN

The Church in Rennes-le-Chateau was still without a priest after Father Lull departed. Even without a priest, the Church was still used by the community. Every Sunday and Wednesday, the faithful congregated in the church to pray. The seven sisters came to clean and talk every Monday, Thursday, and Saturday evening. Some spent more time talking than cleaning, but the others made up for them without too much grumbling or dirty looks.

It was during these cleaning sessions that they discussed what Father Lull had charged them with just before he left Rennes-le-Chateau. Once the vault under the church had been cleared out and loaded onto the Templar's ships, Father Lull gathered the seven sisters together. He had them meet him in the church to share the secret of the underground chamber and its hidden passageway with the sisters.

Father Lull showed them the release by the altar. When he silently swung the heavy pillar on its concealed pivot points, there were appreciative "oohs" of wonder. As they looked down at the ladder leading into the chamber's darkness, several of the sisters grew less excited. Father Lull proceeded the sisters down the ladder. Upon reaching the bottom, he lit a torch that showed the end of the ladder and the landing where he stood. The ladies agreed to climb down once they saw that the ladder only descended six or seven feet. There was one brief issue as Michelle encountered a spider on the third rung and quickly climbed back up. It took some coaxing to convince her to attempt to climb down a second time.

Eventually, they all made it down and were crowded on the landing with Father Lull. As their eyes adjusted, they saw a large cavern filled with mostly empty shelving units and trunks. Things were in disarray, as if someone had hastily ransacked the room. They could see a few scattered coins, scrolls, pieces of parchment, broken bags, and wooden boxes, among other refuse.

Father Lull told them that although the coins and other valuables that remained in the cavern were technically the property of the Knights Templar, he felt they would not mind the Church taking possession of the few items that were left. "Besides," Father Lull said, "I don't believe they will be returning this way. You can consider whatever was overlooked during the hurried packing as rent for the space the Templars used."

The morning after Father Lull had left aboard one of the Templar ships, the seven sisters met in the Cavern. They began to straighten, collect, and then catalog all the leavings. Patricia, Sueann, Michelle, and Judith were tasked with searching for everything of value. Francis and Elaine did all the sorting. Margarette was responsible for logging all the items once they were gathered and sorted.

When they completed their respective duties, the coins they had discovered amounted to a King's ransom. They found several small bags of gold and silver coins that appeared to have been completely overlooked as the cavern's wealth was removed. The neatly organized valuables filled two of the shelving units in the cavern. There was another shelving unit filled with parchments, a couple of handwritten and bound logbooks, and other objects of unknown use or value.

As the seven looked at all they had gathered, Margarette said, "Well, we could turn our little Church into a Cathedral if we wish."

Patricia added, "And have enough left over to care for every widow and orphan between here and Paris."

Michelle said, "We could build a beautiful garden with an outdoor Stations of the Cross, which will attract pilgrims."

Elaine looked at Michelle and asked, "What is a 'Stations of the Cross'?"

Michelle said, "Father Lull told me about it. He said that when pilgrims would visit the Holy Land, they would often walk the places from where Pontius Pilate condemned Christ to the tomb where He was buried. Along the way, they placed devotional areas where significant events of Christ's path to the cross and burial were. Recently, some holy men have erected garden paths where they place statues or other remembrances that depict the various stations. Some returning pilgrims, after visiting these stations of the cross, have recreated them here in France with a garden pathway and statues depicting each station."

Judith said, "I agree we need to use this money to further God's Kingdom, but we need to think about it and spend it where it will do the most good."

Frances said, "I don't think Father Lull wanted us to make the secret of this chamber public knowledge. So how do we decide where the money is spent if it is to remain a secret? We can't ask the entire church. Should we consult our husbands?"

There was a unanimous cry of "NO!"

Sueann said, "I don't think we would get very good advice from our husbands. Although they might be Godly men, I'm afraid of what they might choose to do. I can hear it now, 'Most of the apostles were fishermen. We should honor them by purchasing a boat or three."

They all laughed. Then Pat said, "Father Lull chose us for a reason. I believe the seven of us should decide how the money is used. And once a new priest arrives, we wait and see what he is like and then decide if we tell him."

Frances said, "The priest will have to know. How else will we have access to the chamber?"

Elaine replied, "That's no problem. We can easily distract any man with food long enough for one or two of us to access the chamber."

Judith said, "Besides, we won't need to be in here very often. We all need to keep this a secret. As I see it, this money should last for generations. We could decide which of our daughters to tell to keep the secret safe. It would be easy to ensure one or more of our daughters are always kept on to clean the church so they can be in here, alone, without suspicion."

Michelle said, "So, it's 'no' to a Stations of the Cross?"

Frances said, "Not, 'no,' but wait, and we will see."

Sueann said, "I think it would be a mistake to spend the money freely when there is no explanation of where it came from. We will have to be careful."

Margarette asked, "It seems sacrilege just to leave all these blessings from God buried underground I believe there is a parable about that. What if we used just a little of the money to do some landscaping around the church? If we do the work ourselves, no one will suspect anything. And we could buy a fountain or maybe a small statue that could later be used as a marker for a Stations of the Cross." As she said this part, she winked at Michelle. "If anyone asks, we can just say Father Lull left us a little money when he departed with instructions to buy it."

Michelle and Patricia both grinned, nodding their heads in agreement. The other sisters looked at each other and shrugged.

Sueann said, "Okay, but let's not make this a habit. We should be careful. Now let's get out of here. I need to get started on dinner."

As they were leaving, Patricia leaned close to Margarette and said, "I knew you'd figure a way to talk them into something." They both laughed quietly as they climbed the ladder.

Judith said to the group as they slid the pillar over the hole, "If we need to keep going down there, we need to build regular steps and get rid of that ladder."

CHAPTER FOURTEEN

Mary and Derrick decided not to tell anyone about their impending nuptials until after Derrick returned from the expedition to retrieve Sir Jules and his men. Everyone was too busy, and tensions ran too high for them to feel it was a good time to share the news. Derrick found himself occupied getting the archer's supplies prepared to go. He wanted to personally inspect the oilskins that covered the bundles of arrows so the fletching would stay dry in the wet climate. He also ensured each archer had five extra bowstrings.

Mary accompanied Admiral Gregory to David's village and decided to stay with Julie while Derrick was on the expedition. David agreed to accompany the Templars to the village where the renegade Templars were holed up and see if he could aid in the negotiations.

Admiral Gregory asked David, "Do you know anything about the jarl of the village we are heading to?"

David said, "Not much. Even though they are not too far away, they mostly stay away from Bergen and consider us an extension of the city. They prefer to do most of their trading with other villages in the interior. There has been no animosity from them, but also very little contact. I don't even know who the jarl is or how long he has been their leader.

Every man was ready to go on the designated morning, and they headed out at first light. If the weather held, the journey would take less than two full days of riding. The trip was uneventful until the second day, when they were a few hours from the village. As they crested a hill, they spotted two men on horseback riding toward them. These men turned out to be two of the archers Sir Justin had left to watch the village. The two were glad to see the Templar company and immediately began to report to Admiral Gregory.

The first archer said, "You need to come quickly. Something must have gone wrong. Shortly after Sir Justin left to bring news to you about Sir Jules and his men, we noticed a lot of activity in the village. Later, many of the Norwegian men in the village departed on horseback. That evening, just after sunset, there were yells and screams from the village, but we could not see what was happening in the dark. The following day, it looked as though Jules and his men had seized control of the village, but we could not get close as they sent out patrols of men. The patrols were comprised of the former Templars and were in groups of only three or four. We considered capturing one of the groups, but knew that your orders were just to observe. The patrols rode a perimeter about half a mile from the village, so we saw little inside the village that day. Then, last night, there was a large fire in the village. We had assumed that one of the homes had accidentally caught fire. There were no patrols this morning, so we moved closer to the village. We discovered that several of the renegade Templars were being held as prisoners by the villagers. We counted eight of them tied to stakes in a clearing inside the village wall. We saw no other Templars. The meeting hall is the only building that had burned, and we believe the Templars who slept there were killed in the fire."

Upon hearing this report, Admiral Gregory assigned five archers and three knights to remain with the baggage and follow the rest of the column at their best speed. Then he and the rest of the men galloped off toward the village. They arrived in the early afternoon and rode within bowshot range from the wooden palisade surrounding the village. The wall was only about four feet high, but it still created a barrier Admiral Gregory chose to respect.

The Admiral rode a little forward of the line with Sir William on his right and David on his left. Admiral Gregory called out in French, "My name is Governor Gregory, and I command a village about thirty miles west of you. Some of my men stole from me and fled this way. I am told that they have sought refuge here in your village."

There was no response. David then called out in Norwegian, repeating what Admiral Gregory had said. He added that he was the jarl of another Norwegian village who had agreed to accompany the Templars to help resolve the situation without bloodshed.

After a few minutes, a man stepped forward. They could see his head and shoulders over the top of the palisade, and he called back to them in Norwegian, "I am Jarl Ebbe. We took these men in because they told us that they had been the rightful leaders of their village but that another man had misled the people there and stolen their birthright. They wished to stay with us long enough to gather enough warriors to reclaim what was rightfully theirs. They told us they would pay us in gold and help strengthen our village defenses. But these men lied."

Jarl Ebbe continued, "A few days ago, their leader, Jules, asked if I would go to a nearby village to inquire if they wished to join us in helping his men reclaim their village. I agreed and took twenty of my warriors with me. While we were away, the men under Jules' command killed several of my remaining warriors and took control of our village. Then they began taking liberties with our women. One of the boys from our village ran off and made his way to us while we were at the other village. He told us what was happening, so my men and I left immediately. We arrived just after nightfall and quietly entered our village. At first, we thought the boy was mistaken, but then we looked into the meeting hall. We found most of Jules' men drunk and passed out in there. A few of our women were tied and gagged in the meeting hall with them. We quietly removed our women while the drunken fools slept. The women told us what had been done to them, so I barred the doors and set the building aflame. We discovered that some of Jules' men were not in the meeting hall but were in our homes. We rounded up these remaining few and tied them to stakes. Their leader, Jules, is among those still alive...for the time being."

Admiral Gregory asked, "What do you plan to do with the men you still have alive?"

After David translated, Ebbe said, "Our Priest and I have passed judgment on these men for their crimes, and any that remain alive are to be killed in three days."

Admiral Gregory asked, "May I come in and speak to these men?"

After some discussion with Ebbe's men, Jarl Ebbe said, "You and Jarl David may enter our wall, but only you two."

Admiral Gregory looked at David, who nodded his assent. The two of them dismounted their horses and walked to the gate. Ebbe and a few of his warriors led them to where Jules and his remaining men were tied to stakes. Most of the men had clearly been beaten, and one or two appeared to be dead. As Gregory approached the stakes, some of the men looked up and began to call out to him for help.

Ebbe told David, who translated to Gregory, "We are Christians here in this village. Our priest and I spoke to these men this morning. We confronted them with their sins. They each, to a man, denied any wrongdoing. For us, that places them outside the law, and they forfeit any mercy we may have offered them. For trying to take over my village, I could have ordered them all killed, and their bodies dragged away from the village and left in the open for the animals. But these men are also rapists, so I have allowed the women they defiled to take what revenge they feel is justified. Any man left alive by the morning of the third day will be strangled."

After David translated this to Admiral Gregory, David added, "This is an older practice, but many of the local priests still allow it as it reduces the incidence of rape significantly."

Gregory asked, "What would have happened to these men if they confessed to their crimes?"

Ebbe said, "They would have been shown mercy. We are all sinners and fall short of God's glory. They would have been allowed to confess to our priest and be forgiven. Then they would have had a quick and merciful execution by having a seax driven into their heart. After that, we would have buried them in our Church cemetery."

David translated, and Gregory asked, "What if they confess now?"

David didn't even ask Ebbe. He replied, "In a case like this, they must confess immediately, or they become 'outlaw,' and we no longer grant any option of mercy."

Admiral Gregory asked if he could approach the men a speak to them. Ebbe gave his permission.

Admiral Gregory approached Jules, who had been severely beaten, his pants pulled down, and he was bleeding from his groin. As Gregory drew closer, he saw that Jules's penis had been cut off and was lying in the dirt beneath him.

In a weak and unsteady voice, Sir Jules said, "Please, Admiral Gregory, rescue me from these filthy heathens. Their women taunted us, and my men were deceived. I don't deny that some of my men gave in to the wiles of Satan, but I did nothing wrong. Some of my men may deserve punishment, but I did nothing, I swear to you."

Admiral Gregory said, "Jarl Ebbe told me that all of you are guilty of rape and of trying to take over his village."

Jules nearly hissed out, "I raped no one. These women here are not true Christians. They entice men by showing glimpses of their breasts and wicked looks designed to ensnare a righteous man. As for attempting to take leadership here, I was trying to uproot the evil among them by establishing proper Christian leadership."

Admiral Gregory said, "I see. What of your men here?"

Jules said, "These women are nearer to beasts than humans; my men may be accused of lying with animals, but not women. They may be guilty, I can't say, I wasn't with them. I only know that I am innocent. You must get me released before that bitch comes back. Do you see what she has done to me? She is cooking my balls as we speak and told me she will return to make me eat them. You must help me."

Admiral Gregory said, "I will consider what you have told me." Then he went to each conscious man tied to the stakes. He asked each man if they wished to confess. They all denied doing anything wrong. Many gave excuses that the women lured them into having sex with them. Some claimed to have no idea why the villagers were doing this to them. Gregory had questioned enough men in his time to know these men were guilty of the crimes the villagers accused them of. They had broken the laws of God and humanity, yet they didn't feel the slightest bit of guilt.

Admiral Gregory returned to Jules and said, "I will speak to Jarl Ebbe and hear what he has to say."

As Admiral Gregory started to turn away, Jules said, "He will lie. You must force them to release me. They can keep the rest of these men; I am certain many are guilty, but I did nothing. You must get me out of this evil place. We are brother Templars; you must save me from them."

Admiral Gregory approached Jarl Ebbe and asked, "Jules and the others claim they did nothing. Jules admitted that some of his men may have committed the crimes you accuse them of, but he says he is innocent."

Ebbe replied in a voice filled with rage, "I, myself, found Jules in the act of violating my daughter. He had already raped my wife. All these men were found in the homes of the women they had raped and, in two cases, murdered. The only reason I did not kill Jules when I found him was that our priest was with me, and he stayed my hand. The priest convinced me to give Sir Jules and these others a chance to confess their sins and be reconciled with God before we execute them."

Admiral Gregory said, "I am sorry for what these men have done to you and your villagers, Jarl Ebbe. I do not like to see these men who had once been under my command treated this way. Yet, I understand your right to justice for what they have done. I would like to have one last word with these men, and then I will depart."

Admiral Gregory then turned back to the men tied to the stakes and said loudly so they could hear, "You men have been found guilty of heinous crimes. Crimes against these people, the God you claim to serve, and against the vows you took as Templars. Given the abundant evidence suggesting your guilt, I will not attempt to release you from the punishment they have laid out for you. I implore you all to confess your crimes to God, and perhaps He will forgive you and accept you into His Kingdom."

As Gregory turned away, he heard Jules' voice above the others' cries and pleas for mercy. Jules called out, "Go ahead and leave, you coward. You could easily overrun this village and save your brother Templars, but why would I expect low-born scum like you to do what is honorable and right? I call down God's Judgement on you. I pray the King of France captures you and that the Holy Inquisition gets its hands on you. They will make what we endure seem like a holiday."

Admiral Gregory did not look back as he returned to Jarl Ebbe and David. David asked Gregory as he approached, "Jarl Ebbe said they have found some of the gold Jules and his men had, but they think most of it was in the meeting hall, and it will take some time to find it. He said he will return all of it to you except for the amount needed to rebuild their meeting hall."

Just then, two women walked past Admiral Gregory. One was perhaps twelve; she had clearly been beaten, as her arms and face showed bruises. The girl's eyes were red and puffy from crying. The clothing she wore was dirty and torn in places so that it barely covered her. The other woman was older, perhaps forty; she was also bruised and had dried blood on her face and clothes. The younger girl clung to the older one. They both walked toward the Templars tied to the stakes. The older woman carried a bowl of what looked like broth with two globs of meat. Gregory noticed Jarl Ebbe's eyes follow the two women and saw the pain and anger on Ebbe's face.

Admiral Gregory told David, "Tell Jarl Ebbe that he is to keep all the gold these evil men brought into their peaceful village. Tell him that I would appreciate it if he would give some to the priest for the local church and that, if it is fitting, some be given to each of the mistreated women."

CHAPTER FIFTEEN

Louis spent a couple more days recovering his strength and rehydrating. He spent his evenings talking with Dudel about everything from desert traveling to the nature of God. Louis had never met a man so knowledgeable, except for maybe Father Lull. Dudel seemed to know a great deal about many places and people. He explained that his father had been very strict about Dudel's education. His father had required him to learn about other cultures and to determine the truth of things by looking at them from many angles.

At one point, their conversation centered around Jerusalem and the Holy Land. Louis had assumed Dudel would want the European countries to drive out the Muslim armies, but he seemed to think that would be a bad idea. Louis asked, "Don't you believe there would be more peace and safety if the Crusading armies of the Latin countries controlled the Holy Land?"

Dudel looked at the ground and shook his head, "The Latin kings have shown that they only seem to want to come here to kill and pillage and then return to their homes. They leave only a token force that cannot hope to hold the lands they occupy. Over the last three hundred years, they have shown that they cannot rule together. They fight with each other more than against those they had come to our lands to make war with."

Louis said, "What if one of the military Orders ruled here, like the Templars or Hospitallers? They could maintain the peace and keep the Mamluks and other Muslim groups out of Jerusalem and the other cities in the Holy Land."

Dudel replied, "You don't understand how things work here in our part of the world. We need to trade with the Muslims. And most followers of Muhammad are tolerant of us Jews and you Christians. They have even established synagogues for us to worship in. They allow us to trade freely, and, most importantly, their laws protect us almost as equally as any Muslim. The Mamluks allow you, Latins, to conduct your services in many of your churches. There is far more peace and stability now than when the Latin armies ruled."

Louis was surprised by this. He had always been under the impression that the Muslims were wild, crazy men who killed anyone they saw as an infidel. Louis had heard stories of how some Templars had developed respect and even a working relationship with some Muslims. But he assumed that was a rare occurrence. Louis asked, "If not the Latins, then don't you think you Jews should rule Jerusalem?"

Dudel laughed, "We could not rule there. No one would allow that, not at this time. Perhaps, if some of the Rabbis are correct, Jehovah Rapha will return us to govern Jerusalem. I doubt I will live to see that, nor my children or their children. No, in my humble opinion, only God should rule there. We would need a type of administrator to oversee public works. I guess they would then be considered rulers, and they would need some force to support their decisions. You see, it would be very complicated. For this to work, you need a strong yet fair ruler. But as history has repeatedly shown, if you give a man power, he eventually abuses it. Ah, but what if we countered that power with something like the Roman senate? That might work, but...."

At this point in the conversation, Louis knew he would not be able to interject anything. Dudel had done this several times over the last few days. He seemed to enjoy debating a topic with himself. He could continue for some time and usually seemed to forget Louis was even present. Dudel often left the tent while still arguing with himself. Louis smiled at the thought that Dudel did exactly the same thing that Sir William used to complain about him doing.

Three days after the bandages were removed from Louis' eyes, they decided it was time to start traveling again. Louis had seen camels since his arrival in Constantinople, but he never imagined he'd ride one. As Dudel instructed him about riding the beast, Louis interrupted and asked, "Are you sure I couldn't just ride my donkey or even walk?"

Dudel smiled and said, "That would never do. You would not be able to keep up that way. Trust me, my friend, you will learn to appreciate the camel after a day or two. They can travel long distances in the desert, where water is scarce. They are also quite comfortable, and the swaying motion will become quite relaxing as you grow used to it."

With some disbelief in his tone, Louis said, "If you say so. They just look awkward, slow, and stupid."

Dudel laughed, saying, "People have said that about dwarfs too, even about me. Yet, I am quite indispensable to those who do business with me. You will see these camels are far better than riding a horse when in the desert. When one rides a camel, even those of us of small stature will tower above a man on horseback."

They broke camp just before sunup and packed everything onto the camels Dudel used as pack animals. Next, they had to saddle the camels they would ride. Louis spent the first hour trying to force the camel to obey his commands. Louis continued to attempt to control the animal in the same way he would direct a horse. At one point, the camel, who seemed to have had enough of Louis, began to trot off in a different direction from the small caravan. Dudel, with Adi seated behind him on their camel, chased after Louis. When Dudel and his wife finally caught up to him, Louis was pulling the reins hard to one side, making the animal walk in a tight circle. They could hear Louis yelling at the camel, "As soon as I can climb off you, I am going to cook you and find out how a camel roasted over an open fire tastes."

Dudel helped get the camel under control and said, "You must not yell at the animal as you did. Remain calm and guide him, don't always try to force the camel to do what you want as you might a horse. Also, do not tell the camel you will eat him; it will upset the animal. Besides, it is forbidden to eat camels. As the Torah says: 'The camel, though it chews the cud, does not have a split hoof; it is unclean for you.'"

Soon, Louis learned to gently direct the camel using the small stick and the reins. By the second day, Louis crossed his legs over the front of the saddle and rested them on the camel's neck, just as he saw Dudel do. Louis had to admit that Dudel had been correct; the camel was very comfortable to ride once he got used to it. It became hard to remain awake at times as the rhythmic swaying of the camel lulled him toward sleep.

They reached Angora after three days of travel. As they approached the city, they started to notice small groups and caravans heading in the same direction. Dudel told Louis, "This city is somewhat complicated regarding who rules here. Technically, this region is under Mongol rule, but they have allowed the Seljuks to govern. But the city of Angora is ruled by a semi-independent federation of craftsmen and merchants known as the Ahi. The Ahi rule at the forbearance of both the Mongols and the Seljuks. Generally, the Ahi run the city with very little interference."

Louis asked, "Are there many Mongols in the city? Is there someone of rank among the Mongols I might speak to?"

Dudel asked, "Why do you want to speak to the Mongols?"

Louis hesitated only momentarily, then said, "Going to Jerusalem to entomb my comrade's surcoat is only the beginning of my mission. My lord, the King of Scotland, sent me here to attempt contact with an individual known as Prester John. Prester John is rumored to live in the Far East. I believe the Mongols control the lands where I am planning to travel. Some believe Prester John is the leader of a large clan of Christian Mongols."

Dudel stopped his camel, so Louis had to stop and then turn his camel around. Dudel said angrily, "Your information is foolishness, and your mission is completely impossible. This Latin idea of Prester John is a fantasy, like the Golem among Jews. There is no massive army of Christians to help you take the Holy Land. Many of the Khans have been very tolerant of religious beliefs, and some have studied the religions of the lands they have conquered. From my experience, most of the Mongols I have met were followers of the Islamic faith. The Mongols, as a people, control far more of the world than I believe you understand. They are no longer a single group under a single leader. Some lands you are talking about crossing are controlled by hordes that would be antagonistic toward a Christian trying to combine Latin armies with a rival Mongol horde. You should give me your fallen friend's surcoat; I will see that it is buried with honor in Jerusalem. You have plenty of money on your donkey to travel with a caravan back to Constantinople and, from there, take a ship back to your home."

Louis was taken aback by the anger in Dudel's voice. He said, "I am not sure what I said that offended you so much, but I cannot return until my mission is complete."

Dudel, still obviously angry, said, "There is no mission. I have just told you there is no Prester John. If you start asking questions, you will get yourself killed, and if it is known that I brought you to the city, it is possible I will also pay a price for my part. Many armies have fought their wars here: you Latins, Seljuk, Muslims, Fatimids of Egypt, Kurds, Mamluks, the Moors, and the list goes on. You give no thought to us regular people living in this land, trying to make a life in the desert, raise families, seek God in our own way, and have moments of peace to eat, talk, and be happy. We are the ones to pay the price for your wars. Now, I discover you are here to attempt to raise an army of Mongols to attack from the east while you bring an army of Latins from the west. We are the ones caught in the middle. If this land is so sacred, why do you want to spill so much blood on it? Why not make it a land of peace?"

Louis said, "To us Latins, peace seems only possible if we are in control so that we can enforce the peace."

Dudel said, "That is what every army thinks, and it is fonferer! I thought you were smarter than that." Dudel started moving his camel forward as he added, "Please do not approach anyone in Angora. Once we arrive, you should part from our company and find a caravan heading out of the city, I don't care where. From there, it is up to you to decide what path you will take. I would ask that you at least take time to observe the people whose lives your mission will cast into turmoil."

CHAPTER SIXTEEN

The ride back to the Templar village was quiet. They only rode for a few hours before it started getting dark. Admiral Gregory rode up front alone and hadn't spoken to anyone after he and David had returned from the village. Gregory might have ridden through the night had not Cinead ridden up to the Admiral and said, "Admiral, don't you think we should make camp for the night. I don't know about you, but I haven't eaten since breakfast, and I could use a bit of scran about now."

Admiral Gregory seemed to come out of his quiet revelry and said, "Of course. You're correct; we should stop." Then he halted his horse, turned around, and called out, "Sir Justin, let's find a place to make camp for the night and give the men and animals some rest and food."

The men climbed off their mounts, removed the saddles, and brushed the horses down. While the rest cared for the horses, Derrick prepared stew in a large pot hung from a tripod over a fire. After the horses and the men had been fed, Admiral Gregory told the men what had transpired in the village. Most of the men were shocked that Jules and the other Templars could commit such atrocities. A few refused to believe the accusations, thinking the villagers had decided to rob Jules' men and were using that as a story to cover their actions.

David added more evidence against the renegade Templars by telling the men what he saw. David's collaboration and further details convinced more of the men that Jules and his followers had indeed committed the crimes the villagers accused them of. Even among those who believed Jules' men had done what the villagers claimed, some felt Admiral Gregory still should have rescued the men tied to the stakes. Sir Williams overheard one of the men say as much, and he wheeled on the man and said, "Those men were rapists, thieves, and deserters. If we had rescued them, we would have only taken them back to our camp to stand trial and then executed them ourselves."

The knight Sir Williams confronted said, "At least they would have been tried properly. Perhaps they would have sought forgiveness among their own, and we could have buried them on sacred ground."

Admiral Gregory, who had overheard the conversation, said in a commanding voice so that all could hear, "Gentlemen. I am responsible to God for the decision I made. Those men had two chances to confess.

First, when the villagers and their Priest offered an opportunity, and later, when I confronted them. All those alive refused to admit any wrongdoing. Originally, I planned to do whatever it took to get those men who remained alive and retrieve whatever bones survived the fire so we could bury their remains. As I saw the evidence of what these men had done and witnessed the weeping children and the angry and traumatized women, I decided they earned the punishment they bought for themselves. The villagers also deserved the right to exact that punishment.

"If those men had shown any remorse for what they had done, I would have stopped at nothing to take them back. My decision to leave those men has weighed heavily on my heart. I have prayed to God that He would show me I did the correct thing since we left that village. The decision of what to do was mine to make and mine alone. The decision has been made, and that is the end of it."

Although some men still didn't agree with what had happened, for the vast majority, that statement ended the grumbling. The men all made their way to their beds or sentry duty, and the talk ended.

The next day, they broke camp in a cold foggy mist. Sir Justin and Derrick took the lead since the fog made navigating through the forested countryside difficult. There was little conversation as both the events of the day before and the current weather kept everyone's moods dampened. Late in the morning, the fog burned off, and bright sunshine broke through. The warmth and light of the sun lifted the spirits of the men in the column, and the tension of the previous day slowly abated. Late in the day, they could tell they were drawing near to the Templar village.

As they got closer, they saw the village humming with activity. The community was always busy building projects, fishing, farming, and the like, but this looked different. There were many Norwegians present, including several women and children, which was very uncommon. Much of the activity seemed to be focused in and around the church yard. All activity stopped as the column rode into the village, and their gazes all drew toward Derrick. Derrick began to have a bad feeling as everyone seemed to stop talking and glare at him. He felt certain something bad had happened. His mind began to race. Where was Mary? Was she injured, or worse?

As Derrick got off his horse, he saw David's mother, Julie, step out of the church. Upon seeing him, she got a surprised look on her face and quickly ducked back inside the church. Derrick's heart felt like it was in his stomach; he found breathing difficult. He was instantly filled with dread. His only thought was, "Where was Mary?" He had taken about three steps toward the church when Father Lull stepped out of the building and approached Derrick. For a moment longer, Derrick was certain that something awful had befallen Mary. Then he noticed that Father Lull was grinning. Many of the other people around him, both Templars and Norwegians, were also smiling. Father Lull finally reached Derrick, hugged him, and said, "It is about time."

Derrick, still a bit uncertain but starting to feel a little relieved, asked, "What is going on? Where is Mary?"

Julie, who had followed Father Lull out of the church, said, "You will not be seeing Mary until your wedding day, which will be in six days. Mary will be staying here, and you will be spending the days until the wedding in our village."

Cinead, who suddenly appeared behind Derrick, bellowed out, "Wedding?! What have you been keeping from us, lad?" As he slapped Derrick hard on the back.

CHAPTER SEVENTEEN

Father Thomas spent the next two days alone making plans. He decided that getting word directly to King Philip IV would be almost impossible. The King surely would have no idea who Father Thomas was. He wouldn't know about any of the services Thomas had already provided for the Crown. King Philip would have no reason to listen to anything Thomas had to say unless a close intermediary intervened. Perhaps he could get word to Guillaume de Norgaret. Guillaume had been the man who ordered him to spy on the Templars in the first place, and he was a trusted advisor to the King. Father Thomas was certain Guillaume was the person who recommended that the Templars should be arrested in the first place. On the few occasions Guillaume had spoken to Father Thomas about the Templars, Thomas could see the hate for the Order burning behind his eyes.

Thomas knew getting a message into the hands of the king's advisor would also be very difficult. He felt certain that if he sent a written message, it would likely sit on a desk somewhere or be lost and never reach the King's personal advisor. The man was surely busy, and Thomas's message would have to appear as common correspondence. Otherwise, curious eyes might read the letter and betray him to the Templars or the Pope's men. No, he needed to send a message that would raise no suspicion if intercepted. Anything he sent to Guillaume de Norgaret would be seen as suspect. Then Father Thomas thought about Brother Jaye.

Brother Jaye surely retained some contact with Guillaume de Norgaret. De Norgaret and the King entrusted him to bring the signed confessions of the Templars to the Pope. He was also entrusted with the idol of Baphomet, which the Templars were accused of worshipping. The last time he and Brother Jaye had been together, things had not gone well for Brother Jaye. Thomas feared Brother Jaye might have thought Thomas was somewhat to blame for what had happened.

Brother Jaye's presentation to the Pope had not gone as planned. As Thomas replayed the events, he reflected that Brother Jaye could hardly blame Thomas for what had transpired. He had nothing to do with what happened to the skull. Besides, it was Thomas who got the Pope and Cardinals to consider the evidence the King had sent with Brother

Jaye. Thomas had nothing to do with the Pope's decision to retain him at Avignon while sending Brother Jaye away.

Thomas resolved that Brother Jaye was a reasonable man. After all, he was a trained lawyer like himself; surely he would understand that Thomas had done only what had to be done. Brother Jaye would probably welcome him with open arms once he saw the information he was bringing. The location of the Templars hiding in the Swiss Confederacy and the complicit nature of the Pope and His Cardinals in hiding the Templars from King Philip would be of great value to the Inquisition and the King. Brother Jaye must know that this information would surely increase his, and by extension, Thomas's value to the Crown of France.

Now that Father Thomas knew to whom he would send a message, he needed to determine how to deliver it and what to say. The letter must sound harmless to anyone who might see it, yet Brother Jaye would need to be able to discern the true meaning.

As Thomas considered what to write, one of the village boys who was learning to be a squire interrupted him. The young man informed Thomas that he was needed at the church's building site immediately. Father Thomas had no idea why they would request his presence there. The building of the church was the responsibility of Cardinal Soprano, and Father Thomas had not been involved in any way with its design or construction. Father Thomas's duties within the community were limited to accounting for the money the Templars paid out and acquired.

When Thomas arrived at the building site, he found Cardinal Soprano, Sir Henry, Sir Gilbert, and Sir Garrard waiting for him. They all had solemn expressions, and Thomas instantly started to worry that he had let something slip, and they knew he was going to betray them. As soon as that thought crossed his mind, he realized it was foolish. How could they know anything? He had done nothing, only planning, which he did all in his head. He had written nothing and spoken to no one.

He approached the men who stood at the construction site. So far, they had only laid the foundation and started building the wall and support columns. As Thomas reached them, Cardinal Soprano said, "We are all here now. Let me share with you, gentlemen, why I have asked you to gather here with me. I know you are all busy, but this is an important moment. The workers are about to lay the flagstones that will lie beneath the altar. Before we left Avignon, I requested a relic from the Holy Father. Pope Clement V allowed me to retrieve the finger bone of John of Lodi Vecchio, Italy. He was a hermit who later became the Prior of Fonte Avellana. I have decided that we should place the bone under the flagstones beneath the altar. I had the blacksmith make a small reliquary to place the bone in." Cardinal Soprano pulled from beneath his robes a small metal container. He then placed it in a crevice in the stones that made up the subfloor. After setting the reliquary within the gap, he led the men gathered in prayer. Then the workers placed the fitted flagstone over the top.

As the three knights thanked the Cardinal for inviting them and began to leave, Father Thomas attempted to exit quietly, but Cardinal Soprano stopped him. "Father Thomas. Please stay a moment. I would like to speak to you."

Thomas patiently waited. As Sir Henry was leaving the church, he walked past Father Thomas. Henry looked Thomas in the eyes as he came close to the priest; Thomas saw in them the hatred he always witnessed when the two made eye contact. Thomas tried to keep his expression calm and impassive. Inside, he was smiling and thinking about how this arrogant fool would soon be back in the King's dungeons, experiencing the hospitality of the Inquisition.

Cardinal Soprano interrupted Thomas' revelry. "My good Father Thomas. We have not spoken for a couple of days, and I had grown used to our daily discourses."

Even though no questions were specifically asked, Father Thomas knew he was being asked what he'd been doing. Honestly, Father Thomas hadn't thought about the fact that since they had left Avignon, he and Cardinal Soprano had met together to talk at least once a day. It wasn't a scheduled meeting; they would just get together at some point each day and talk. Father Thomas had come to enjoy most of those conversations. During those discussions, Thomas felt he did not need to be on guard constantly. Thomas believed he could be honest with someone for the first time in many years. It had been very liberating and pleasant. Now that Thomas had determined to contact King Philip's men and expose what was happening, he desperately wished to avoid the Cardinal. Thomas knew he could no longer feel at ease talking to the Cardinal, given the scheming he was undertaking.

Father Thomas replied, "I am sorry, Your Eminence. I honestly had gotten so busy with my duties that I hadn't realized I hadn't taken the time to speak with you."

Cardinal Soprano replied, "I don't want you to feel obligated to meet with me if you don't want to. I just thought it was helpful for us to lean on each other spiritually. As the Scriptures say: 'Do not forsake the fellowship of the saints.' Sometimes when we spend too much time with only our own counsel, we convince ourselves of the truth of falsehoods placed in our path by the deceiver. We need to be ever watchful of the wiles of the evil one."

Father Thomas feared momentarily that the Cardinal had somehow divined his thoughts. He said, "Your Eminence is, of course, correct. I just got wrapped up in my duties and failed to give proper allowance for my spiritual nourishment."

Cardinal Soprano gave Thomas an appraising look as if he sensed deception, then said, "Think nothing of it. We all get distracted by what we think is important and sometimes overlook the truly critical aspects of life. Are you free to go for a stroll in town and chat?"

Father Thomas did not want to add to the Cardinal's suspicions. Still, he was so unnerved by the man's uncanny ability to see through him that he did not feel he could talk with him now. Thomas decided he needed time to get in the correct frame of mind before he spoke with the Cardinal. Thomas finally said, "I am sorry, Your Eminence, but I need to complete a time-sensitive task. The banking system the Templars have established is performing much better than they had expected. It appears some of the brothers have made errors in their math, and I need to correct the mistakes. Perhaps we can get together this evening before Vespers?"

Cardinal Soprano happily said, "I look forward to it." Then the Cardinal left the church. Father Thomas watched him go and thought to himself that he would need to be very careful. Perhaps he could devise an excuse to leave Lucerne for a time.

CHAPTER EIGHTEEN

Julie told Derrick, "You should leave now with David and go to our village. Your presence isn't needed here until the day of the wedding." Then she walked back to the church.

As his friends congratulated him, Derrick stood there confused; he and Mary had agreed not to tell anyone until he had returned. Father Lull noticed the look on Derrick's face and said, "Mary is worried you will be upset with her for having told Julie about your proposal. She asked me to tell you that it just slipped out."

Cinead said, "Derrick, my boy, you'll find women can't keep secrets from other women. Once they start blathering together, they get diarrhea of the mouth, and everything just comes out."

Derrick finally said, "Tell Mary it's okay, but why must I leave?"

Father Lull replied, "Once Julie knew about the impending nuptials, she took over. Apparently, it is a Norwegian custom that the groom can't see the bride for several days before the wedding. Julie is insisting that you two must follow this tradition. I'm sure David will be able to tell you more. I need to get back to the church before Julie decides to drape seaweed across the altar or some other nonsense." Then Father Lull walked rather rapidly back to the church.

The next day in David's village, David told Derrick, "As Father Lull said, in Norway, the bride and groom are separated for several days before the ceremony. The bride is kept with only the women in the village, while the groom is sequestered with the other men. Weddings are only held on Fridays, so the wedding will be in five days. Between now and then, we need to do a couple of activities before the wedding."

Derrick asked, "What do these activities entail?"

David replied, "You will find out." Then he laughed and started to leave Derrick alone in the meeting hall, where he was supposed to wait until the other men retrieved him later that evening.

Just as David was exiting the lodge, he said, "One of the women will come by tomorrow and make sure that you have proper, clean clothes for the wedding." Then Derrick was alone.

David returned to the meeting lodge just after sunset and said to Derrick, "It's time. Follow me."

Derrick went outside and found what appeared to be most of the adult men from the village standing around a large bonfire. David stood in the forefront and said, "Derrick, since you wish to be wed to Mary, you have a task you must first complete. You must prove your manhood by retrieving your family sword; in the process, you must die and then be resurrected. As you have no family sword, we forged one for you. This will become your family sword hereafter, and you will give it to your bride at the wedding ceremony if you can retrieve it and return alive and whole. Your sword is in a crypt guarded by a dead man who will not relinquish it to you until you have proven your manhood."

Derrick was certain this was all a big show, but a small voice reminded him that these people, although Christian, did not always do things like French Christians do. These people seemed to retain some of their ancestors' old mystical and more nature-based spiritual practices. He was pretty sure he would not be fighting a dead man, but he wasn't certain.

David took a torch in his left hand, stepped up to Derrick, took hold of Derrick's left arm, and began to lead him out of the village's front gate. All the other men followed, and several of them also carried torches. They walked about a quarter mile into the woods until they came to the mouth of a large cave. David handed Derrick the torch and pointed toward the cave entrance without saying a word. Derrick looked back at all the other men standing quietly behind David. He could see the faces of some of the men in the flickering torchlight. Those he could see all held stern, serious expressions. None appeared to be taking this as a joke.

Derrick decided he had no choice, so he ducked and stepped into the cave. After entering the mouth of the cave, it opened enough for Derrick to stand upright. The cave was quite large inside, and there was the sound of trickling water. His torchlight flickered orange and yellow along the cave walls and ceiling; this still left most of the cave in shadows. It took Derrick a couple of minutes to search the chamber before he noticed what looked like a pile of fur lying on the floor along the back wall of the cavern. He approached it slowly and quietly. It wasn't until he stood almost within an arm's length of the bundle of fur that he could make out that what he thought was a formless pile was a heavy coat worn by a man who appeared dead. In the torchlight, Derrick could see that the man's face was white with black circles around his closed eyes. The man was lying on his back, holding a sword against his torso with both hands gripping the hilt.

Derrick assumed he was supposed to unwrap the dead man's fingers from the hilt and take the sword. Derrick slowly reached down, and as his fingers touched those of the hands gripping the blade, the dead man's eyes suddenly opened, and he quickly rose to his feet. Horrified by the movement, Derrick stepped back several steps and dropped the torch. Luckily, the torch stayed lit. The flickering flame cast an eerie light from the ground, leaving the dead man's face mostly in shadow but making the eyes seem to glow. The dead man was much taller than Derrick. He slowly raised the sword upward as if he were about to swing it down upon Derrick's head. In that instant, Derrick thought of running, but then the sword that the dead man was still raising struck the cave ceiling with a soft clink sound, and the dead man said, "Crap." Then in a loud, theatrical voice, the dead man added, "Gaze upon your destiny as I cleave your thieving head from your shoulders."

Derrick knew that voice. He suddenly realized that the "dead" man was Leif. Derrick's apprehension fled, and he whispered to Leif, "What am I supposed to do? Do I fight you for the sword?"

Leif whispered back, "No. Just say something about not being a thief and that this is your family sword."

Derrick cleared his throat and said loudly so the men outside would hear, "I am no thief. That is my family sword."

Leif lowered the sword and said, "I can see you speak the truth. I have long held this sword until the rightful owner could be found." Then he held the sword out for Derrick to take.

As Derrick exited the cave, the men all cheered and congratulated him. Then they all walked back to the village in a party mood. David explained to Derrick that the confrontation with death in the caves symbolized his death as a boy. Returning with the sword showed his resurrection as a man ready to take responsibility for his household. David also asked that he not speak of what happened in the cave to the unmarried men back in the village. They wanted all the future grooms to enter the cave with trepidation so that they might experience the ritual fresh before their wedding.

Derrick asked David, "Am I to keep this sword?"

David replied, "Yes, it's now your sword. Normally, the sword the groom retrieves from the tomb is a family sword passed down to the firstborn son. If a man is lucky enough to have more than one son, he has a sword made for each of them. But, knowing you don't have a family sword, I purchased this one from our smith."

Derrick looked more closely at the weapon. It was a one-handed sword with a double-edged blade about three feet long. The pommel was heavy steel, and although Derrick knew very little about swords, it seemed well-balanced. He asked David, "I don't know much about using a sword."

David said, "This particular sword is going to be a gift you give to Mary during the wedding ceremony. She will also give you a sword that my mother is providing for her. Most of us hang the swords on a wall in our homes. They have become more of a symbol as we no longer go off to raid. If you wish to learn how to use it, Leif could teach you, or I am sure any of your Templar friends would." Derrick figured he'd probably not learn how to use the weapon. He'd just stick with the bow.

Back in the village, the unmarried men, who were not allowed to accompany them to the cave, had set up a small feast. The drinking and feasting lasted until early in the morning.

CHAPTER NINETEEN

The city that appeared so close was still miles away. Sir Louis still had trouble judging distances in the desert. Louis rode slightly behind Dudel and Adi after their conversation about Louis' mission. Louis felt bad about having angered Dudel and was considering what Dudel had said. He asked himself for the first time: Why do I want to take the Holy Land from the Muslims? Louis knew that originally, the crusades into the Holy Land had been because of the supposed atrocities committed by the Muslims against Christians. Now he was wondering if that was the truth. Louis had never been here before; the only person he knew well who had been to Outremer was Sergeant Bertrand. The sergeant had not told him details, but he had strongly indicated that the situation in this part of the world was not what the Clergy wanted them to believe.

Louis didn't want to be responsible for creating more bloodshed and suffering. Especially if he was making decisions based on what he had been told by men who might have ulterior motives. At the same time, he had been sent here by King Robert the Bruce, and Louis had sworn to obey him. From what he knew of King Robert, he would also want to know the true nature of the situation. Louis decided to discover as much as possible about the people of this land so that he could make a full report to King Robert upon his return.

Louis urged his camel to a trot and caught up with Dudel and his wife. Louis told Dudel, "I am terribly sorry I offended you. I would appreciate it if you would continue educating me on the situation in the desert. I see that I have been overly hasty in many regards and would like any corrections you can offer. I promise to take it all into account before I decide to head East from Jerusalem."

Dudel was quiet for a moment and then said, "I will help you if you listen and truly attempt to see and understand what is around you."

Louis could tell Dudel was still angry, so he simply said, "Thank you." Then he slowed his camel and dropped back behind the one that Dudel and Adi rode on. Louis felt it best to leave him alone and allow Dudel time to get over his anger.

They entered Angora, which was not a large metropolitan city like Constantinople but was still quite substantial. To Louis, the city seemed to spread out in an open layout, unlike European cities, whose buildings seemed clustered tightly together. Dudel led them to a large residence with a high wall around it. After entering the ornately wrought metal gate, several servants came out to help Dudel and Adi off their camel and lead the other camels and Louis' donkey away. Louis was a little concerned as he watched his remaining possessions being taken away with the other animals. It must have shown on his face because Dudel walked up beside him and said, "Do not worry, my friend, I will have my servants take your possessions to the guest quarters."

Just then, a young woman dressed in blue silks and wearing nothing on her feet ran across the courtyard. She fell to her knees before Adi and embraced her tightly. Dudel walked up to the pair, and the three hugged. Then the girl leaned back and began speaking to them in the same language Adi used. The girl wagged her finger at the two and seemed to be chastising them. Then, with tears in her eyes, she hugged them once again.

Dudel finally broke the embrace and made the girl stand. Dudel motioned toward Louis, and the three walked over to him. Dudel said, "This is Louis de Champagne. Louis, this is my daughter Seraphina. Dudel's daughter was young and very pretty, with dark black hair and large brown eyes. She was perhaps five feet tall and slender. Louis dropped to one knee and said, "I am pleased to meet you, Lady Seraphina."

To which Lady Seraphina hit him on top of his head with her shoes, which she was carrying in her left hand. The shoes were made of some soft material, so Louis was not hurt in the least, but he was shocked. Dudel and Adi both started yelling at Seraphina. Louis regained his feet as Dudel said, "I am sorry, my friend, but she is cross with me for being late in returning home. Apparently, she blames you since she misunderstood when I told her you were the reason for our late return."

Louis said, "No harm done." Then he looked at Seraphina and said, "I am sorry I kept your parents from you. It was my fault for attempting to cross the desert so ill-prepared. Your parents saved my life, and I am indebted to them and you for the trouble I have caused."

Louis had assumed Dudel would translate what he said. Apparently, there was no need, as Seraphina said in French, "I would hope you are ashamed. You caused me to worry so much that I thought I might die. I was about to send men out to find them. They were supposed to be home three days ago. Not only was I worried, but they missed my fifteenth birthday."

Louis said, "Again, I am sorry."

Dudel said, "That is enough, Sera. You have made your point, and Louis is not to blame. We will celebrate your birthday tomorrow night. Do not worry; all is well. Your mother and I are safe, and we did very well in our trade negotiations, very well indeed."

Dudel, Adi, and Seraphina excused themselves and entered the large central building. Dudel had one of his men show Louis to a small two-room cottage. One room was occupied mostly by a bed. The other room had a table and two chairs. On the table was a pitcher of water and a bowl of fruit. All his belongings from the mule had been placed along the opposite wall of the table.

Louis sat on one of the chairs, despite feeling tired, and the bed looked very soft and inviting, but it also seemed very clean. After so many days in the desert, he felt it would almost be a sin to get on the clean bedding. He was just about to take a nap on the floor when there was a knock at the door. The knock was immediately followed by a young man opening the door. The young man entered and said in perfect French, "My master asked me to have a bath brought to you so you may refresh yourself."

Two larger men hefted a huge kettle into the room as he said this. Other men began bringing in buckets of hot water. After the men had filled the kettle, they all departed except for the young man who spoke French. He carried a bundle of clothes, which he handed to Louis. He then said, "Master Dudel said that after you bathe, you should put these clothes on so that we may clean yours." The young man then indicated a clay jar that the men had also brought in and said, "In this jar is a mixture of ash, sand, and some fragrant oil for you to use to help scrub the grime off yourself. After you are cleaned and dressed, you can leave your dirty clothes outside your door. Dinner will be served in about an hour, and master Dudel asks that you dine with him in the shade outside his dwelling."

After Louis was as clean as he could make himself with the warm kettle of water, he put on the clothes that the young man had left for him. The clothes consisted mostly of a long flowing garment that went down to just above his feet and had long, loose-fitting sleeves. The material was much softer than the rough spun clothing Louis was used to.

Feeling much better after cleaning himself and putting on fresh clothes, Louis walked to Dudel and Adi's home. Louis assumed the entire area inside the high stone fence was owned by Dudel. There was a stable area in one far corner and four large buildings that Louis took for warehouses. In the center of the property was a short wall that enclosed a small pond surrounded by trees and plants. Louis' room was part of a building that appeared to have many apartments like the one he was staying in. Louis assumed this building was where Dudel's servants dwelt. Dudel and Adi's home was in the center of the property. The structure was a two-story home with balconies on several of the second-floor windows. Most of those windows were now open, and the slight breeze that accompanied the sun's setting was rustling the curtains. Louis noticed Dudel was already seated at a table in front of his home. As Louis approached, Dudel indicated the chair across from him and said, "Please take a seat."

He seated himself and said, "Thank you. You have a very nice place here. I thought you were a simple trader?"

Dudel smiled and said, "I am a simple trader. But I am a successful, simple trader. I have done well over the years. I have been blessed, which has allowed me to expand my business."

Louis said, "Well, you seem very prosperous to me. I never would have guessed that you had any servants before arriving here, but you appear to have an army of them. Why were you out on the road with just your wife?"

Dudel replied, "Firstly, the people who work for me are not just servants. They are employees, and some of them even own small portions of my business. I have found that people work harder when they are treated and compensated fairly. As to why it was just Adi and me on this trip, I had business to take care of in Constantinople that I needed to attend to personally. I could have brought several attendants who would have cared for Adi and myself. I also could have rented a well-appointed home to stay in while we conducted our business there. Sometimes I do that, but in some situations, it is best to approach negotiations from a humble standing. So, I chose to appear as a man struggling to establish trade for those negotiations."

Louis asked, "What type of negotiations were you conducting, if I may ask?"

Dudel said, "I was setting up a trade route to Muscovy, which will also allow me to establish a trade center there."

Louis asked, "Where is Muscovy?"

Dudel said, "It is one of the principal cities of Rus, a confederation of cities far to the East. The Mongols of the Golden Horde control Rus. In Turkey, the Mongols allowed local leaders to govern their territories as long as they paid the taxes due to the Khan. Muscovy is fast becoming the center for trade in that part of the world."

Louis asked, "Will you go to Muscovy to set up your trade center?"

Dudel said, "I will, as soon as I gather the necessary merchandise and personnel. I hope to be ready to depart within six months."

Louis wondered if Muscovy might be a good place to search for Prester John since he is rumored to be in the Far East. He asked Dudel, "I know you are not thrilled with the idea of me nosing around for King Robert of Scotland, but do you think I could travel with you to Muscovy? I promise to keep an open mind. With me traveling in your company, you will have the opportunity to instruct me in my ignorance. I would, of course, first need to attend to matters in Jerusalem, but I believe six months gives me plenty of time for that."

Dudel sat quietly for a moment, considering Louis' proposition. Then he said, "If you are still willing to consider the lives of those of us who live in the desert, the very people that your actions will affect most, and you still wish to go when I have made my preparations, I will allow it. You will be able to go to Jerusalem and back easily before I depart for Muscovy. As it happens, I will be sending some retainers to Jerusalem in a couple of days to gather some items from my trade center there to take them to Rus. If you wish to travel with them, they will see that you arrive and return in relative safety."

CHAPTER TWENTY

Father Lull and Julie had a few heated discussions about how the wedding would be conducted. Julie wanted the wedding held outside so that everyone could attend. Father Lull explained that in order for the marriage to be sanctified, it would need to be held in the Church. Julie wanted the exchange of swords and insisted that a goat should be sacrificed before the wedding, and its blood should be sprinkled on the couple to bless them. At this request, Father Lull nearly lost his temper. When Father Lull said something about "pagan rituals," Julie looked like she might strike him. Mary decided she had had enough of their squabbling and stepped in. She informed both of them that it was her wedding, and she was going to make the decisions on how it was done.

Mary said, "The wedding vows and ring exchange will take place in the church just as Father Lull prescribes. Given the limited space in the church, only those I invite will be able to attend that part of the ceremony. When we leave the church, we will go in a procession to the head of the tables set up outside for the wedding feast. We will conduct the sword exchange in front of all who wish to attend, as Julie described to me. I will change the kransen that Julie has graciously provided for the crown that the blacksmith has made. There will be no blood sprinkling, and the only goats killed will be those used for the feast." Julie and Father Lull attempted to argue a bit more, but Mary shut them down. From that point on, the preparation proceeded as Mary directed.

While Mary was busy with all the wedding preparations, Derrick had little to do. The men in David's village had attempted to distract him with activities, but it had not worked. They hunted, fished, drank, and told stories late into the night. To Derrick, time seemed to drag, and his thoughts continually drifted to Mary. The Norwegian men had a good time, but Derrick wished they could get the wedding over with. Derrick had not seen Mary since he had gone with Admiral Gregory to the village Sir Jules had attempted to take over. He had this unsettling fear that something terrible would happen to her before they could be wed, and he would never see her again.

The morning of the wedding broke clear and bright. The men from David's village escorted Derrick back to the Templar camp just after sunup. Derrick found himself standing at the front of the church with

Father Lull. The Church was filled to capacity with all their close friends. As Mary entered the church, Derrick felt his knees go weak and thought he might stumble. He also felt a huge lump in his chest and feared he might cry. He fought to bring his emotions under control. He had just succeeded when Father Lull leaned over to Derrick's ear and whispered, "That beautiful woman is a gift that God has given to you." When the father said that, Derrick almost lost it again.

 Derrick was completely in the dark about the entire ceremony. He simply stood wherever they instructed him and repeated whatever words they told him to. He didn't seem to mind, especially whenever he gazed at Mary. When the couple left the church an hour later, it appeared that every Templar and person from David's village was waiting for them. Mary and Derrick exchanged swords, and the kransen bracelet Julie loaned Mary was exchanged for a crown made of thin rods of steel woven into an intricate pattern. The crowd erupted with cheers when the crown was placed on Mary's head, and the feast began.

The Templars noticed that there were occasions when one of the Norwegian men would get Derrick to step away from the celebration area. Whenever this happened, many Norwegian men would rush to where Mary was and kiss her on the cheek. Later, one of the Norwegian women would lure Mary away, and the other Norwegian women would rush to kiss Derrick on the cheek. After witnessing this a few times, several of the Templars joined in with the game.

As the afternoon grew toward evening, the bride and groom were loaded into a cart pulled by two horses. The cart was led away from the festivities by Julie, David, Sir William, Sir Justin, and two Norwegian women, who were all riding horses. Cinead was supposed to be a part of the procession, but he was too drunk to stay on the horse, and Sir Justin volunteered to replace him. The small group rode away from the Templar settlement, generally heading toward David's village. David rode his horse alongside the cart and explained, "We have a cottage somewhat apart from our village. The cottage is isolated, so the two of you will have privacy. We will not bother you for one cycle of the moon. We have provided you with food to last for a month. Some people have also left wedding gifts for you that they placed in the cottage."

Mary's eyes began to tear as she said, "I don't know how to thank you all for what you have done for us. This wedding has been like something out of a dream."

The party reached a clearing just as the sun was nearing the horizon, and the sky was changing from blue to orange. There was a small brook that flowed in front of the cottage. The cottage had been decorated with strips of colored material woven in an intricate pattern over the front of the door. The party halted as Derrick and Mary gazed at the scene before them. Mary's eyes glistened with tears as she turned to face the group that had conducted her and Derrick to this beautiful and peaceful spot. She tried to speak, but no words would come; instead, she hugged each person in the party. The last person she hugged was Julie. She was finally able to speak and simply said, "Thank you."

Derrick shook hands with each person, thanking them. As he turned his horse to lead the others away, David said, "We have also provided you two with enough honey mead to last you the moon cycle. We call this special time, for those who have been newly married, a honeymoon for that reason.

Back at the Templar community, things were winding down as people drifted away from the festivities. Admiral Gregory had told them they would clean up the area used for the reception in the morning. The last few days, the focus had been on the wedding, which helped take everyone's mind off the situation with Sir Jules and his men. Admiral Gregory was grateful for that, but he knew he still had to get a grip on the status of the Templars here and set some long-term goals. As Sir William had said, they needed a clear objective beyond hiding from the monarchs of Europe.

CHAPTER TWENTY-ONE

Sir Henry was taking an early morning walk along the streets of Lucerne. He rarely found time to go outside the Templar grounds. For the moment, things seemed to be progressing well. The church was being constructed under the watchful eye of Cardinal Soprano. Sir Garrard had the military arm of the brothers well in hand and had a fine group of young squires being trained. Sir Gilbert seemed to be making good progress on loans to local farmers, with seven parcels of land already under contract. The banking section Sir Gilbert oversaw had already purchased a bakery, a bowyer, and a tanner shop that the Templars now operated in the town.

Before being sent to Rennes-le-Chateau on that fateful mission with Sir William de Sevrey, Sir Henry loved the martial aspects of being a Templar. Yet now he found that he rarely thought about his military training. He realized it had been weeks since he had taken time to practice with the other knights and sergeants. He made a mental commitment to speak to Sir Garrard and set up regular daily practice time. He reconsidered as he continued his walk; maybe three days a week would be enough. Even with things moving along smoothly, he had much to oversee. He knew he would never find time to train every day. He wondered, 'Really, who would I be training to fight?' He would not be going to the Holy Land to fight. There were minor incursions into the Swiss lands around Lucerne from the Austrians, but he was unlikely to be involved as a soldier.

That thought started him down another line of thinking. They had been sent here to establish a place where the Pope could send other Templars. A place where they would be free from King Philip. The community they had set up seemed safe. Cardinal Soprano had sent word back to Pope Clement V to say as much, but they had heard nothing in response, and no new Templars had arrived. Henry also wondered if they were really "Templars" anymore. Some of his men thought they should become a new Order, perhaps one that rented out their service and warriors to other countries.

Sir Garrard said that he felt the Swiss Confederacy might pay them to send patrols into the mountains around this part of the Confederacy to keep tabs on any incursions into their lands. Sir Henry did not like the idea of becoming a band of mercenaries. Yet, at the same time, they were a military order, and there was little chance of them using that skill in any other way. The Seneschal of Lucerne had been very impressed with the fighting skill of the men under Garrard's command. He had told Garrard that Lucerne's leaders were wondering if Sir Garrard would be willing to train some of the men of Lucerne. The seneschal explained that the Confederacy was very concerned by the recent actions of the Austrians and felt certain they needed to prepare for a full invasion.

Sir Henry hated how these thoughts seemed to crowd into his pleasant walk on a beautiful sunny day. To make matters worse, Sir Henry noticed a familiar figure in priest's clothing just down the street, talking with a local priest. Sir Henry had not trusted Father Thomas from very early in their relationship. As he got to know the man, he trusted him even less. Then the father betrayed him and his squire, Odo.

Additionally, Sir Henry was certain that Father Thomas had more to do with the death of Odo than he had admitted. Henry didn't care how much Cardinal Soprano believed Thomas had changed; he would never trust the man. As Henry watched the father talk with the other priest, he couldn't shake the feeling that Thomas was up to no good.

Sir Henry stepped into a blacksmith's shop, pretending to examine some of the wares as he kept an eye on Father Thomas. The blacksmith was busy working at the anvil, making that ringing rhythm with his hammer that is constant in any blacksmith shop. Soon, the smith noticed Sir Henry, stopped hammering, wiped his coal-covered hands on his apron, and stepped toward him. The smith said, "May I help you with anything, Sir?"

Henry had been so focused on Thomas that he was somewhat surprised by the man's question. Henry said, "No, just looking." Although Henry said this, he was clearly not looking at anything in the shop; he was intent on watching Father Thomas.

The blacksmith said, "I know who you are, Sir. I would like to show you something."

Henry was caught off guard by the man saying he knew who he was. Did the smith know who Henry really was? Suddenly, a short wave of caution and paranoia swept over Sir Henry. He looked around quickly but saw no one except the smith in the room. Henry asked, "What do you mean that you know me?"

The smith, somewhat perplexed, said, "I don't presume to mean that I know you personally. I meant that I know you are the commander of the monks and soldiers who defeated the Austrians in the mountains near our village."

Henry's uneasiness abated, and he said, "I am sorry. I didn't intend to sound so gruff. My mind was elsewhere when you spoke. What is it you wish to show me?"

The smith said, "I recently spoke with a couple of your soldiers who were looking at my halberds. They pointed out that they were fine weapons against an unarmored man on foot, but they would only be effective against an armored opponent on horseback if he rode straight at you. They felt the only practical use of a halberd against cavalry would be purely as a defensive weapon. And only if you had a trained squad of men armed with them who could stand in a formation to keep any enemy on horseback at a distance."

Sir Henry said, "Yes, that is the way of halberds. All weapons have their strengths and weaknesses. Halberds are fine weapons for guards and small group patrols in confined areas."

The smith said, "Yes, sir, but I thought if I added a billhook opposite the axe blade, it could be used to pull a man from his saddle as he rode past. Then I thought that adding a bit more length and weight to the axe head would make it better at chopping. The smith then handed Sir Henry one of these redesigned halberds.

Henry was impressed by the feel of the weapon. It was a couple of feet longer than most of those he had used, and the billhook looked effective as long as the footman could keep it in his hands once he hooked the man on horseback. Henry said, "I am not an expert with this weapon, but it looks like it would be more effective under the right circumstances. Would you sell this one to me so that I can have some of my men evaluate it more properly?"

After paying the smith for the halberd, Henry looked around for Father Thomas, but the priest was nowhere to be seen. Berating himself for having been distracted by the blacksmith and losing sight of Father Thomas, Henry decided to return to the commandry and give the halberd to Sir Garrard. Walking up the street, he tried to forget about his concern regarding Father Thomas. Sir Henry attempted to regain his calm by telling himself that the priest could not do anything in Lucerne that could really harm Henry or his men. It was no use; Henry could not relieve himself of the thought that Father Thomas was up to no good, and that if he did not do something about the bastard, he was going to destroy everything they had begun in Lucerne.

CHAPTER TWENTY-TWO

The day after Mary and Derricks's wedding, Admiral Gregory met with Sir William, Father Lull, Cinead, and Master Acel. He started the meeting by saying, "We need to make some plans. This village is reasonably self-sufficient and operates somewhat smoothly. A few knights and sergeants wish to be released from their vows. They believe that the Templar Order has reached its end. Additionally, several squires, craftsmen, and masters wish to be allowed to leave the service of the Templars. These men wish to find their own way here in Norway or some other location. A few have indicated a desire to return to France."

Sir William interjected, "Can we allow that? If we allow men to return to France, eventually someone will talk, and King Philip's men will come here seeking us out."

Gregory said, "I agree, but as we are all aware, this village cannot be our long-term objective. As we discussed earlier, this place will ultimately be discovered. A Norwegian fisherman will say something, and eventually, the monarchs of Europe will hear about us. We need to do what Sir William and I both believe Grand Master Jacques de Moley intended for us to do. He sent Sir William and his small band to Rennes-le-Chateau to bring the map to me and Father Lull.

"Many people believed our Grand Master ignored the signs that King Philip was about to move against the Templars. Personally, I believe he knew full well what was about to happen. I also think he knew that, as Grand Master, he could never hide. I am certain he sacrificed himself to give some of us a chance to escape. He sent this map, which has been hidden safely for many years, to those he thought would understand its purpose."

Cinead, still hungover from the night before, interrupted, "My head still feels like a ship tossed in a gale, so could you tell me plainly what you think your Grand Master wishes you Templars to do?"

Gregory said, "I believe Grand Master Jacques de Moley wants us to use the map to take as many Templars as possible to this new land in the west. Once we are there, we are to establish a Templar community. From this remote and hard-to-reach location, we will finally be free of interference from the Crowns of Europe. We can grow and establish a community."

Father Lull interjected, "I, for one, agree with Governor Gregory."

Cinead asked the Father, "I know I'm not a good Catholic, but Father, won't this move also put you in opposition with the Holy Roman Church and outside their area of authority?"

Father Lull said, "No, the Church is universal. Just because there are no cathedrals or priests there, it does not mean this new land is apart from God or the Church. Regarding being in opposition to the Church, I have prayed about that since the arrests first started. I believe the Holy Father has acted the way he has because of the pressures and lies originating from the King of France. Pope Clement V is not a strong-willed man. He owes a great deal to King Philip IV for his position as the head of the Church. Pope Clement knows King Philip will stop at nothing to get what he wants.

"Even though I am sure the Holy Father knows this move by King Philip is basically a money grab, the accusations Philip leveled against the Templars must be addressed. At the start, I think the Pope was unaware of how far this would go. Then at some point, self-preservation caused Pope Clement to give in to King Philip's demands. If the Pope were a stronger man in a more secure location, I believe he would have fought for the Templars. I am sure the Pope would be happy to see us establish a safe location for his warrior monks."

The good Father's remarks did not convince Cinead, but he let it drop.

Sir William said, "You all know I support this plan to establish a base in the land west of Greenland. I am certain if the Grand Master could get a message to us, he would tell us himself that we need to do this."

Master Acel said, "I can see how you Templars came to this conclusion, but there are a few things you men need to consider. What will you do with all the men who do not wish to go? We know very little about this new land to the west, and most of what we know comes from the Norse Sagas, which are not entirely reliable sources. Lastly, but maybe most importantly, we have only one woman amongst our band of men, and she was just married off. I assume you all know where babies come from. So, with only one woman and with you all taking vows of celibacy, we might be expecting a little too much from Derrick and Mary if you plan to build a growing community."

90

Cinead laughed and said, "I've taken no vow of celibacy. If it helps, I shall impregnate any women we can convince to accompany us."

Father Lull said, "Cinead! You are a married man. That is beneath you."

Cinead grinned and said, "Beneath, on top, or in front, makes no difference to me."

Admiral Gregory cut in before this got further out of hand, "Cinead, we appreciate the sacrifice you are willing to make on our behalf. But I assumed you would return to your home rather than accompany us on this adventure."

Cinead said, "And pass up the chance to see this new land? No, I will be coming with you."

Sir William added, "There are a great many decisions we need to discuss, not the least of which are the ones Master Acel has brought up. I fear we must discuss much of this privately unless we think we can persuade everyone to join us. We don't want men returning to France with information that could help the King locate us before we can establish ourselves in the West. I don't want King Philip to know anything about where we are until we are ready to confront him about his accusations against the Templars."

CHAPTER TWENTY-THREE

As it turned out, Sir Louis arrived in Jerusalem just over two weeks after departing Dudel's home. The merchants' men, with Louis riding along, led a caravan of several camels to the town of Seleucia, on the southern coast of Turkey. Dudel's men and Louis left the camels in Seleucia, where they would be needed to carry the trade items back on the return trip. They boarded a ship Dudel had waiting for them. The ship took them to Tripoli, where a man Dudel had hired met them with a train of donkeys and camels to take them on the last leg of their outward journey. Louis traveled with this new caravan to Dudel's trade center in Jerusalem. Once they arrived at the trade center, Dudel's men got to work sorting and preparing the items they needed to take on the return trip. Louis took his leave of his traveling companions, assuring them he would return to the trading center within three days. With Sargent Burtrand's surcoat, Sir Louis started his search for a suitable place to deposit the token of the warrior and teacher he had grown to respect.

Louis spent a day wandering in the city, visiting many of the Holy sites. Most of the sites appeared to have been abandoned. To Louis' surprise, he found that the Church of the Holy Sepulcher had Latin priests present. As Dudel had told him, they performed the Latin liturgy there with the Mamluk Sultan's permission.

Louis went to confession, and after doing his penance, he went to mass. Later, he met with one of the priests. Louis informed the priest that he wished to bury the surcoat of Sergeant Bertrand in a place that would do the Sergeant's memory honor. The priest told Louis that he could stay in one of the clergy cells for the night, and the next day, he would help Louis with his task.

The priest met Louis outside the main doors in front of the church the following morning. Louis had the surcoat wrapped in a waxed piece of canvas to conceal and protect it. The priest approached Louis and said, "May God be with you."

Louis replied, "And also with you."

The priest continued, "Many pilgrims bring bones to bury here in the Church of the Holy Sepulcher so that their loved ones can be laid to rest near the empty tomb of Jesus. Usually, they make a sizable donation to the Church for such a privilege. I realized this is more of a token than human remains, but it would still take up space within these limited grounds."

Louis had not anticipated he would need to pay to bury the surcoat. He mentally calculated what he had with him. He said, "Well, I'm unsure how much I have. What would be expected as an appropriate donation?"

The priest replied, "There is not a price that we could put on having this item entombed near our Lord's burial and resurrection place. This is also near the location where Christ made the sacrifice on the cross for the elect. We must also consider that the item you wish to lay to rest here is one to which some people may take offense. It does represent an invading army among the locals and an Order which has presently fallen out of favor with the Church."

Louis took the leather pouch of money out of his tunic. He opened the purse, showed the priest its contents, and said, "This is all I have."

The priests looked in the small pouch and said, "That would not be an acceptable donation for what you are asking of us." Then the priest stood and turned toward the church doors.

Louis said, "I can arrange to send more to you later. I wasn't expecting to need to pay for this."

The priest did not slow or look back at Louis as he said, "It is not a payment; it is a donation you would freely give." Then the priest entered the church and let the doors close behind him.

Louis walked away from the church, unsure where he should go. The attitude of the priest angered him. Louis knew that the church often "accepted donations" to receive certain considerations. Usually, it was not so obviously a payment for services. The priest didn't even seem to consider that Sergeant Bertrand had been a Templar and a warrior-monk who committed his life to protect others. As Louis thought about it, he grew angrier and frustrated.

Louis walked for several hours, wandering through the streets of Jerusalem, until his anger diminished. Eventually, he sat down near a well. A young boy approached Louis with a clay vase and handed it to Louis, indicating he should drink. Louis was thirsty after walking around in the hot sun for several hours. Louis took a long drink without really considering the wisdom in drinking what this boy handed him. The cool water was immensely refreshing. As he lowered the vase and returned it to the boy, he said, "Thank you. That was very kind of you, young man." Knowing the boy would not understand French, Louis also touched his hand to his forehead and bowed slightly as he had seen others do.

The boy indicated with gestures, asking if Louis wished for more water. Louis shook his head and said, "No."

The boy left and joined a group of three other children under the direction of a woman, gathering water from the well. The four of them soon left. Louis sat there for a minute or two, then stood to leave. As he was departing the area of the well, a man approached Louis and said to him in passable French, "Are you French?"

Louis paused and looked at the man, who was clearly not a local resident. The man had blond hair, blue eyes, and pale skin. The man spoke French but with a strange accent. Louis said, "Yes, I am. I am Louis de Champagne."

The other man said, "I thought I heard you speak French to that boy. I don't hear French spoken here very often. My name is Georges Weber. I am here with my father purchasing supplies for our tailor business back home in Luxembourg. I noticed you have been sitting here by the well for some time. Are you lost?"

Louis said, "No. I was just thinking, attempting to work out a problem."

Georges said, "I see. Is there anything I can help you with?"

Louis said, "I doubt it. I have a token here of a friend of mine who has passed away. He once was here in the Holy Land as a soldier. I had hoped to leave it here in the city, but have not located an appropriate location."

Georges replied, "Come with me. I know just the spot you are looking for."

Louis asked, "I do not have much money. Will this cost much?"

Georges said, "It will not cost you anything. There is an old crusader cemetery just outside the city walls. Many pilgrims bring mementos of loved ones who fought in the Crusades and left them there. There is a low wall along one side. You can bury your item beside the wall."

Just before sunset, Louis buried Sergeant Bertrand's surcoat beneath a foot of soil just outside the wall of Jerusalem. He felt relieved to have completed that task. Sergeant Bertrand had not requested that anyone do this for him, but he was in no condition at the time of his death to make such a request. The sergeant always talked about the fighting he did in Outremer. Although Bertrand often expressed disagreement with how and why the fighting was done, Louis still felt this act in some way honored the man, and that was something Louis believed he owed him.

CHAPTER TWENTY-FOUR

The principal leadership members in the Norwegian Templar community met to discuss plans to relocate to the lands west of Greenland. Admiral Gregory opened by saying, "In the past, we could have had this discussion among all the Templar brothers in one of our private meetings. But I fear that we need to limit who is present when discussing our intent to move under the present circumstances. Some of our brethren's commitment and willingness to follow orders has slackened somewhat."

Sir William interjected, "We can hardly blame them. Even though we have an established leadership here with Governor-Admiral Gregory, other aspects of our leadership and legitimacy remain in question. According to the most recent information we have received, Grand Master Jacques de Molay is still alive. He has recanted his earlier confessions and is still locked up in King Philip's dungeons. There is also talk that the Pope may dissolve the Templar Order. Some of our brethren believe we are akin to outlaws and should disband and blend into the world as individuals or in small groups. Others, fearing excommunication, feel we should journey to Avignon and throw ourselves on the mercy of the Holy Father."

Cinead replied, "Excommunications come and go; dinna fash yourself with that. I thought ya lot were soldiers. You're in charge here, Admiral Gregory. You tell the bastards what to do, and they damn well should obey."

Admiral Gregory said, "In the past, that would be true, but as Sir William has said, leadership at the moment is somewhat precarious."

Cinead said, somewhat quietly, "Hang a few bastards, and the rest will do as told."

Sir William said, "I am afraid this is more than just disobeying orders. There is a real crisis of faith involved. We have sworn oaths to the Church. Now the Church is involved, to some degree, in this attack against us. Many are unsure what to believe and how to behave."

Cinead said, "Aye, but this is the same Pope who was supposed to be your only authority here on Earth. Yet it's pretty King Philip who's got ya by the balls, and the Pope is not holding up his end of the bargain. Ah dinnae ken, ya need to establish authority and tell the bastards what to do."

Father Lull said, "It seems to me that in our present situation, we should tell the men what we intend to do, and if they choose to remain here, we allow them to. It will divide the company somewhat, but maybe we could establish a joint command. Admiral Gregory would be in overall leadership with two sub-lieutenants, one overseeing this community and the men who remain, the other supervising preparation for our departure to the west."

Admiral Gregory said, "That brings up two other issues. First, I do not feel we should tell the men of our ultimate goal. I believe we should inform the Templars, squires, craftsmen, and other members of our community that we intend to relocate to Greenland. I have been told that the Greenlanders would not be happy with our attempt to establish a community there. Jarl David said Greenland can barely support the few inhabitants that reside there now, and they are less than welcoming to visitors. Once in Greenland, we will inform everyone that we cannot remain there due to its inability to support any additional population. With no other place to go, we let the Greenlanders know we are taking our group back to Norway.

"The captains of each ship in our fleet will be told the truth about our true destination. Once the flotilla is back at sea, the captains will inform everyone on their ship that we are heading to lands further to the west. The hope is that if any word got out that Templars escaped to Greenland and King Philip's men followed us there, it would be assumed that the flotilla must have met with disaster and sunk while trying to return to Norway.

"The second matter is that I believe it would be best for Sir William to take command once we reach the lands in the west. I will remain in command of our fleet of ships, but William should be in overall authority. I have spoken to Sir William, who has agreed that if the men select him as commander, he will accept the responsibility."

Sir William added, "I think we should have a meeting of all knights and sergeants as soon as possible and present both the plan to relocate to Greenland and the change in leadership once we reach our destination. Once we know who will be staying in Norway, the men will need to elect a new leader for those who choose to stay. Those two leaders would become the sub-lieutenants that Father Lull mentioned."

By the end of the week, the community had two new leaders who answered to Admiral Gregory. Sir Dubois oversaw those who would remain in Norway, and Sir William was in command of those who would head west. Things worked very smoothly with the new command structure. Admiral Gregory focused on getting the fleet ready and settling conflicts in the allocation of the men and materials between Sir Dubois and Sir William.

Some of the men under the command of Sir Dubois wished to be set free from their obligation to the Templars and be allowed to leave. At the request of Admiral Gregory and Sir Dubois, these men agreed to stay in the Norwegian community for one year more before departing. After that, they were free to go where they wished, but they were asked to remain quiet about those in Norway and Greenland.

Six months after the meeting that effectively divided the Templars of Norway into two groups, those who followed Admiral Gregory and Sir William were ready to sail west. The plan was to first sail to Iceland, then, as soon as they could resupply, they would head to Greenland. In Greenland, they would again resupply as best they could from that harsh land. Then they would start the last and most dangerous leg of their journey. There was a lot of discussion about what to bring. Farming, carpentry, masonry, and metalworking tools were of primary concern. Many of the knights and sergeants-at-arms wanted to bring horses. Due to the space requirements and the difficulty of transporting horses on open seas, Admiral Gregory rejected any talk of taking horses.

By the time all preparations had been made, nearly a quarter of the Templars chose to remain in Norway. Most of the craftsmen, farmers, and other contract workers who had come to Norway with the Templars also decided to stay in Norway. They had all heard tales of the harsh conditions in Greenland. Many had found Norwegian women and wanted to stay and start a new life.

The group that was leaving had nine ships in its flotilla. Each of the vessels had some of the Templar treasure that had been in Rennes-le-Chateau stored in their hold. They left about a fourth of the treasure with the group remaining in Norway. Most of the leadership was going, including Admiral Gregory, Sir William, Father Lull, Master Acel, and Sir

Justin. Cinead, Derrick, and Mary were also among the group making the voyage. About thirty-five Norwegians chose to accompany them; this included several women. David, who Admiral Gregory had told about their true destination, asked if he could inform Leif where they were really headed. Leif had long wanted to visit and explore Vineland. Admiral Gregory and Sir William reluctantly agreed. When David told Leif, he instantly requested to accompany the group.

CHAPTER TWENTY-FIVE

Father Thomas had spoken to several people in Lucerne to discover if there was anyone he could trust to carry a message to Brother Jaye in France. There was no one. Everyone he spoke to had expressed gratefulness for the band of monks and warriors that had come to Lucerne. Thomas believed he needed someone who had some reason to dislike or mistrust them. Father Thomas wondered how grateful they would be to them if they knew they were Templars. He almost considered letting it slip to a fellow priest he had met the other day, but he realized that could backfire, and the priest might tell Sir Henry.

He was at a loss until he devised a new plan that would get word to de Norgaret and get himself away from Cardinal Soprano. Thomas started laying the foundation for this scheme while talking with the Cardinal during their evening walks through the village. During these sojourns, Thomas told the Cardinal that he was conflicted. He explained how he felt his faith was a sham and was uncertain about his calling into the priesthood.

Cardinal Soprano told Thomas this was common for all men of God. He said, "Father Thomas, we are all tested at times. You must prayerfully seek God and listen for that small, still voice. Faith often feels like the tide of the ocean to me. Sometimes it is high and sometimes low, but it is always sufficient."

One cool evening as the two men walked in the twilight, Thomas said, "Your Eminence, I believe I should take a pilgrimage to Assisi, Italy." This was going to be the most difficult part of Thomas' plan. This was the part where he had to lie to the Cardinal openly, and Cardinal Soprano had the uncanny ability to see through most of Thomas' lies.

The Cardinal was quiet momentarily and then said, "I have had several individuals come to me saying they felt compelled to make a pilgrimage. Most of them had not truly considered what that decision entailed. Many just wanted to get away from the responsibilities they felt were overwhelming. I typically recommend that these men spend a week in a cell praying and fasting. This usually cleared their minds and bared their souls to God. This often changed their minds about going on a pilgrimage. I know you are a man who usually calculates and plans before he does anything. Tell me why you think a pilgrimage would bring more glory to God."

Father Thomas said, "You are correct. I have been considering this for some time. When I came to Avignon with Brother Jaye, I was convinced of the truth of what I was doing. You helped me see that much of my righteous zeal was due to my pride, fears, and lust for comfort. Since then, I have attempted to allow God to remove those feelings and desires from me, but I still struggle with them. I know all of us struggle with desires and thoughts, for we are men, and we all fall short of the glory of God. Yet this seems to be something deeper in me. I want to be esteemed above others, have fine robes, and eat the best foods served to me on gold platters. I know this is wrong, but I still desire it. If I could leave this place as a beggar with nothing but the clothes on my back and walk to Assisi, I hope to learn the humility God wishes me to know. In Assisi, I will pray to Saint Francis and Saint Clare to teach me the humility and disdain for material pleasures that those two holy Saints knew."

Cardinal Soprano was again silent for a bit. He finally said, "I will miss our conversation, but if you feel this is what God would have you do, I will not interfere. Before you depart, you must go to Sir Henry and request permission to leave, as he is in overall command here in Lucerne."

Father Thomas had not considered that. He was momentarily concerned that Sir Henry would interfere with his plans. Then he thought how much Henry disliked him. Perhaps Sir Henry would see this as a way to be rid of Thomas.

Thomas said, "I will go and speak to Sir Henry now. If he approves, I will find you to receive your blessing and take my leave immediately."

Thomas found Sir Henry in the practice yard sparring with the other knights and sergeants. Thomas waited until Sir Henry took a break, then Thomas approached him and asked, "Sir Henry, I am sorry to interrupt you, but I need to have a word with you."

Henry didn't look at Father Thomas but instead watched the other soldiers practice while he drank some water. Sir Henry then said, "What is it, priest?"

Thomas fought to control his anger. What right did this buffoon have to speak to him in this manner? Thomas' anger flared within him. He wanted nothing more than to lash out at Sir Henry de Creon. But right now, he needed to sound contrite in order to receive permission to leave. Controlling his anger, Thomas said, "I have received permission from Cardinal Soprano to go on a pilgrimage to Assisi, Italy. Now I just need your permission to take my leave."

Sir Henry slowly turned to look at Thomas. He gazed at him momentarily as if trying to see inside the man. He slowly and carefully said, "Father Thomas, it is no secret that I do not like you, and I opposed you coming with us on this mission. As a matter of fact, I believe you should be held accountable for your past actions. You are free here with us in Lucerne because Cardinal Soprano argued that your actions were misguided and that you only did what you thought was correct at the time. So, my decision may come as a surprise to you. I will not permit you to leave. I do not want you traveling around stirring up some new evil. I want you where I can keep an eye on you."

Father Thomas could only stare at Sir Henry. How could he refuse him? Thomas needed to leave; how could this mere knight have the authority to stop him from going on a pilgrimage? He could plead with Henry and explain that God wished him to go to Assisi, but he was sure it would not work. Perhaps he could get Cardinal Soprano to talk to Henry or even supersede Sir Henry's refusal. So, Thomas, as contritely as possible, bowed his head and said, "As you wish, Sir Henry. I will leave you to your practice." Then Thomas turned and left, his heart filled with hate and murder.

Thomas walked until he got his emotions under control. After composing himself, he went to Cardinal Soprano. Thomas said, "Your Eminence, I spoke with Sir Henry, and he refused my request to go on a pilgrimage. I realize he is the commander of this expedition, but I wondered if you might have a word with Sir Henry. His hatred for me is understandable after what I did to him. In this case, I think his dislike for me has blinded him to the spiritual necessity of my going on this pilgrimage."

Cardinal Soprano said, "I am not surprised by his refusal. I will speak to him."

CHAPTER TWENTY-SIX

The trip from Norway to Iceland went smoothly. There were no storms, and the winds were steady. The days were mostly sunny, although the temperature grew colder as they made their way across the North Atlantic. Resupply in Iceland was hampered due to a bad harvest that year among the Icelanders. Still, they filled the water casks and purchased plenty of salted fish. The fleet remained in Iceland for three days and then set sail for Greenland.

As the flotilla approached Greenland, the temperatures became much colder, and the wind grew in intensity. As expected, the sight of several ships filled with people landing on their shores did not make the Greenlanders very welcoming. There was nearly a battle between the two groups until Sir William and Admiral Gregory told the inhabitants that they would depart and head back to Norway as soon as they could be re-provisioned.

The Greenlanders showed them where to fill their water casks, but said they had no food to spare. Admiral Gregory and Sir William had expected this reaction and had even counted on it as part of the ruse. Admiral Gregory and the other leaders had planned to stretch their provisions to reach the lands further west without food from Greenland. After patching some leaks in three of the ships and waiting for a storm to pass, the Templars set sail for the mysterious lands to the southwest of Greenland.

On the second day after departing Greenland, it began to storm, and the sea grew very rough. It became difficult to judge how far they traveled, and even the direction of their travel grew problematic with the storms raging about them. The ships of the flotilla had been sailing close to one another, but as the sea grew worse, the vessels began to spread out. This was partly for safety, as the ship's movements were more erratic in the rough seas, and because each ship had to focus more on staying afloat than remaining together.

After a week of continuous rough weather, the wind finally began to die down, and the clouds cleared. Of the nine ships that had left Greenland, only four other ships could be seen from Admiral Gregory's vessel. The Admiral had the five ships draw closer together. Then he requested that the captain or first officer of each vessel in the reduced flotilla come to a meeting on his ship.

Three of the captains and one first officer rowed over. They met in Admiral Gregory's cabin. The meeting included Sir William and Father Lull. Cinead, Leif, and Derrick were helping with repairs to the ship, and Mary was below deck trying to sleep. She had been terribly seasick during this journey. Surprisingly, William had been fine since they left Norway; he seemed to have finally gotten his sea legs.

Admiral Gregory opened the meeting, "First, I want a report from each of you about the condition of your ship and crew and what you may know about the four missing ships."

As it turned out, each of the five remaining ships suffered some damage, but only one seemed severe. The first mate who came over for the meeting said, "I am First Mate Corgan. My captain sent me in his place because he wanted to oversee the repairs personally. We sprang a few leaks, but we are managing to keep the flooding under control. The real issue is that our main mast is cracked, and the shipwright is attempting to repair it, but is unsure how strong he can make it until we can beach her."

Only one of the captains had any news of the other ships. He told the others, "I saw Captain Anderson's ship go over. They were only a few hundred yards off my port quarter. Her main mast snapped like a twig and fell into the sea. The crew attempted to cut loose the lines, but a wave struck her amidship, and I witnessed her layover. The mast appeared to keep her from righting, as I could see her keel lying flat to the sea. That was the last I saw of her. A large roller came between our two ships, and when my ship rose on the next crest, there was no sign of her."

In a voice almost too quiet to be heard, Father Lull said, "Captain Anderson's vessel carried all the Norwegians except for Leif."

After a moment, Admiral Gregory said, "No one saw anything else?" None spoke up, so he added, "Well, they all had the same map as the rest of us; perhaps we will link up again at sea or at our destination."

All the seamen knew this was a faint hope, but there was little else to do but hope and keep a lookout for the others. Admiral Gregory looked at the first mate from the ship with the damaged mast and said, "I will send a couple of carpenters to aid you in repairs. How soon before you can raise sail?"

The first mate replied, "I believe we can have all the repairs that can be managed at sea completed in three hours, Sir."

Admiral Gregory said, "That should be fine. I want to be under sail as soon as possible. We will adjourn this meeting so you all can return to your ships and prepare to get underway. As soon as I receive word that all ships are ready, I will hoist my main sails, and we shall move out. First Mate Corgan, I want you to tell your Captain that I want his ship behind mine so that I can keep her in sight. I want everyone to keep a weather eye out for our missing ships."

The flotilla was underway a few hours later, but just before the sun set, a storm engulfed the ships again. This time, it seemed the winds and waves were seeking vengeance on the vessels that had survived the first storm. The captains did their level best to keep in sight of each other. Soon, each ship's captain realized he needed to focus his attention on keeping his ship atop the waves and just survive. The ships moved further apart one by one as each vessel fought its solo battle with the sea.

One of the men on watch reported to Admiral Gregory that he saw one of the ships that had been running behind them just disappear as if the ocean had swallowed them. That was the last reported sighting Admiral Gregory had of any of the ships in his fleet. As the sailor returned to his station, Gregory thought to himself, I guess I'm no longer an Admiral. Can't be an Admiral with just one ship. I'm Captain Gregory again. Unless this storm lifts soon, I doubt I'll even be that.

The following evening, waves heaved the ship up and down across its surface, and the wind lashed the men on deck with icy pellets. Above the crash of thunder, Captain Gregory heard a man yell, "Land off the starboard beam." Lightning flashed just as Captain Gregory looked to starboard, and in the afterimage of the lightning, he saw that, indeed, there was land. The question now was whether he should approach it amid the raging storm. As he considered his options, a sailor found him and said, "Admiral, the water is collecting below faster than we can keep it out."

Captain Gregory made his choice, a choice which held in its balance the lives of everyone on board. He strode to the helmsman and said, "I'll take over. You get all the men on deck and find me a place to beach."

CHAPTER TWENTY-SEVEN

After Louis returned from Jerusalem and arrived at Dudel's home in Angora, he remained there for two months until Dudel had everything ready for the journey to Muscovy. Small caravans arrived with supplies and merchandise to fill the trade center Dudel would open in Muscovy. Everything had to be inventoried and repacked for the long trip to Rus.

A few days before leaving, Louis asked Dudel, "Is your wife coming with us?"

Dudel replied, "No, I would not take Seraphina on such a long trip, and I cannot separate Adi and myself from her for so long."

Sir Louis said, "How long do you expect to be gone?"

Dudel said, "I hope I will be able to return home within two years."

Louis said, "That long? I didn't expect it would take that much time to open a store."

Dudel replied, "After we arrive, I must make arrangements with the local administration to open the store. Luckily, I was able to get tentative approval from a Muscovy official in Constantinople. Then I will need to ensure everything is running smoothly before departing."

Adi and Seraphina said a long, tearful goodbye as the caravan prepared to leave. Dudel repeatedly had to extricate himself from the hugs of his wife and daughter. Dudel felt relieved once he was in the saddle and out of reach of the two women.

The caravan was large. Thirty-five camels carried merchandise, and nineteen men attended to the camels. Two other men seemed to oversee the overall operation as they traveled. Louis later learned these two men would manage the trading post in Muscovy once Dudel had everything established. Another twenty men also rode on camels, acting as scouts and guards for the caravan.

While in the desert, the daily routine was to travel until noon, then set up a temporary camp for a few hours of rest and refreshment. After the hottest part of the day, they would continue their journey until it grew dark, and they could no longer travel safely. The camels could see well enough at night, much better than horses. The concern was the possibility of bandits attacking in the dark while the caravan was stretched out. Therefore, once the sun set, they would set up camp for the night.

Louis spent most of his time during the middle of the day while they rested, talking with Dudel about life in the desert. He also continued to learn Arabic from Dudel and the other men in the caravan. Most of the men who worked for Dudel were Muslim. Louis had found that these men were very devout and didn't seem to harbor any ill will toward Dudel for being a Jew or Louis for his Christianity.

As Louis' fluency in Arabic grew, he began talking to the Muslim men about their lives, beliefs, and feelings about the Latin crusades. He found that their lives seemed to be like those of most of the common people back in France. They had families they wished to care for. They paid little attention to all the squabbling for power that transpired around them unless it directly affected them or their family members. Even when a new governor, prince, king, or amir did affect them, there was little they could do about it. Their focus was on their God and their family.

They all seemed to respect and like Dudel and didn't understand why Louis thought they should care if he was a Jew. If Dudel did not demand that they forsake their God or interfere with their worship, they didn't care. As for Louis being a Christian, they had met few and interacted with far fewer still. Most of the men knew that in the past, the Latin armies had attempted to seize control of lands in the desert, but they did not feel they were a threat to their way of life any longer.

Louis discovered they were more concerned about the Mongol Hordes than Latin knights. They had heard that the Mongol and Latin armies had attempted to work together to defeat the Seljuks at some point in the last few years. That joint operation fell apart before it could even start. Dudel's men explained to Louis that the Mongol Hordes mostly left the Muslims alone as long as they paid their taxes. Still, there was always a lingering threat when the Hordes were around.

Louis did find a few of the guards in Dudel's caravan who felt differently. These few men had fathers and uncles who fought against the Crusading soldiers. These men seemed to feel some anger toward the Latin kingdoms. They believed the soldiers of Europe had no right to be in their lands, as the crusaders wanted only to convert or kill the inhabitants of the desert. Yet, they showed no anger toward Louis, believing he was not connected to those Latin armies that had been driven out just because he was from that part of the world. Louis wondered what they would think if they discovered he was here to look for allies for another crusade that would again disrupt and maybe destroy their way of life.

It took nearly three months to reach Muscovy. Louis saw little on the trip north that would make him think there would be any allies in that part of the world until they reached Muscovy. The city seemed to burst with people and new businesses. Dudel was not the first merchant to have the idea of opening a trade center there.

After arriving, Dudel needed to make his presence known to the city's rulers and find a warehouse and location for his shop. Dudel rented a temporary place for his men and the caravan, then arranged a meeting with the local authorities. He was given a scheduled time to meet with the prince on the following day. Dudel decided to take Louis with him when he went to meet Prince Yury Dailovich.

CHAPTER TWENTY-EIGHT

The wind was causing the waves to break over the ship's sides. And the rain was falling in sheets that stung as it struck the skin. Captain Gregory had only the vaguest idea of where the beach was and had no clue about the surrounding waters or the composition of the beach. He was steering the ship on instinct based on his lifetime spent at sea. In a flash of lightning, Gregory had glimpsed what might be a clear stretch of sand where he hoped to beach the craft. He was reasonably certain he was still heading in the correct direction. He prayed that there were no rocks or a reef or a thousand other things that could rip open the ship and drown them all before he could get his vessel wedged onto a good bottom.

Suddenly, there was another flash of lightning, and in the blaze of brightness, Gregory saw trees almost as if they were reaching out to him. As the light vanished, all he saw was the afterimage of trees and branches. Then he felt the keel hit bottom. The ship suddenly slowed, throwing everyone to the deck who had not been holding firmly onto something. The vessel continued its progress forward for a few moments, and then she literally ground to a halt. Gregory yelled to the men to lower the sail before the wind tore the mast off the ship. He then had the men take soundings and check below deck for damage. He had to determine the likelihood of the ship staying together until morning, when they could attempt to transport everyone and everything to shore.

At the ship's prow, the soundings showed a depth of the water to be about 6 feet. The vessel seemed solidly grounded in sand or small gravel, and although there were several leaks below the water line, it wasn't as if the ship would sink. As a matter of fact, the water coming in only added ballast, which would help to keep her settled on the bottom. He ordered the men to start bringing everything below decks up and begin preparation to take everyone and all the provisions ashore at first light. Believing the ship was in no immediate danger, he went to the aft castle, where he knew William, Cinead, Father Lull, Leif, Mary, and Derrick would be waiting.

Before they could ask any questions, Captain Gregory said, "We appear to be soundly grounded, and at first light, we will start to ferry everyone and everything ashore."

Father Lull asked, "Do you think this is the land talked about in the Norwegian sagas?"

Captain Gregory said, "I can't say for certain. I believe the storm pushed us further south than the sagas described. But, unless this is an island, I believe it is part of the same large land mass that the Norsemen claim to have discovered. If you look toward the shore and wait for a flash of lightning, you will see that the land is quite close, and after a short stretch of beach, it appears heavily forested. Which I hope will provide most of the materials we need to make repairs to the ship."

William asked, "Since we are so close, should not a few of us go to shore now to establish a camp and base of operations on land?"

Captain Gregory said with his first smile in days, "No, Sir William. I know you do not enjoy being at sea, but even a short ride in our small rowboat in this storm, and on a pitch-black night, would be foolhardy. Besides, we are firmly aground, and the ship hardly moves even in this storm."

William, a bit crestfallen, said, "Honestly, Admiral, I've grown used to being at sea and have found I even enjoy it now, as long as the wind and waves are not trying to kill me. I wish to go ashore first, not for relief from shipboard life or fear of the ship breaking up. Rather, as I will be in command once we are ashore, I feel I am responsible for ensuring the shore is safe."

Admiral Gregory replied, "I see. Yes, of course. You will certainly be on the first boat to shore, but that will not be until first light."

The next morning, the storm was still active but was no longer raging. Even though the skies were overcast, the sun's light was comforting compared to the unknown, inky blackness of night. The rain had slowed to a steady drizzle, and the wind was mild.

The first group to be taken the eighty yards to the beach included three sailors, Sir William, Derrick, and Father Lull. As soon as William, Derrick, and Father Lull exited the small boat, the three sailors started back. Father Lull knelt on the ground to pray. Sir William knelt beside him, and contrary to what he had told the Admiral just a few hours ago, he was very thankful to be on land again. At least until he stood up and found he had trouble walking. William had experienced this before, but this time it was far worse. His legs were certain the ground was still moving, even though his brain knew it wasn't. It was so pronounced that he was forced to make his way to a log just a little way up the beach and sit down.

Father Lull came and sat beside him and said, "The last couple of days were rough, but we will regain our equilibrium soon. I love being at sea, but I am relieved to be on solid ground. Do you think any of the other ships made it?"

William had closed his eyes briefly, thinking that would help, but it did not. He opened his eyes, looked at Father Lull, and said, "I pray that some of them have, but I fear it is a forlorn hope. I am surprised we made it, and Admiral Gregory is far more skilled than any of the other captains."

While Father Lull and Sir William were talking, Derrick disappeared into the woods. As the two looked up from the log they sat on, Derrick emerged from the woods with another man. William and Father Lull quickly stood and waited for Derrick and the other man to approach them.

The man with Derrick was dark-skinned, although not as dark as some sailors Father Lull had previously met among Phoenician sailors. The man's skin was also more reddish-brown than black. The man wore a leather breechcloth and had leather leggings. He wore nothing to cover his torso, had long black hair, and had a leather strap tied above his eyes. The man carried a strange-looking bow. The bow seemed to have a small bow face in the opposite direction of the main limbs. The longer limb portion of the bow was like a more traditional style bow. The string went all the way around both the large and small bows. The man carried a few arrows that appeared to be tied with bone.

Father Lull smiled broadly at the newcomer and said in both French and English, "May God bless you. I am Father Lull."

The man stared at him blankly, and Derrick said, "He speaks a different language. When I met him in the woods, he said something to me, but I didn't understand it. He used sign language that indicated he and I should return to the beach. I saw four others with him. I believe he has several more companions in the woods that I did not see, but I felt their presence."

Father Lull then tried Latin and got the same blank response from the man. Father Lull said to Sir William and Derrick, "This man must be one of the Vinlanders that the Sagas about Leif Erikson mention."

111

The newcomer then pointed out the ship and the smaller boat that was rowing toward shore, containing Admiral Gregory, Mary, and a fourth sailor. The Vinlander said something none of them could understand.

Father Lull pointed to the ship and said, "Ship."

As Father Lull continued trying to communicate with the man, William took Derrick by the arm and guided him toward the incoming boat. As they walked toward the ocean, William said quietly, "How many do you think there are in the woods, and are they all carrying weapons?"

Derrick said, "I can't say with any certainty, but I would guess maybe ten. They appear to be very comfortable in the woods, so there could be many more, and they only allowed me to see the five of them. From what I saw, they all carried a bow, like our new friend, or a spear with a bone tip. I also saw some knives."

William said, "I don't like this. Who do you think they are? The language is like nothing I've heard before. They appear to have been waiting in the woods for us to come ashore. We are completely exposed here on this beach, and there are only a few trained fighting men amongst us. With Admiral Gregory coming ashore, we will have only two swords and no armor with which to defend ourselves."

Derrick said, "I do not believe they mean us any harm. They seem to be mostly curious and cautious. I believe they are a hunting party who happened upon us."

Admiral Gregory, Mary, and the sailor approached Sir William. All three gazed curiously at the dark-skinned man with Father Lull several feet up the beach. Gregory said, "It appears we have already met one of the locals."

William replied, "Yes, and Derrick saw a few others in the woods. He seems friendly, but we need to be cautious. We are very exposed here and have only five men ashore so far."

Gregory said, "I agree that caution is called for, but given that we are few even after we have all our men ashore, I think we must attempt to make friends. We will likely need their help if we expect to make our home here."

Just then, the group heard Father Lull laugh loudly and excitedly, saying, "Truly amazing!" Father Lull then turned to face the others of his party and called to them, "Come here, all of you. This is most amazing."

As the group from the shore walked up to Father Lull and the other man, Father Lull said, "I would like to introduce you to Nattesg'g. At least, I believe that is his name and not his title. His people are called the Mi'kmaq. Although I don't think I am pronouncing it quite correctly."

Nattesg'g was grinning broadly and said as he held his hand to his chest, "Nattesg'g." Then to their surprise, he pointed to Father Lull and said, "Lull." Then, pointing to each in turn, he said, "Gregory, William, Derrick." He then pointed at Mary and the sailor, looking at Father Lull quizzically.

Father Lull laughed and pointed to Mary and said, "Mary." Then, to the sailor, and said, "Philip."

Nattesg'g said, "Mary, Philip."

Father Lull told the group, "Nattesg'g has a clear aptitude for language. He may learn our tongue long before I can learn his."

Admiral Gregory said, "I don't suppose you learned anything about their intentions regarding us?"

Father Lull said, "No, names are as far as we have gotten."

Derrick interrupted and said, "The others are coming out."

As they all turned toward the woods, they could see twenty or so others dressed in leather like Nattesg'g emerging from the woods.

CHAPTER TWENTY-NINE

Cardinal Soprano met with Sir Henry in the clergy cell Sir Henry used as an office and sleeping chamber. The cell was slightly larger than the ones the other men had since he needed a small table and chair in his, but it was just as plain as any other monk's cell. Sir Henry said, "Your Eminence, I know why you have come, and as much as I would like to be rid of Father Thomas, I do not want that man out from under my control. I fear what new mischief he could stir up if left to his own meager principles."

Cardinal Soprano said, "I understand your feelings toward Father Thomas, but there are things regarding the father I would like you to consider. Men do change; it is uncommon, I will admit, but it does happen. Father Thomas has shown that he understands, at least intellectually, the evil he has done and admitted to his errors in judgment."

Sir Henry couldn't help but interrupt, "Errors in judgment? I am sorry, Your Eminence, but he took an oath when he became a member of the Templars. Even though that oath is not as binding for a priest as it is for a knight, it still obligates him to us. He betrayed the Order, he betrayed Odo and me, and I am certain Father Thomas had more to do with Odo's death than he has said."

Cardinal Soprano said calmly, "Be that as it may, he has displayed remorse and appears to be trying to change. As I was saying, we need to consider more than just our feelings. I know you do not trust Thomas, and I must admit I do not fully trust him either. He has done much evil, leaving a stain on his soul that is most difficult to clean. I understand your desire to keep him under your watchful eye, but you cannot do that for the rest of his life. The only way we can determine if a man is truly trustworthy is to trust him and see how he does. I think this may be a good opportunity. We allow the father to go on his pilgrimage. Suppose he completes his journey and returns to us with a humble heart? In that case, we have added an asset to our group here, and we may both be able to relax our watchfulness over the good Father. If Father Thomas fails, we have an answer of a different sort, but still an answer."

Sir Henry said, "I do not like him being out there without someone watching him. We will have no way of knowing what he is truly up to.

Yet, I will release Father Thomas to go on this pilgrimage if you think it is for the best."

Cardinal Soprano said, "Thank you, Sir Henry. Rest assured that God's will shall be done; how could it not? We must also remember that no one is completely alone, and God sees all that we are up to, even those things we think are hidden in our hearts."

Sir Henry said, "I just can't shake the feeling we are turning loose a fox in the hen house."

Cardinal Soprano took his leave from Sir Henry and went directly to Father Thomas' cell. Father Thomas was there waiting to hear the outcome of the Cardinal's meeting with Sir Henry. The Cardinal said, "Sir Henry has decided to allow you to go on your pilgrimage."

Father Thomas said, "Thank you, Your Eminence. I am relieved to hear that. I am very eager for this next step in my spiritual journey."

Cardinal Soprano asked, "When do you plan on departing?"

Father Thomas replied, "I see no reason why I should not leave immediately, as I am taking only the robe I am wearing. I need not pack anything. I have no duties to wrap up here. If you will give me your blessing, I will start my journey immediately."

Thomas knelt before the Cardinal. Cardinal Soprano placed one hand on Father Thomas' head and raised his other hand as he said, "God our Father, be with this man on his pilgrim's journey of faith. Give him the grace and courage to step forward in faith and hope on the road ahead. Blessed Virgin Mary, open his eyes to see your face in all those he encounters. Open his ears to hear your voice in those who are often ignored. Lord, bless this man that he may be an instrument of Your divine mercy. In the name of the Father, the Son, and the Holy Spirit."

Father Thomas said, "Thank you, Your Eminence, for all you have done for me. There are a few hours of sunlight left, so I believe I will begin my journey. God be with you, Cardinal." Then Father Thomas departed.

As Cardinal Soprano watched Thomas walk away, he said in a low voice to himself, "May God be with you too, and may the eyes of those who watch over you be diligent."

CHAPTER THIRTY

Within a week, Sir William's group had established a small base just beyond the tree line from where the ship was beached. At first, the party was extremely apprehensive about the Mi'kmaq. They always appeared without warning and usually in large numbers. The Mi'kmaq quickly made it clear to everyone that they wished to be friends. All the members, except Sir William, soon began to trust and befriend the Mi'kmaq. William appreciated their help but remained skeptical of their good intentions. He had trouble explaining why he remained cautious when the other members of his party asked him. The Mi'kmaq did nothing even remotely aggressive and were also eager to help. They brought food to the group and even helped them build their settlement. They showed the Europeans where to find fresh water and took Derrick, Leif, Sir Justin, and some of the other men hunting.

Captain Gregory immediately began repairing the ship while Sir William focused on building and supplying the camp. Leif, Sir Justin, and Cinead often joined in to help Captain Gregory with repairs. They hoped to have the vessel seaworthy in another week. Captain Gregory planned to sail the coast looking for the other ships and explore the coastline. Until the ship was ready to sail, Sir William had sent two groups of men, accompanied by some Mi'kmaq, to follow the shoreline both north and south to search for any sign of the other ships.

One afternoon, Captain Gregory came to Sir William and said, "The ship will be ready to sail in the morning. I propose that I take her north and search the coastline. I should return in about two weeks. I will take a skeleton crew, so you have enough men to continue building our camp and gathering winter supplies. I would like to take Cinead, Sir Justin, and Leif, as they are able seamen and will be handy when we go ashore."

Sir William said, "That sounds like a worthy plan, Captain. Do you think you will need to go to shore much? I would hate to lose all three of them; they are all very skilled at hunting and tracking. We still need to gather a great deal of meat before winter sets in."

Captain Gregory replied, "I don't ask for them lightly. I realize that winter stores are important, but they have skills I will need. We will likely need to go onto the shore a few times to examine the beach and nearby forest if we locate a natural harbor. If we find any signs of the other ships, we may need to travel inland to locate survivors if they were foolish enough to leave the shoreline. I will need someone who can track. The best trackers are Derrick, Sir Justin, and Leif. I don't think I could get Derrick to go unless Mary were allowed to travel with us, and she doesn't appear to have recovered from the last sea voyage."

While considering the request, Sir William said, "We are lucky Leif chose to sail on our ship rather than with the rest of the Norwegians on Captain Anderson's vessel. Could you make do with taking only Leif and Cinead?"

Gregory thought momentarily, then said, "They should be fine if they do not need to travel inland too far. A rope of two strands is stronger than one, but still far more likely to fail than a rope of three strands. Although I suppose we can make it work."

Sir William said, "Good, we should be fine with both Derrick and Sir Justin hunting. We also have Nattesg'g and a couple of his fellows helping us hunt periodically. Sir Justin has become quite the tracker and hunter, almost as good as Derrick. I wish we had more men. I constantly have to pull men from one job to complete another. I know we must search for the other ships, but I'm anxious to finish the camp. We just don't have the manpower to do everything as thoroughly as I would like."

Captain Gregory said, "All the more reason for me to get my butt out to sea where I can search a broader area more quickly. If I can find any of the others, it will add significantly to our manpower."

William asked, "What do you truly think the likelihood is that any of the others survived?"

Gregory said, "That is difficult to say. If any of the other ships made it through the storms, the chance of finding them close to where we landed is slim. Some may have weathered the storms, but could be many leagues north or south of us. Some of the ships may have even returned to Greenland after the first storm. We may never know the fate of the other ships, but we must search for them."

Sir William said, "Well, we will pray God directs you."

Father Lull, Mary, and Derrick had spent most of the week among the Mi'kmaq. Derrick had befriended Nattesg'g and found the man to be one of the finest hunters he had ever met. Their double bow configuration was brilliant. It added significant power while keeping the bow short and easy to carry through the thick woods.

Whenever Nattesg'g was not hunting with Derrick, Father Lull was learning the Mi'kmaq language from him. Although no matter how much Father Lull worked, Nattesg'g seemed to be learning French quicker than Father Lull could pick up the Mi'kmaq language.

Mary, who had been seasick the entire passage from Norway, seemed no better now that they were on shore. She was vomiting several times a day. She claimed she felt better after each time she was sick, but a few hours later, she would be nauseous again. One of the Mi'kmaq women finally solved the mystery of Mary's nausea. The Vinland woman very matter-of-factly indicated that Mary was pregnant. It seemed all the Mi'kmaq women had known this, but it wasn't until they learned enough of the French language that they realized Mary was unaware she was with child.

Mary was at the same time frightened and excited. When she told Derrick, he was unsure how to respond. He knew that her becoming pregnant was likely to happen, and there was a sense of joy in having a baby. At the same time, he wondered what type of father he would make and what their life would be like here in this new land. When he told Mary about his fears, Mary said, "Don't you worry about that; as long as we love this child, things will work out."

Derrick took a little comfort from that, but a voice in the back of his mind whispered, *"Your mother and father loved you and your sister too."* Derrick knew better than to voice any further concerns, so he hugged Mary and said, "I know things will be fine. I just want the best for our child."

The others in their group would also have been more excited if things were not so tense. Preparations for winter were going well, but they all felt an undercurrent of worry. Vinland was abundant with game and plant life of all sorts. It seemed to contain everything they needed. Yet, at the same time, the land around them seemed so wild it often left them with a feeling of foreboding.   Everyone was also concerned about the fate of the other ships. They all felt their party was too small in this unknown land. They had a few farmers among their group, and some craftsmen, chief among those, Master Acel. They had the knowledge and experience to build a community, but did they have the numbers to establish a permanent base of operation?

The Mi'kmaq's summer settlement was a two-hour walk northwest of where the Templars settled. The Mi'kmaq encouraged the Templars to build their settlement further inland, but Sir William and Admiral Gregory wanted to be closer to the sea to watch for the other ships. There was a little concern when Sir William discovered the Mi'kmaq would leave their summer settlement in a few weeks and travel further inland to the winter settlement. Nattesg'g explained that the winter was less severe, and winter hunting would be better if they traveled inland. Sir William believed they would be fine this winter and maybe consider a winter camp inland next year. He also knew they could not hope to set up a second camp before winter struck.

Captain Gregory and his crew were finally ready to set sail. Before Gregory departed, Sir William said, "I hope you find some other survivors. Have a safe voyage."

Captain Gregory slapped Cinead on the back and replied, "We will be fine. I have Cinead with me; what could possibly go wrong with him around?" Cinead smiled but remained uncharacteristically quiet as he climbed into the small rowboat, waiting to take them to the ship. Those on shore watched as the sails unfurled and the ship steered north, then they all got back to work. There was much to finish before the snow started to fall.

The Templars had built a longhouse in the Norwegian design in a small clearing just inside the tree line from where they had first landed. They also began to lay in stores of meat and fish. The Mi'kmaq gave the Templars some fruit, vegetables, and a little grain from their winter stores, but they had little to spare.

Nattesg'g continued hunting with Derrick and Sir Justin. When he was not hunting, he could be found with Father Lull learning French and teaching the priest his language. Father Lull learned the language the Mi'kmaq spoke was called Mi'kmawi'simk. He also discovered that Nattesg'g's name meant "to chase" or "to hunt." Nattesg'g became the spokesman for the Mi'kmaq among the Templars. With Father Lull's help, he continually increased his ability to communicate with the Templar party. After Nattesg'g's vocabulary grew and he could speak more fluently, he again encouraged Sir William to relocate their camp further inland. Nattesg'g told Sir William, "The wind and storms will be much stronger close to the sea. Hunting and fishing will become very difficult, and even going outside could become hazardous."

Sir William replied, "This will only be a temporary camp until the rest of our ships arrive. I believe we will make it through one winter. We have lived in Norway, which also has very cold winters." The matter was settled for Sir William, and he went back to work on their camp. Nattesg'g tried a few more times to convince William, but to no effect.

The longhouse was built large enough for all the Templars to winter together. They added a couple of interior walls to give Mary and Derrick a private space, but the rest of them would all sleep in the main open room. In addition to the main building, they dug a root cellar and built a cold house to store their perishables.

Sir William also had Master Acel construct an underground chamber to keep the treasure that their ship had carried. Sir William pulled Master Acel aside and told him, "I want you to make sure that none of the Mi'kmaq know anything about the treasure chamber."

Master Acel could not make the chamber as deep as he would have liked due to flooding once they dug down to about fifteen feet. He created a cleverly hidden trap door under the central fire pit using a large stone set with an internal pivot pin.

One day, when Nattesg'g and Derrick were out hunting, Nattesg'g told Derrick in broken but understandable French that he was concerned for the Templars this winter. He felt they would have a very hard time of it. He told Derrick that he tried to convince his people to take the Templars in for the winter, but they refused, believing it would stretch their food supplies too far. Nattesg'g added that he had convinced his people to allow Derrick, Mary, and Father Lull to live with them if they wished. Derrick thanked Nattesg'g but said, "I don't think Mary and Father Lull will agree, but I will talk to them."

When Derrick told Father Lull and Mary about Nattesg'g's offer, Father Lull said, "I do not feel like I should leave the Templars. I have come to love the Mi'kmaq people, but I can't just leave. I am concerned about Sir William discounting Nattesg'g's warnings regarding the camp's location. However, I believe the log house should be warm enough, provided the winter isn't as harsh as we experienced in Norway, and we

120

will have enough food stored. Yet I wish Sir William did not distrust the Mi'kmaq as he does."

Mary seemed to be considering the offer more, but she finally said, "I agree with Father Lull. We should stay with the Templar camp and help through the winter. The Mi'kmaq women said they do not believe I will have the baby before the spring." Derrick was less certain. He had grown to trust Nattesg'g and was concerned by Nattesg'g's continual worry about the harsh winter. Derrick also feared the baby coming with no woman around to help with the birth.

Two weeks, almost to the day after Captain Gregory had left the settlement, the ship returned. Captain Gregory and most of the men came ashore. Sir William called an open meeting with the rest of their party so that Captain Gregory could tell them all that he had discovered.

Gregory said, "We sailed nine days north and saw no sign of ships nor wreckage at sea or along the shore. We saw no other people and only put ashore twice. Both times, we checked the composition of the beaches in areas with a natural harbor deep enough for our ship. We found a harbor about three miles north that may be a good place for the ship to lie in anchor this winter. I think we still have a bit of time to search further. I propose that the crew and I sail south and see what we may find in that direction. The weather shows no sign of turning yet, so I believe we should be safe for at least a couple of weeks."

Sir William asked, "How soon do you propose to leave, and how long do you expect to be gone?"

Captain Gregory said, "I would like to leave tomorrow and should return within two weeks." Sir William indicated that that would be acceptable.

The temperature dropped two days after the ship sailed south, and the wind blew hard from the north. Then it started to snow. Nattesg'g indicated that the snow and cold temperatures may continue all winter or clear tomorrow and warm back up for a while. He told Sir William there was no way to know about the weather this time of year. The settlement collected more firewood while Derrick, Sir Justin, and the other hunters focused on hunting, fishing, and trapping.

It did not warm back up, and the snow continued to fall. Each day, Sir William and the others prayed that the ship and Captain Gregory would return, and every day they were disappointed. One morning, as he looked at the steel grey clouds heavy with snow, William reflected that they had left Norway with over three hundred people. Now they had less than forty if Captain Gregory and his men returned. Without the Captain and his sailors, there were only twenty-eight members of his party to start a new base of operation for the Knights Templar. Of those twenty-eight, there were only five knights and six sergeants-at-arms.

CHAPTER THIRTY-ONE

As they walked through the city, Dudel told Louis, "You must be very careful around Prince Yury Dailovich. I was told he can sometimes be erratic and has had many people put to death for apparently minor offenses."

Louis asked, "I assume he is the Prince of Muscovy. Is his father the king of Rus?"

Dudel replied, "Honestly, I am a bit confused by some of these titles. He is married to the sister of Uzbeg Khan, who is the commander of the Golden Horde. From what I was led to believe, Uzbeg Khan made him the Grand Duke of Vladimir after he married his sister. This made him the highest-ranking non-Mongol authority in all of Rus. I also have heard he is not well-liked by the populace, but that can be said of most royalty."

They arrived thirty minutes before their appointment at the city's government building. The administrative office was one of many inside a large complex of buildings and courtyards. The whole collection of structures appeared to be designed to act as a military fortification if necessary. Dudel had been told that the grounds also housed the administrative center for Muscovy as well as the local residence of Prince Yury Dailovich and some of his senior staff. He was told there was a massive open courtyard in the center where the prince held outdoor parties and even military exercises.

Presently, a wall was being constructed around the outside of the entire compound. Louis and Dudel got directions to the government offices from an officious-looking man inside the outer wall. Most of these outer buildings were connected in a ring about thirty feet inside the outer wall that was under construction. Louis presumed the sandstone buildings would become an inner wall when construction was complete. The two walls would create a killing field between them if an enemy breached the outside wall.

Louis and Dudel went through a heavy door to the offices they had been directed to. Inside was a large hall with benches lining the walls. There must have been forty people seated on the benches waiting. Louis and Dudel walked to the gallery's far end, where a man sat at a desk. Behind the man seated at the desk, two soldiers stood to either side of a door. Dudel introduced himself and told the man at the desk he had an appointment regarding the establishment of a trade center. The man wrote Dudel's name down and told him to have a seat on one of the benches. They waited for over two hours while others were called forward and then ushered through the door that the soldiers guarded. It was early afternoon when the man at the desk told everyone in the hall to return the following day, as Prince Yury and his advisors were too busy to see anyone else today."

Dudel did not appear upset or even surprised as he stood up to leave. Louis told Dudel as they walked toward the outer door, "You act as though you were expecting to be told to return later."

Dudel replied, "It is not uncommon, especially in a city where I am new and have not discovered who I need to pay in order to receive preferential treatment. As yet, I am nobody to the ruling authority. It may easily take a month of coming here every day before I am given an audience unless I can find someone to recommend me to the right person."

Louis asked, "What if I explained that I was a knight sent as an envoy from the King of Scotland? Do you think that might get me an audience? Then I could bring you with me, and you could conduct your business."

Dudel did not have time to answer before one of the soldiers who was herding everyone out of the hall suddenly took Louis by the arm and asked, in French, "Did you say you are a Scottish knight?"

Dudel said, "We are very sorry to disturb you, sir, but we were..."

The soldier interrupted and said, "I am not speaking to you, little man."

Louis did not like the tone of this man, so he straightened to his full height, drew a step closer to the big man, and said, "I was not speaking to you. I was talking privately to my friend here, whom you have just insulted."

The large man looked into Louis' eyes as if gauging his abilities. Then he smiled and said, "I apologize to your little friend; I meant nothing hostile. I thought I heard you say you were a knight from Scotland, and if that is true, I would like to have words with you."

Louis was still uncertain of this man's intent, but saw no need to deny that he was a knight. He said, "Yes, I am a knight under the command of King Robert the Bruce of Scotland. I am Sir Louis de Champagne."

The big man's smile broadened, and he said, "I am Kirill Volkov. I am the chief guard to Prince Yury. What business do you have with the prince?"

Louis said, "My friend here, master Dudel Askenazic, is here to see about setting up a trade center here in Muscovy."

The big man looked down at Dudel and then back at Louis, "But, I heard you say you were here at the request of the King of Scotland."

In Louis's mind, he could hear Sergeant Bertrand saying, "Your mouth is going to get you killed, or worse."

Louis said, "Yes, but my business is secondary to master Askenazic's. I was only trying to get my friend in to see your Prince."

Kirill said, "So, you are not sent here by the King of Scotland?"

Louis said, "Yes, I mean, no. Yes, I have been sent here by the King of Scotland and have business with your Prince, but my business is secondary to Dudel's."

Kirill said, "We will let the prince decide whose business is secondary. Follow me."

The three of them walked through several doors guarded by men carrying spears and wearing light armor and furs. Dudel nearly had to run to keep up and was about to ask them to slow down when they exited the building. Dudel and Louis found themselves in a large courtyard where the prince's soldiers were practicing. The soldiers seemed to be sparring in small groups scattered around the open area. The ground was mostly flat and open, with few trees. On the opposite side from where they stood was a viewing area where several important-looking men were seated on a raised platform. Kirill led them across the yard to where these men were watching the soldiers practice.

As they approached, one of the men wearing a high conical hat glanced at Kirill and said, "What do you wish, commander?"

Kirill said, "These men have business with Prince Yury."

The man in the conical hat said, "The prince does not have time for any further business today."

Kirill said, "I believe the prince will wish to make time for these men. This man is Sir Louis de Champagne, a knight sent here from the King of Scotland."

Several of the men looked away from the practicing soldiers they had been watching and turned to gaze at Louis, who suddenly felt very conspicuous. One of the men rose. He wore a flowing robe and a fur hat. He had a beard that covered much of his face. This man said, "You are a knight? Where are your armor and weapons?"

Now, everyone, even many of the soldiers nearby who had been practicing, stopped what they were doing and stared at Sir Louis. Louis assumed this man was Prince Yury. Louis bowed and said, "Your Royal Highness, I did not believe it would be appropriate to wear my armor and bear weapons when meeting royalty. I did not want to give the wrong impression about the nature of my visit."

Prince Yury replied, "I see. Who is your little friend? Your squire?" This drew a few laughs from those around Yury.

Louis was about to introduce him when Dudel stepped in front of Louis and said, "Your Royal Highness, I am Dudel Askenazic, a humble merchant of fine goods who wishes to open a trade center in your wonderful city of Muscovy. I have a letter from...."

Prince Yury held up a hand, indicating Dudel should stop talking. He looked down at Dudel and then up at Louis. He seemed to be considering what to make of this pair. He finally said, "Does the King of Scotland wish to open a shop in Muscovy?"

Louis bowed his head slightly and said, "Your Royal Highness, I am sorry. My friend Dudel and I are here on separate business. He is here to work out the details for his shop, and I was just accompanying him at this time. I planned on seeking an official audience later after Dudel finished his business."

Prince Yury looked to his left, raised his voice, and said, "Boris, take Master Dudel here and see to his needs. Make sure he has a good location for his shop."

A man stepped forward and indicated that Dudel should follow him. As Dudel and Boris went to an unoccupied table several feet away, Yury looked back to Louis. He said, "Your friend's business is being taken care of. Now, I would hear why the King of Scotland has sent a knight to speak with me."

CHAPTER THIRTY-TWO

The temperature began to plummet, and the hunting and trapping produced sparse results. Just getting enough water became a grueling daily chore. What weighed heaviest on Sir William was that Captain Gregory and his men had not returned. The ship was almost a month late, exceeding the expected two weeks; the captain indicated he believed the trip would take. Sir William prayed they were safe and would return once the weather warmed up. He hoped they had found a safe inlet to harbor the ship and had been able to find enough food to sustain them until they could return.

The long house stayed reasonably warm, but any venture outside the lodge had to be cautiously taken. Being outside in the wind and cold for a few minutes could cause unprotected skin to become frostbitten. They had thought they would be prepared for the cold since they had spent two winters in Norway. This was worse than they expected; the winds blew constantly, and they had to send men out every day to clear snow drifts from the entrance to the door and the holes in the roof that allowed smoke to escape.

Sir William believed the stores of meat they had laid up in the cold house would see them through the winter if they were careful. They had a few fruits and vegetables, but he thought it would be enough. Their contact with the Mi'kmaq became very rare.

One day, Nattesg'g showed up at the longhouse with a sack of groundnuts and some smoked salmon. It was not much, but all the Mi'kmaq could spare. Nattesg'g stayed for three days showing the Templar band how to ice fish and better methods for winter trapping. Nattesg'g again encouraged Derrick, Mary, and Father Lull to return with him. He said, "Winter is just starting. It could be four to five more moon cycles before spring. Many of the elders among my people believe there will be a lot of snow this year. With the way the snow is accumulating, it may soon be impossible to travel between your camp and our summer camp. Mary needs more food. Father Lull could teach more French. Most of my people have already traveled to the winter camp. Only a few of us remain nearby."

Mary and Father Lull were unwilling to consider it. Then Derrick said, "I know you do not want to abandon these men here, but you need to consider a couple of things. By our departure, we may increase the chance of everyone's survival. The others who remain will have three fewer mouths to feed. Also, no one here knows anything about delivering a baby. The baby is supposed to come in the spring, but what if it comes before the thaw? Wouldn't it be better for Mary to be with the Mi'kmaq women who can help her?"

Father Lull said, "Perhaps. Those are good points. Maybe we should talk to Sir William."

Sir William listened silently as the three explained what Nattesg'g was offering and Derrick's reasons why they should consider it. William was feeling a bit trapped. He had already lost Captain Gregory, who was his primary confidante. Now to lose these three, whom he had come to rely on for advice. At the same time, he saw the wisdom in having the three of them go, particularly Mary. Many of the Templars were very uncomfortable having Mary in the longhouse with them. What would it be like during the birth?

At last, he said, "I agree with Derrick. Although I will miss the three of you terribly, I think it would be best for all of us if you wintered with the Mi'kmaq."

Two days after the discussion to go to the Mi'kmaq village, the sun shone brightly on the frozen landscape. Nattesg'g said the weather was as good for travel as they could hope for this time of year. The four of them left the Templar camp and began the trek through the snow. Before they left, Nattesg'g told Sir William, "About thirty of my people have decided to remain in the summer camp. If you need help, try to reach the camp; we will do whatever we can."

Sir William said, "Thank you, Nattesg'g, but I believe we will be fine. "

The trip usually took two hours, but with Nattesg'g and Derrick having to cut a path through the higher snow drifts, it took almost eight hours. Many of the drifts were more than waist high, and Nattesg'g said they were likely to get much higher, making travel very difficult, if not impossible. By the time they arrived, they were all exhausted and very cold.

Nattesg'g's people took the three into their community happily. All three had visited the Mi'kmaq's village several times previously. The three had befriended many of the villagers and demonstrated they would make a good addition to their community.

Although it was apparent that the village was not overburdened with food stores, they were in a better position than the Templar camp. There were several wigwams rather than one communal longhouse. The Mi'kmaq cleared most of the snow in the camp so that movement between wigwams was easy. This made it feel like they were less trapped than remaining in the single structure of the Templar base all the time.

Derrick was the first to note that there were far fewer wigwams than the last time they had visited. Derrick asked Nattesg'g, "How many of your people have already gone to the winter camp?"

Nattesg'g said, "The majority left during the first snow. Normally, we would all have gone, but those of us here chose to stay. We wanted to be closer to the Templar camp, to help if we could."

Derrick asked, "Help in what way?"

Nattesg'g shrugged and said, "I am not sure. If the snow gets too deep, we may not be able to reach the Templar camp, even from our summer camp. The winter village is three days inland when the weather is good. Now it would take many days to reach it. Too far if your people need help. Sir William should have listened to me and made your camp near our winter camp. I fear they may not survive winter."

The days of winter passed slowly. Derrick learned many new trapping skills. Father Lull spent his days teaching French and learning the Mi'kmaq language. Father Lull tried to convert many of the villagers. Although they enjoyed his stories and listened intently to what he said, they showed no desire to convert. In response to Father Lull's Bible stories, the Mi'kmaq told him their creation stories and tales about Kji-Niskam. Father Lull was very interested and asked many questions. Eventually, the questions he asked seemed to make no sense to the Mi'kmaq, so they told Father Lull, "In the spring, you should ask our Puoinaq; he is with the winter camp. He will teach you."

Mary was made to feel very welcome by the women who had stayed at the summer camp. They eased her mind a great deal as three of the women were experienced at aiding with childbirth. The women showed Mary how to weave a papoose for the baby and helped Mary make clothing for the soon-to-be-born infant.

CHAPTER THIRTY-THREE

The drop in temperature and the never-ending wind made things increasingly difficult for Sir William and his men. Trapping and ice fishing provided the group with nothing except cases of frostbite and frustration. They knew the trapping and fishing would slow, but they hoped they would still get some game to add to their meat stores. Eventually, the ice flows on the shore grew so thick that they could no longer cut through the ice.

One morning, about three months after Mary, Derrick, and Father Lull had left, the Templars found that the cold house they had built to store the meat for the winter had been discovered by mice. The mice had chewed on several pieces of the frozen meat. It didn't look too extensive, but they would need to attempt to seal it off better, or it could worsen. Sir William had known that things would grow tougher as the winter continued, but none of them expected it would get this bad. They all felt trapped by the ice and snow. Each of them dreaded going outside in the blustering cold weather, but they also felt cooped up in the longhouse.

Sir William was beginning to believe he should have listened to the Mi'kmaq about moving further inland for the winter, but there was nothing he could do about that now. Today, he was going to go with the team to collect more firewood while other men tried to make the cold house more mouse-proof. When William returned from the bitter cold of hauling wood to the longhouse, he found that the crew working on the cold house had discovered that it was not just mice eating at the meat stores. Rats and apparently some other larger animals had found their way into the meat storeroom. At some point, before the ground had frozen solid, some animal had burrowed under the outside wall of the cold house. The men had filled in and sealed that hole, but found numerous other places where the mice and rats had made their way into the cold storage.

As the men dug down through the meat stores, they discovered more of it had been chewed upon. They estimated they had lost about a week's worth of their stores. When Sir William arrived, the men were discussing bringing the meat into the longhouse. Someone suggested they put the meat along the peak of the roof, just under the thatching. They believed that the freezing temperature outside would keep the meat frozen. They also thought the smoke from their ever-present fire might help preserve the meat. William doubted the smoke would have much effect, but it was very cold just under the thatching. Perhaps that would work.

William wished Derrick were still with them. William thought the young man's experience would be able to guide them. In the end, Sir William decided to do as others recommended. They brought all the meat from the cold house and placed it along the roof of the longhouse. Getting the meat wedged up into the thatching was a chore, and it took several hours. As they brought the meat in, they discovered even more meat that the rodents had gnawed on.

That night, as they slept, the two men standing guard heard rustling from the ceiling. One of the men stirred the fire to provide more light. When they gazed at the ceiling of the longhouse, it appeared to be moving. They quickly realized the roof was full of mice and rats crawling amongst the meat. The two guards cried the alarm and woke the others. As the men saw the rodents feasting on their winter meat store, they grabbed sticks, swords, arrows, whatever was at hand, and tried to drive off the vermin.

At one point, William saw a creature he initially thought was a small bear up in the ceiling. On second look, he realized it seemed more like a weasel than a bear. As a man swung a lit torch near the creature, it showed its large teeth and hissed ferociously. After a few moments, it became obvious that the men's attempt to chase off the creatures infesting the lodge ceiling had little effect. William was about to order the men to climb up and remove the meat. Before he could give the command, one of the men swung a torch too close to the dry thatch. Before anyone could react, a fire was spreading rapidly across the ceiling.

Sir William instructed the men to gather whatever they could and throw it outside the lodge. In moments, embers were dropping to the lodge floor; animal hides and clothing caught fire. Soon, the room was full of smoke, and Sir William ordered everyone out of the growing inferno. The twenty-five remaining members at the Templar camp watched as their shelter burned to the ground. William could not believe the number of mice and rats he saw fleeing the flames.

William wondered what they would do as the flames died, and the red embers glowed in the dark of early morning. They were out of supplies, and their only shelter was gone. He wondered if they should make for the Mi'kmaq village, but was unsure if they would be welcomed or seen as an unacceptable burden.

All had been silent until one of the men yelled, "What were you thinking, Albert? You dumb ass, you have killed us all by waving that bloody torch around and lighting the ceiling aflame."

Albert replied, "It wasn't me; it was Kendal. He was slinging his torch at that baby bear, or whatever it was. He hit the dry thatch; I saw it."

As Kendal began to deny that his torch had done it, Sir William yelled at the men, "That will be enough of that! There is no time or need to lay blame. I decided we should put the meat in the thatching. It is my fault. Right now, we need to decide what to do. I have no doubt we can build a small shelter, but what are we to eat? There are still several weeks of winter left."

Sir Justin spoke up, "Sir William is right. What's done is done. We need to decide what to do now, and we need to decide soon."

William said, "First off, is anyone injured from the fire or falling debris other than minor burns?"

No one spoke up.

William continued, "Good. I think our only choice is to pack up what supplies we have left and make our way to the Mi'kmaq village. Nattesg'g said they did not have enough supplies for us, but maybe they could take us in, and with their help, we might be able to trap or hunt some game further inland. Nattesg'g said the hunting was a little better there during the winter."

There was some mumbling among the men, but they soon quieted and got to work packing up what they had salvaged from the fire and prepared to head out. They decided they would travel for a few hours, attempt to build a fire, warm up as best they could, rest for an hour, and then start out again. They decided they would travel day and night. The nights were much longer during winter, and they didn't think they could afford to only travel in the daylight.

Before they started the trek through the woods, Master Acel asked Sir William, "What should we do about the treasure we have hidden in the stone chamber below where the long house had stood?"

Sir William said, "I think it will be safer where it is for now. It will do no good to pack it with us in this wilderness."

As the first rays of sunlight peeked bleakly through the heavily overcast skies, the band of twenty-five men began to push a trail through the deep snow.

CHAPTER THIRTY-FOUR

Thomas had been pilfering money from the Templar community for the last few months, knowing he would need it at some point. Given the Templars' extensive involvement in new business activities, it was not difficult for Thomas to skim off a substantial amount of money. A few days before he left Lucerne, Thomas had hidden the money in a dead tree just off the roadway south of the town. On the first night, after departing Lucerne, he had recovered the money. Thomas carefully sewed it into his robes to keep it concealed. Father Thomas spent the first week of his "pilgrimage" walking the roads toward Italy, begging for food when he encountered anyone, and offering a blessing. On the seventh day after leaving Lucerne, Father Thomas entered the village of Engelberg.

Once Thomas arrived in Engelberg, he found an inn, got a room, and ordered a meal. The next day, he purchased a horse and supplies. The following morning, Thomas, dressed in riding clothes, rode generally west toward France. The ride was uneventful, but Thomas felt exposed riding alone through the mountains. He was constantly looking over his shoulder, expecting to see bandits.

By the time Father Thomas reached the city of Bern, he had decided he had had enough of traveling alone through the Swiss mountains. While purchasing more supplies, Thomas considered hiring a man or two to accompany him as protection against thieves. As luck would have it, Thomas discovered a group of merchants on their way to Troyes, France. Father Thomas put his priestly robes back on and asked the merchants if he might accompany them.

Father Thomas left Bern the following morning in the company of over a dozen traveling companions. Thomas decided he should not use his real name just to be safe, so he told the merchants his name was Father Dion. The only problem Thomas encountered on this leg of his journey was a monk who was also in the company. The monk was also originally from France and decided that he and Father Thomas should be friends. The monk's name was Alfred. He was a bit rotund and very talkative. No matter how much Thomas attempted to avoid Alfred, the monk seemed to always be at his side.

One morning, as Thomas rode along with the group of merchants, Alfred, riding a donkey, trotted up next to him. In a cheerful voice, Alfred said, "Good morning, Father Dion. What a wonderful day for traveling our Lord has given us."

Thomas kept his eyes on the road ahead and grunted a noncommittal response.

Alfred told Thomas, "I have not returned to France for eleven years. I am very excited to see my homeland again. When were you last there, Father Dion?"

Thomas knew he could not escape the conversation without seeming rude, which might draw unwanted attention. With little choice, Thomas decided to talk with the brother. He replied. "I was last there two years ago."

Alfred said, "Oh, so you were in France during the excitement with the Templars?"

Thomas, trying to evade this topic, said, "I was in France, but I was traveling around the south and heard only rumors. There were not many Templars down there."

Alfred said, "That's too bad. I would love to hear what went on. I have met only a few Templars, and they seemed like good fellows, not at all like I would assume a heretic would act. Did you know any Templars, Father Dion?"

Thomas sighed, wondering if this monk always ended his statements with a question. Thomas answered, "No, I have never met any Templars."

Alfred said, "I hear they are fearsome warriors and tremendously wealthy. It's fortunate that King Philip IV discovered their malicious activities before they could cause more harm. I often wondered what became of all the Templars' treasure. I have heard it said they had more money than the Kings of France and England combined. What do you think happened to all their money?"

Thomas said, "I have no idea."

Alfred said, "Makes one think, doesn't it? I suppose they couldn't have arrested them all. There are so many of them, literally an army. Still can't understand; if they are such great warriors, how did the King's men best them and place them under arrest? How do you suppose they did that, Father Dion?"

Thomas was becoming increasingly annoyed with the topic and decided to try to change the direction of the conversation. He said, "I don't know. Perhaps the Templar's abilities have been overstated. Why are you returning to France, Brother Alfred?"

Alfred said, "Oh, some Cardinal somewhere mentions his shoes are uncomfortable. A Bishop hears this, so he tries to seek favor by appointing a committee to investigate making more comfortable shoes for Cardinals. Next thing you know, priests and deacons everywhere are scrambling to do something about uncomfortable Cardinal shoes. An Abbot gets an idea for a new design for slippers to cover the feet of Cardinals. Before you know it, we lowly clergy get shuffled around to accommodate the new practice of making comfortable slippers for Cardinals."

Thomas looked down at the monk riding the donkey and, for the first time, he was interested in the conversation. Thomas asked, "You are being sent to France to make slippers?"

Alfred laughed, "No, I have no idea why I am being sent to Troyes. I was just saying I'm a servant, and I go where I am told, usually without knowing why. Why are you returning to France, Father Dion?"

Thomas wanted to throttle the monk. Controlling his anger, Thomas said, "I have business with another brother that must be handled personally."

Alfred said, "That sounds interesting. I don't suppose you can tell me what the business is?"

Thomas said, "I am sorry, but no."

Alfred said, "Probably for the best. Since you must handle your business personally, I would assume it's not for everyone's ears. Is the man you're meeting in Troyes?"

Thomas said, "I am not sure where he is."

Alfred said, "What is the brother's name? Perhaps I can help you locate the man."

Thomas thought for a moment and decided it wouldn't hurt anything to name whom he was searching for, and besides, maybe it would frighten Brother Alfred. Perhaps that would keep the monk from talking to him so much. Thomas said, "His name is Brother Jaye. He is a ranking man in the Holy Inquisition."

Alfred was quiet for a bit and then said, "Well, I doubt I will have an opportunity to meet with a brother like that. It has been nice chatting,

Father Dion." Then Alfred trotted his donkey toward the front of the line. Father Thomas smiled.

CHAPTER THIRTY-FIVE

Mary felt like a giant, ungainly beast. Her feet seemed to be twice their normal size. It was a chore to stand up, and she waddled when she walked. She felt hungry at odd hours and seemed to need to eat constantly. The Mi'kmaq women told her all this was normal, but she felt certain they would say that even if it wasn't. They informed her that she was further along than they originally thought. They felt certain the baby would come before spring, making Mary thankful she wasn't still at the Templar camp.

On three occasions, Mary believed the baby was coming. She had cramping that seemed to come in waves. Bineshii, one of the Mi'kmaq women, had taken charge of Mary's birth preparations. Bineshii was older than the other women, well past childbearing age. She had helped deliver many babies among the Mi'kmaq. Bineshii examined Mary each time she had these cramps and informed her that it was not yet time. She told Mary that these pains were just her body preparing for the birth.

One evening, Bineshii was sitting with Mary when Mary felt water between her legs. At first, she thought she had peed herself. Since becoming pregnant, Mary had found she had trouble holding her urine. Bineshii checked the liquid and made sure it was mostly clear and not bloody, then she helped Mary to the log house where they had prepared for her to give birth.

Bineshii was calm and clearly in control of the situation. She helped Mary get comfortable, then sent for the other women who were to help with the birth. Derrick and Father Lull soon discovered all the activity and appeared at the log house where Mary was. One of the Mi'kmaq women told Derrick that he was not needed. They would take care of Mary and the baby, and it might be many hours before the baby was born.

Nattesg'g guided Derrick and Father Lull to one of the larger teepees and waited. Derrick felt worried, almost to the point of being sick. At first, Father Lull tried to offer words of comfort, which only seemed to increase Derricks's anxiety. He told Derrick that God would watch over the birth and that they should pray for God's will to be done. He and Derrick knew that childbirth was very dangerous for women, and there was little they could do but pray.

138

Nattesg'g noticed that Derrick was thinking too much about the possible bad outcomes of the birth and that the Priest's words only added to Derrick's fears. Nattesg'g said, "Sakom Lull, I think we should talk of different things. My brothers are preparing some food for us while we wait. Perhaps we should talk about what type of man the child will become."

Father Lull looked up at Nattesg'g and asked, "What makes you think the child will be a boy?"

Derrick, who had been staring at his feet, slowly raised his gaze to Nattesg'g, obviously interested in his friend's response.

Nattesg'g smiled and said, "One has only to meet the parents to know that the first child will be a strong, healthy boy. Besides, the women all said they know it will be a boy by how Mary carries the child and other signs they have noticed."

Derrick asked, "What other signs?"

Nattesg'g, realizing that he had finally pulled Derrick away from his silent fears, dove into the topic to keep him distracted. "There are many signs that foretell a male child. Mary craves savory foods over sweet ones, a clear sign that she carries a boy. When a little girl grows within the mother, the baby girl steals her mother's looks. When carrying a girl, the mother looks less healthy and often gets pimples. When they carry a boy, the mother looks healthy, and her skin shines."

Father Lull slapped his knee and said, "You had me going for a minute, Nattesg'g. I thought you were serious."

Nattesg'g looked intently at Father Lull and said, "I am most serious, Sakom. Why would I joke about such a thing? Nature provides us with many clues about the future. We know the seasons change as the sun shifts along its path relative to the horizon. We know hunting is better when the moon is full. We smell rain on the wind. The animals of the woods tell us of dangers approaching, dangers of other animals, people, and nature's dangers. We know the best time to separate a suckling baby from a mother's breast is at full moon. Nature always tells us what to expect if we listen."

Father Lull said, "I have heard wives ' tales about determining the sex of an unborn child, but they are only guesses. They seem to be wrong as often as right."

Nattesg'g said, "If one only looks at one sign, you may be wrong. There are many different signs the child gives. Sometimes, the child does not want anyone to know their sex, and the child confuses the signs, so no one can be certain. This usually happens with a tricky, laughing, or deceitful child. Mary and Derrick's child has made it clear he is a boy."

Now fully attentive to the conversation, Derrick asked, "Have there been other signs?"

Nattesg'g said, "Yes, there are many. There is no doubt that you will have a son."

"What other signs were there?" Derrick asked.

Nattesg'g grinned big and said, "One sign we noted is from you, Derrick. When a woman is pregnant with a girl, the father tends to gain weight during the pregnancy. You have clearly lost weight. Another is that Mary is calm and pleasant to be around while pregnant, a sign that she carries a son. Most telling, the women prepared a stew a few weeks ago, especially for Mary. The stew they served Mary contained a lot of wild onions. Not only did Mary hungrily eat the stew, but afterward, the women said they could not smell any onion on her breath. That is a clear sign that a boy will be born."

Father Lull was still unconvinced and started to say something, but just then, several men from the village entered the teepee. They brought with them bowls of food and pipes for smoking. The Mi'kmaq smoked dried red willow bark, bearberry leaves, and a plant called tmaqan. The mixture they called kinnikinnik. Derrick and Father Lull had tried it. Derrick didn't enjoy it as much as the Mi'kmaq did, but he didn't mind it in small amounts. On the other hand, Father Lull grew dizzy and sick to his stomach the first time he tried it and refused to smoke it again.

CHAPTER THIRTY-SIX

As the men all seated themselves in a wide circle around the central fire in the wigwam, they began to eat and smoke. Nattesg'g noticed that Derrick was again growing withdrawn with worry for his wife. Nattesg'g raised his voice above the chatter and said, "Friend Derrick, it is traditional that while the women attend to the mother giving birth, the men gather and tell stories. I will tell the story of the Great Lord Glooskap and his brother Malsumsis.

Nattesg'g waited as the men quieted and then started his tale, "Before their birth, the two brothers discussed how they would enter the world of the people. Great Lord Glooskap, being just and good, chose to be born of a woman as regular men are. His brother, Malsumsis, felt it was beneath him to be born as a common man, so he chose to burst from his mother's side. At their births, Lord Glooskap entered the world in peace and light, but Malsumsis entered in death and darkness, killing his mother.

"The two spirits had powers beyond that of man, and each had a secret on how they could be killed. One day, Malsumsis, the young wolf, asked Glooskap how he could be killed. Glooskap, thinking about how Malsumsis entered the world by killing his mother, decided it would not be wise to share his secret with his younger brother. Yet, he felt it would be good to know Malsumsis' secret, so the great Glooskap agreed to tell his brother if Malsumsis would do the same. So, they decided to exchange secrets. Glooskap told his brother he could only be killed by being struck with an owl's feather, which was untrue. Malsumsis said that for him to be killed, he must receive a blow from a fern root.

"In after-days, Malsumsis was tempted to kill his older brother Glooskap. Malsumsis was enticed by Miko, the squirrel, or perhaps from the evil within himself, for in those days, all men were wicked. So, Malsumsis took his bow, shot Ko-ko-khas, the Owl, and took one of his feathers. While Glooskap was sleeping peacefully by a stream, Malsumsis snuck up to him and struck Glooskap with the owl's feather. Glooskap woke in anger, but being crafty, he said that it was not an owl's feather that would kill him, but rather it was being struck by a pine root that he would die.

"Many days later, Malsumsis led his older brother deep into the woods for a hunt. Again, Malsumsis struck his brother while he slept, but smote him with a pine root this time. Glooskap woke unhurt, but in his anger, he drove Malsumsis away. Then Glooskap sat beside a small pond, and considering all that had happened, he said to himself, "Nothing but a flowering rush can kill me." But a beaver was hidden among the reeds, and having heard the words of Glooskap, he rushed to Malsumsis to tell him. Malsumsis promised to give the beaver whatever he wished since he told him his brother's secret. The Beaver thought and said he wished to have wings like a bird. Upon hearing this, Malsumsis laughed and said, 'What would you, with a tail like a rough paddle, want with wings? Get away from me."

The beaver was angry, so he went to Glooskap and told him all he had done. Glooskap's anger rose deep within him. He dug up a fern root and sought Malsumsis deep in the dark woods. He discovered his younger brother sleeping and crept up to him, striking him with the fern root. Then Malsumsis, the younger brother, died. Glooskap then lamented and cried over the death of his brother. Malsumsis, being dead, was turned into the Shick-Shoe Mountains."

Derrick had listened intently to the story and was somewhat uncertain how to interpret it. It seemed to him that both characters in the story were deceitful, and neither was a good role model. He was also taken aback by the abruptness of the ending. So, he asked, "Is there a lesson in the story I missed? Both brothers seemed to be dishonest."

Nattesg'g grinned and said, "It is a story. It tells us how the Shick-Shoe Mountains were created. I have noticed that many of the tales Father Lull tells tend to portray men as either entirely evil or entirely good. Especially the Jesus person. Do you really think men are that way? Isn't there evil and good in all of us?"

Although the question was directed at Derrick, it was Father Lull who answered, "Men, as God sees them, are evil, and only through the grace of God can they do any good. Jesus, while being a real man, was also God. He lived a perfect life and became a holy sacrifice to pay for mankind's sin."

Nattesg'g smiled and said, "Did we not do good for your people when you came to our shores? Yet we had never heard of this god of yours."

Father Lull said, "God knew you, even though you did not know Him. He shows grace on whomever he chooses, even if the man does not know Him by name."

Nattesg'g slapped his knee and laughed, "Your god seems like a man who cannot make up his mind and makes his choices like the blowing of leaves on a high wind."

Father Lull, who had discussed theology with the Mi'kmaq enough to know that it would do no good to continue the conversation now. So, he grinned along with Nattesg'g and said, "I can understand how you would think that."

One of the other Mi'kmaq said, "Now you tell us a story. Friend Derrick, tell us how you got your powerful scar; that must be a great story indeed."

Derrick was at a loss; he really had no desire to tell the story of the death of his parents and sister. Father Lull, knowing Derrick did not like talking about himself, said, "How about if I tell you a story?"

The Mi'kmak who asked for Derrick to tell a story said to Father Lull, "You can, as long as it is not a story trying to convince us to let you drown us in a river or worship the man-god your people killed."

Father Lull, a little hurt that he had so little success converting these people, said, "I believe I have a story you will like. It is a true story that involves the Templar Knights."

CHAPTER THIRTY-SEVEN

For a moment, Louis was uncertain how to answer the prince. He had not expected to speak to him so soon. Honestly, Louis hadn't yet decided if he would attempt to meet with any of the officials of Muscovy. He was still confused by everything he had experienced since his arrival in Constantinople. He had met many friendly, helpful, peaceful, and hardworking Muslins. They were nothing like the crazed heathens, who wanted to kill all Christians, he had expected.

Then there was Dudel and Adi. They were Jews; they were the killers of Jesus. Louis knew there were Jews in Europe, but he had never met any, much less gotten to know them. He had always been told they were deceitful and conniving. Dudel had saved his life and been nothing but friendly.

He had not met many Christians in his time in the Holy Land, but those he had met did not seem to be mistreated. Louis was starting to think that another Crusade would do no good and make things more difficult for those who lived here. He thought perhaps it would be better to return to King Robert and suggest that, rather than a crusade, they should seek a treaty with the existing rulers. Yet, he was under orders to try and discover if Prester John existed and, if so, to attempt to contact him.

Prince Yury waited expectantly. Louis finally said, "Your Royal Highness, I was sent here by His Majesty Robert the Bruce, King of Scotland. I am to inquire about an individual known to us as Prester John, who is reportedly the commander of a large Christian army. We have been led to believe that he is in this part of the world or perhaps even further to the east."

Prince Yury was thoughtful for a moment, then he said in a somewhat clipped tone, "I was unaware there was a King in Scotland, but I will assume you are telling us the truth regarding this King Robert the Bruce. I have never heard of this Prester John either. Why did your King think I would know about him?"

Louis replied, "Your Royal Highness, I was not sent to seek you out in particular. It was a happy coincidence that I could seek wisdom or guidance from your court. I am sure King Robert the Bruce would chasten me quite harshly if I had not sought Your Highness out and conveyed greetings on His behalf."

Prince Yury looked at Sir Louis sternly for a moment. Then he laughed, "If your fighting skill is half as good as your abilities in court, you must be an impressive warrior. Now that we have established that neither your King nor I have any knowledge or concern for the other and that you are here by chance, we can relax and perhaps help one another. I will have my advisers see if they know or can discover anything about this Prester John. Meanwhile, I was wondering if you would mind providing us with a demonstration of your martial skills?"

Louis was taken aback but said, "I would be pleased to, Your Royal Highness, but may I ask why? You seem to have many fine warriors here." In truth, most of the men Louis saw in the courtyard seemed to be half-trained farmers forced into service as soldiers.

Prince Yury said, "I am planning a campaign for which these men are training. They are far from real soldiers, but we are instructing them. We have some great warriors in my army. Some are true Bogatyr. Additionally, my brother-in-law promised me that some Mongols of his Golden Hoard would join my forces. They are great horsemen and archers. But I have heard that a knight of the Latin armies is very impressive in battle. I would like to witness your skill at arms."

Louis asked, "What type of demonstration does your Royal Highness have in mind?"

The prince said, "Perhaps we could put on a tournament. Like the ones I have heard about in Europe. We couldn't handle the jousting, as you're the only one trained in that area, but we could cover other events. What would you suggest?"

Louis had never seen a tournament, but he knew the basic events. He said, "We could do a passage of arms. In this event, a contestant would challenge another in single combat on foot or horseback. There is also the melee, where teams of soldiers would fight either on foot or horseback. We could also hold archery or wrestling contests."

The Prince of Muscovy said with great enthusiasm, "That sounds wonderful. Let us do all those tomorrow!"

Louis said, "Tomorrow? Your Royal Highness, most tournaments are planned for months, giving contestants time to travel to the tournament's location. The events are spread out over several days so that the soldiers have time to recover so that they can compete in multiple events."

Prince Yury smiled and said, "Perhaps you are right, we should prepare, but I cannot wait months, and it cannot last for days; I have a battle to get to. My advisors will make all the arrangements. I'm sure we can have everything prepared in three days. You and my soldiers will be the contestants, so there is no need to wait for anyone to arrive."

Louis feared this was getting out of control, but had no idea how to rein in Prince Yury. Before he could think of anything, Dudel and the prince's advisor rejoined them. The prince asked Dudel, "Master Dudel, did you and Boris make arrangements to your satisfaction?"

Dudel replied, "Yes, Your Royal Highness. I will have my shop open and be sending you taxes for my sales in no time. I am very pleased."

The prince then shifted his interests to observing his soldiers' practice, saying, "Sir Louis, please come back tomorrow so that you can help my advisors plan the tournament, and I will have whatever information we can discover about this Prester John presented to you."

Dudel and Louis bowed and were led by Kirill back the way they had come. As Kirill was about to leave them, he smiled and said to Louis, "I look forward to trying myself against a Latin knight." Before Louis could reply, Kirill turned away and departed.

Dudel looked up at Louis and said, "Never have I gotten arrangements made so fast and so favorably. You have worked a wonder, my friend, and I am indebted to you."

As Louis and Dudel returned to where they were staying in the city, Louis said, "You saved my life, friend. I can never repay that. I am glad things have worked out so well for you." To himself, Louis wondered if he was lucky or unlucky because of what transpired between him and Prince Yury.

CHAPTER THIRTY-EIGHT

Father Lull started his tale of the Knights Templar, "About one hundred and thirty years ago, in the year of our Lord 1177, the enemy of the Christian army, Saladin, was intent on taking back the holy city of Jerusalem. Several years before, the Christians assembled a great host of devoted men to retake the Holy Land from the infidels. Jerusalem was the Holiest of the cities in the Holy Land and was the seat of the Christian King, Baldwin IV. King Baldwin IV was a young man, almost a child, and was stricken with a disease called leprosy that weakened him and made movement painful. Yet this young, sickly King was a devout man of God and noble warrior who commanded his army with great skill.

"Saladin, the Sultan of Egypt and Syria, brought a great host of soldiers. His fighting force consisted of thirty thousand men and siege machines capable of destroying thick stone walls. The Muslim army also had a massive baggage train with them to provide for the army's needs. In addition, Saladin brought his personal force of Mamluk bodyguards, who were known to be great warriors.

"King Baldwin's army had about three hundred fifty mounted knights and only a few thousand foot-soldiers. Even though Saladin's host vastly outnumbered the Christian army, Baldwin was committed to stopping them from reaching Jerusalem. Grand Master Odo de St. Amand of the Knights Templar commanded a separate small force of only eighty Knights Templar. These Templars were riding from Gaza to link up with Baldwin and the rest of the Christian army.

"Baldwin's army, being vastly outnumbered, retreated to the city of Ascalon, as Saladin's army slowly made its way toward Jerusalem. To further slow Saladin, God caused the skies to open, and heavy rains fell. The roads became muddy, and Saladin's army slowed even more as his siege machines became stuck near Montgisard. Saladin rode to the rear of his army in an attempt to speed up the baggage and siege engines creeping through the sodden ground. Saladin was surprised when he noticed a small force of Christians had arrayed itself on a hill behind his army. This was the Knights Templar led by Grand Master Odo, who was still attempting to link up with King Baldwin. Saladin noted the small number of men under Odo's command and chose to ignore them as they were too few to bother his massive army. Saladin rode back to the front and put the small force of soldiers at the rear of his army out of his mind. The Muslim army continued its slow movement toward Jerusalem.

"King Baldwin, sensing he had to move now if he had any chance of stopping Saladin before his army reached the walls of Jerusalem. The king prayed and asked God for guidance. Baldwin then moved his army out of Ascalon to interpose it between Saladin and Jerusalem. Saladin was taken off guard by the suddenly appearing army in front of his main body of forces. Even though Saladin clearly outnumbered this meager force, he was concerned because his army was in disarray. Saladin's army was spread out because of the slow-moving baggage train and siege weapons. Several of his soldiers were also out foraging in the countryside for supplies. Even so, Saladin was not worried; he greatly outnumbered these Christians. The Sultan gathered his elite troops around himself, which numbered about fifteen hundred well-trained warriors. Saladin's nephew, Taqi ad-Din, who was in command of the main body of soldiers, attempted to move the army into a proper defensive position rapidly. But, before the Muslim army could complete its deployment, the Christian army attacked.

"Grand Master Odo and his eighty Templars attacked at the same time as King Baldwin. Having never linked up, the two Christian armies attacked from different directions, confusing the Muslim army further. Grand Master Odo struck at the very center of Saladin's forces. Even though the army of Saladin was much larger than that of the Christians, the ferocity of the attack against their hastily organized defenses forced the Muslim army into further disarray. Seeing Saladin's personal guards, Grand Master Odo led his Templars straight at them. The Templars crashed through the Muslim defense of Sultan Saladin's elite warriors.

"Saladin himself admired the ferocity with which the Templars attacked with their much smaller force at the heart of his best warriors. Although the Sultan's guards outnumbered the Templars twenty to one, these few powerful men of God scattered and crushed the Sultan's elite force. Saladin fled the field on a camel with a few remaining members of his personal guard. Saladin's forces were all but destroyed that day. Only about one in ten of Saladin's army made it back to Cairo. After witnessing the bravery and fighting ability of the Knight Templar, Saladin would never again underestimate the power of these dedicated warriors of God."

When Father Lull finished the tale, Nattesg'g said, "That is not a very good story. What are we to learn from that? Why do they fight over a city? Just move the city to another location to hide it from the other army. You tell us that Odo and Baldwin are brave, but you tell me nothing of their personal feats in battle. Attacking a foe who outnumbers you can be brave, but it can also be foolish. Are these Muslims not Christians? Do they have a spirit they follow? What is a camel? I am sorry, Father Lull, but I do not like your story."

CHAPTER THIRTY-NINE

The sun was just breaking the horizon. The morning looked as if it would be a clear and cold day. The men sitting vigil with Derrick had been telling stories all night long. Derrick could not concentrate much on the shared stories, but he appreciated the distractions they provided. They had heard screams a few times and some yelling, but the men assured Derrick those sounds were all quite normal in childbirth and encouraged him not to worry. Derrick had previously believed he was very calm under stress. He had discovered he could stop and think clearly when other men could not. Now, he was lost in worry and could not concentrate on anything but his fears. He worried about Mary, the baby, and all the responsibilities of becoming a father.

One of the Mi'kmaq was telling stories about Lox. Lox seemed to be a somewhat evil character at times, but was very tough and courageous. In the tales, Lox often seemed like a demon; later, he would become the butt of a joke. There also appeared to be no way to kill Lox, or more accurately, no way to keep him dead. Lox would die in many stories, but would later be alive again.

Father Lull asked, "This Lox seems somewhat like the Norwegian god of mischief named Loki. I would like to hear more about his...." Just then, the men in the wigwam heard the clear sound of a baby crying out.

Nattesg'g smiled broadly, slapped Derrick on the back, and said, "Your son is here."

Derrick was on his feet and out of the wigwam in a second. He didn't recall feeling the cold, although he hadn't bothered to put on his fur coat and hat before he rushed out into the bitterly cold morning. He reached the log house before any of the other men had even exited the wigwam. Derrick opened the door, stepped into the log house, and stopped. The scene before was etched in his mind for all the years of his long life. The room was warm and lit by the central fire. There were two women besides Mary in the room, cleaning up after the birth. Mary was seated, wrapped in a fur blanket, holding the baby. Derrick moved to Mary and said, "Are you okay?"

Mary replied with a happy but tired voice, "Yes, I am fine. They tell me the birth went very well. However, they did have me drink a mixture of ground rattlesnake rattles and ground root bark, boiled in water. They told me it would speed up the birth. It was not very pleasant to drink."

Darrick looked at the cherub-like face of his child and asked, "And how is our son?"

Mary looked astonished and said, "He is wonderful. How did you know he was a boy?"

Derrick reached a hand toward his son and said, "Apparently, everyone in the village knew it was going to be a boy." His son raised a small hand and gripped one of Derricks's fingers. Derrick felt tears well up in his eyes. Just then, the door to the log house opened, and Father Lull entered, followed by the other village men. One of the Mi'kmaq women interposed herself in front of the men and said, "It is not time for the mother and child to have visitors. They both need rest. Leave and come back tomorrow." The men knew better than to argue, so they turned and left. Then the Mi'kmaq woman went to Derrick and said, "You should leave too. We will care for your wife and child. You go let the other men congratulate you and consider what you will call the boy. Mary and the baby will need sleep."

Derrick kissed Mary and the baby on their foreheads and departed. He stood outside the log house, still somewhat dumbstruck, until the cold made him move. He went to the wigwam, where he had spent the previous night half-listening to stories. Inside was only Nattesg'g, who sat smoking a pipe as if waiting for Derrick. Nattesg'g said, "The others have all gone to their wigwams for some sleep. You can sleep here; I am sure you are exhausted after the long night's vigil. I must go to my wife and my wigwam, but I first wanted to congratulate you and Mary." Derrick didn't recall saying anything in response to Nattesg'g. He felt a sudden exhaustion overtaking him. Derrick fell into a deep and dream-filled sleep. He did not remember any of the dreams. He woke feeling a level of happiness, joy, and relief like he had never felt before, but he also recalled thinking, "Don't be too happy." Remember what happened to your parents and sister. There is no telling what the future will bring.

CHAPTER FORTY

Father Thomas hoped that he had sufficiently frightened Brother Alfred away during their last conversation by bringing up Brother Jaye and the Inquisition. He was mistaken. Brother Alfred seemed unnerved by the discussion at the time, but it didn't last. The very next day, Alfred found Father Thomas and began chattering away.

As Alfred trotted his donkey up alongside Thomas' horse, he said, "Good morning, Father. Did you sleep well?"

Thomas sighed to himself and said, "I slept fine."

Alfred said cheerfully, "I am happy to hear that. I, for one, did not sleep well. I hate to complain, but how can the ground be more uncomfortable than the slabs of a monk's cell? Maybe I am still getting used to sleeping outdoors. I haven't had to travel much as a monk, and before I bound my life to serve God, I was the son of a prosperous merchant and slept comfortably on a straw-filled bed. No offense to the merchants we travel with, but I greatly prefer a monk's austere life to a merchant's. My father was training me to take over the business. I hated all the tedious inventories and profit/loss calculations. I couldn't stand the fake friendliness toward people I didn't like just to make a little more money."

Thomas couldn't help himself and said, "Surely you still must put up with individuals you don't like? I know I do."

Clearly ignoring the hint, Alfred said, "There are people I interact with that I may not like, but I don't have to be fake. I just show them the love God feels for them. As a merchant, I had to seek out people I didn't like and put on a show of friendship just to make business deals. Now I seek out those who need my help or those with whom I enjoy talking, like yourself. What did you do before you entered the priesthood?"

Thomas felt he would never be rid of the monk, no matter what he said or did. He sighed again, this time audibly so Alfred would hear. Then he said, "Nothing in particular. I decided to be a priest early in life

Alfred said, "You must have been very thoughtful and faithful in your youth. I was quite wild and willful as a youngster. I chased women, drank far too much, and squandered much of my father's money. I had much to confess when I finally decided to become a monk. I am much happier now, but sometimes I miss those wild times. Father Dion, do you miss anything about your previous life?"

Thomas very truthfully said, "No."

Brother Alfred said, "Yesterday, you said you were seeking out a Brother Jaye, who was in the Inquisition. I was wondering, where do you know this man from? Were you in the Inquisition?"

Father Thomas was quiet for a moment, deciding how to reply. Then he said, "No, I was not in the Inquisition. I was trained as a lawyer by the Church. In the past, I had some dealings with Brother Jaye."

Alfred waited to see if Thomas would continue. When he did not, Alfred said, "I see. So, why are you seeking, Brother Jaye? Just to rekindle an old friendship?"

Thomas said, "I have some business to discuss with him, private business."

Alfred said, "Oh, yes, I recall now that you had mentioned that. Private issues must be kept confidential. We all learn that as members of the clergy. We are repeatedly told we must not reveal secrets, except to another member of the clergy. As I am also a clergy member, perhaps you might want to tell me. I may be able to offer some guidance or a nugget of wisdom. Don't you think it might be a good idea to tell a fellow member of the cloth?"

Thomas looked down at the chubby monk riding beside him and said, "No."

Alfred said, "Oh, I see. I am sorry if I intruded. I only meant to help you carry the burden of what you feel you must tell the Inquisition."

Thomas interrupted and said, "It is not a burden to me. And I am not telling the Inquisition anything; I am talking with a colleague, who happens to be a brother in the Inquisition."

Alfred continued as if he hadn't heard Thomas, "Ah, yes, I see. Your training as a lawyer must make you comfortable with sharing information with the Inquisition. Those fellows frighten me, and I have never even spoken with them. Truthfully, I have only seen members of that Order once. And that was just when they stayed one night in a monastery where I lived. You are not intimidated by having to have dealings with the Inquisition, Father Dion?"

Thomas said, "No. There is no need to fear them unless you are guilty of something."

Alfred said, "Aren't we all guilty of something? I would just be fearful they might think me guilty of something they thought was bad, even though my intent was only to glorify God."

Thomas said, "Sometimes men think they desire to glorify God, but in reality, they are only attempting to glorify themselves."

Alfred said, "I think it may be difficult for one man to decern another man's intentions. Can the Inquisition know a man's true motivation? Perhaps, this is what has happened with the Templars. What do you think, Father Dion?"

Thomas stopped his horse, causing Alfred to stop a few feet in front of Thomas and turn his donkey to the side so he could see the Priest. Thomas then said, "What exactly do you mean, Brother? Are you saying the Templars are not guilty? They lost us the Holy Land. They are confessed idolators, heretics, and sexual deviants."

Alfred swallowed, "Like I said earlier, I know little of the Templars. I was just meaning, isn't it possible one man may think another is being impious because they don't truly know what is in the man's heart?"

Thomas said, "That is why the Church has the Order of the Holy Inquisition. They are trained to discover what is in a man's heart. It is God who guides them to determine the truth."

Brother Alfred continued, "Yes, I understand the purpose of the Order, but don't you think their methods may cause a man to confess even if he is not guilty?"

Thomas sneered, saying, "Only a truly weak and obviously untruthful man would confess to things he has not done, no matter the consequences."

Alfred said, "Perhaps, but I fear I am too weak to hold to the truth under such questioning."

Thomas nudged his horse forward and went around the monk as he said, "Then perhaps you should reevaluate your commitment to God."

Brother Alfred sat astride his donkey, watching the Priest, who called himself Dion, ride up the road. Alfred wondered what he should do. It would take several days to get word to Cardinal Soprano and longer to receive a reply. Alfred knew the final decision would be one he would have to make himself. Besides, he mused, the Cardinal would probably not approve of what Alfred believed he would have to do. He said in a low voice only he could hear, "Perhaps it's best if I just take care of this without the good Cardinal knowing until it was too late."

As Thomas rode, he decided he would soon need to inquire about Brother Jaye if he hoped to find him. Father Thomas concluded not to ask around until he reached France. Once in France, Father Thomas would excuse himself to pray whenever they reached a village or town large enough to have a church. While at the church, he would ask, as surreptitiously as possible, about the Inquisition in general and Brother Jaye in particular.

CHAPTER FORTY-ONE

Sir William knew the trek to Nattesg'g's camp would be tough, but he believed his men were all hardened to the conditions of this land. He figured the trip would take a day or two at the most. It was only a couple of hours' walk in good weather, so they should make it in good order even with their slow pace through the deep snow. Or so he thought the first day.

They had only traveled about two hours before they ran into a snow drift so deep and large that they could not get through it or find a path around it. By the time they backtracked and found a place to cut to the side, they were almost back at the camp. They started off again at a slightly different angle, hoping they could find a way through. They soon discovered that the group of men blazing the path through the snow could only effectively work for about twenty minutes before they needed to be relieved. After a few hours, the entire group needed to stop and rest. On the few occasions, they had the energy to find and gather some dry wood, they would try to build a fire. The fire was constantly being put out by the snow melting around the flames, as they didn't expend the energy to create a proper foundation for the fire.

The men's spirits stayed strong the first day, yet they only traveled a few hundred yards. They were often forced to dig out channels of snow eight to ten feet deep so they could pass. At some point during the second day, they discovered wolves were tracking them. They only saw the wolves twice on the second day, and they were just glimpsed in the distance. They had no idea of the size of the pack, but judging by the howls, it sounded as though there were enough wolves to surround the group of Templars.

That night, the group located a rocky outcropping where they could clear the snow and build a good-sized fire to keep themselves warm. They also gathered a few long, straight branches and sharpened one end of each to make spears. The group had a few swords and bows with a small supply of arrows, so the spears were a nice addition. The wolf pack moved in closer at night, and the howling grew more incessant. The Templars would occasionally see glimpses of movement in the dark or see the firelight glinting off a pair of eyes between the trees.

The men knew wolves rarely attacked humans, but hunger and the apparent struggle of the humans seemed to have emboldened the pack. One of the men with a bow shot an arrow at a pair of eyes he saw in the darkness. This produced a yelp of pain and a tumult of yips, barks, growls, and howls from the darkness. Soon, it sounded as though all the wolves surrounding them were congregating in the area where the archer had fired the arrow. The cacophony of animal sounds tripled in volume and excitement.

The group of Templars all strained to see what was happening in the blackness beyond the glow of their campfire. Sir William told the group, "It appears the arrow found its mark, but I would warn against further shooting into the dark. Any arrow we shoot at night will be lost to us for good, and we have a limited supply. Although the pack is reduced by one, they are also better fed and stronger than before, and they have the smell and taste of blood that could drive them to boldness." The men, who had been encouraged by the apparent death of the wolf, now saw the wisdom in what Sir William told them.

They only stayed around the fire for a few hours. Most of them slept at least a little, but none felt truly rested or warmed much by the fire. Some of the men began to wonder if they would ever feel warm again. It was still dark when they decided to push on. As they left their fire behind, a few men collected some burning brands to carry as torches, even though they were little more than glowing embers. Within a few minutes, the winds, which had increased, blew out the feeble torches, and the men tossed them aside.

As the sun started to rise on the third day of their trek, it brought little light and no heat through the heavily laden skies. The men tried to press on with as much vigor as they had on the first day. They encouraged one another, but the difficulty in cutting a path through the snow and the constant badgering of the wolves weighed against them. As midday approached, they could still see the rocky outcropping behind them where they had camped for a few hours the night before. Sir William called a halt, and they ate some of the rapidly disappearing rations. No one attempted to start a fire, as none had the strength.

The wolves seemed a bit bolder as they pressed in closer, and the men saw more of them between the trees, slowly circling the group. William kept the men focused on the job and told them that soon they

157

would be among the Mi'kmaq and have shelter, warmth, and food. In less than an hour, the men started plowing through the snow again.

The depth of the snow seemed to be less along the low ridge they were traveling. The winds had carried much of the powder away, and the Templars' travel rate increased. The relative speed and ease of advance bolstered their spirit. They decided not to break to rest but continued to push ahead, feeling more encouraged for the first time since they started the journey. The wolves seemed to notice the change in their quarry's attitude and kept a little further afield, howling less.

As daylight started to fade, Sir William called a halt and said they would need to take some rest and food. The group was still on the ridge, but the snow was growing deeper. They attempted to dig and tramp their way down to solid ground for a fire pit, but soon gave up the attempt. They then tried to build a platform of green branches to lay the fire on, but the melting snow kept extinguishing the flames. Eventually, they stopped trying to make a fire and just huddled close together for warmth. As the light in the sky diminished and they were left with only the feeble light of the moon, their high spirits from earlier in the day also dwindled. Each man felt the weakness that was overcoming them. Weaknesses caused by a lack of food, little sleep, and constantly fighting the cold and harsh winter conditions.

The wolves drew in closer as darkness overtook the sky. The howling grew in volume, and the yipping grew more insistent. The wolves seemed to be making tentative movements closer to the bunched-up Templars. The men began to sense that the wolves were preparing to attack, but they were so cold, tired, and hungry that they didn't have the strength to rise up against them. The wolves, sensing this, crept in closer.

Like the others, Sir William had been lulled into nonaction by fatigue and cold. Suddenly, he felt the hair on the back of his neck stand up. He then heard the voice of Sergeant Bertrand say, "Get your ass up, you damn fool boy!"

Sir William forcefully roused himself. He stood and said in a loud, clear voice, "Men of the Temple, it is time to rise and force off this foe."

The knights and sergeants rose immediately, taking up what weapons they had. The rest of the men grudgingly followed. A few men seemed to be in a daze and rose more slowly as if unsure of what was happening. As the men drew into a protective ring shoulder to shoulder,

William could feel the apprehension among the group. The ring of men holding swords, spears, knives, and bows faced outward. They all peered into the dark night and saw glimpses of shapes circling them on silent paws. They could hear the ominous growls rumbling from the beasts.

Sir William said loudly for all to hear, "You men are all my brothers. We have fought and struggled alongside each other over the last few months and years. Some of you may not be trained warriors, but you are all men who have been tried and proven. You are strong and brave. Now stand beside me in this dark night and fight off these beasts. You are all my brothers to the end."

The ring of knights, sergeants, farmers, and craftsmen said loud and clear into the cold, dark night, "Brothers to the end!"

The wolves must have felt their opportunity was slipping away and decided to attack at that moment. The first few attacks came as dashes forward by a few wolves darting in and nipping at a man, spear, or sword point, then dashing back into the darkness. Several arrows were launched, but either due to the low visibility or the frozen fingers, none seemed to find the mark. Then, as if a sign had been given, it appeared as though all the wolves attacked at once.

Sir William would never have guessed there were so many wolves in the pack. Each man standing seemed to have at least one wolf lunge or leap forward and attack him. As a man attempted to fend off the wolf confronting him, one or two more would dart in to snap at the man's legs, trying to drag him off his feet.

The fight grew into a mass of snarls, yells, grunts, and screams from both men and beasts. Sir William felt warm blood wash across his face, which momentarily blinded him. He slashed and jabbed with his sword, aware of men fighting to either side of him. Master Acel was to his right, and William saw him go down as fur and teeth flashed from the darkness in front of them. William drove off the two wolves that had been atop Master Acel, but the man did not rise to his feet. William feared they would all succumb to the mad attack by so many wolves, then he heard a wild roar from the darkness beyond the wolves. The roar made the wolves pause momentarily, giving the men a brief second to press into the attack on their canine foe. The Templar soldiers moved with precise movement honed by years of training. As a unit, they stepped toward the wolves who had momentarily paused their assault.

At that moment, the wolves appeared lost in indecision, unsure if they should continue their attack on the men or turn to face the roaring threat behind them. Then a large creature, at least seven feet tall, stepped out of the black shadows of the trees and into the partial light of the moon. It roared again, this time louder and more ferocious. The wolves decided as one that they had had enough, and they leapt away into the night with yips and barks.

Sir William shifted his attention to the brown-furred creation standing about ten feet to his front. On the one hand, he was thankful this beast had chased off the wolves, but now they had a bigger and seemingly more ferocious threat to fight. Two men carrying wooden spears moved to stand beside William as he pointed his sword at the beast. William assumed the archers had already used up their few arrows, or they would have fired.

At first, the creature did not move or make a sound as it stood before them. Then it raised a furry arm and pushed back the hood that hung over the face of Leif the Norwegian.

CHAPTER FORTY-TWO

The next morning, Louis woke to the sounds of Dudel yelling at his men. The sun was already up, and Louis was surprised he had slept so late. He was in the habit of rising well before the sun. Louis got up and quickly dressed. He found Dudel departing to take possession of the building that would become his trade center in Muscovy. Dudel was walking out the door when he noticed Louis. Dudel said, "Louis, dear friend. My men and I are going to begin the task of setting up and doing inventory for my new shop. Two of my servants will remain here, so you don't need to worry about your possessions while you visit with the prince's men."

Louis didn't have time to reply before Dudel closed the door and was gone. He thought about eating something, but his stomach didn't feel settled enough to eat, so he decided to head to the fortress and his meeting with the prince's advisors. As he walked through the city, Louis tried to recall all he knew about tournaments. He had never fought in a real tourney or even witnessed one. He knew what the events entailed, but that was all. Some of his training as a squire was closely related to tournament events. He supposed that gave him a little experience. Still, he felt totally out of his depth. He really wished he had not been manipulated into this.

Louis was unsure where to report, so he headed to the same administration building he and Dudel had visited the day before. He told the man at the desk that he was supposed to meet with some of Prince Yury's advisors. Louis was instructed to take a seat on a bench and wait. He glanced at the soldiers guarding the door; since Kirill was not among them, he sat on one of the hard, wooden benches. He began to feel stressed as he waited on the bench. He was uncomfortable, his back ached, and his skin felt warm. He became acutely aware of all the people crowded into this stuffy hall. He wished he could leave to get a breath of fresh air and perhaps a cool drink of water, but was afraid they would call him forward while he was absent.

Finally, they called his name. As Louis stood up, he felt momentarily dizzy and had to steady himself before walking up to the desk. The man at the desk pointed to the door, which one of the guards held open. Once he went through the door, the guard closed it, and he was alone in a long hallway. He began walking in the direction he was sure he had gone the day before. Louis soon discovered he had no real idea how to reach the inner courtyard. He couldn't recall the path Kirill had led him on through the labyrinth of doors and hallways. He tried to remember the route, but he was having trouble concentrating. Louis wandered around, searching for someone to guide him, but the hallways appeared deserted. Louis thought he should probably retrace his steps back to the stuffy waiting room and ask for assistance. As he started to head back, he soon realized he could not even recall the few turns he had made since leaving the waiting room. He couldn't seem to concentrate on anything. Louis noticed he was sweating, his skin felt clammy, and the dizziness had also returned. He just wanted to find a way out of the building and get outside into the fresh air. He was randomly walking down passageways and trying every door he came across. His efforts became more frantic as he yearned to get outside into the open air.

He knew he wasn't thinking clearly. He encountered some people, but he couldn't seem to communicate with them. By pure chance, he found a door that opened to the outside. It wasn't the courtyard where he had met the prince the day before, but at least he was out of those hallways. It seemed hotter outside than he recalled, but at least he could breathe. He took two deep breaths, which calmed him a bit. But soon, the dizziness returned, and everything spun around him. He reached a hand toward one of the walls but missed. He then collapsed to the ground and passed out.

When Louis came to, he felt like he was soaked in sweat. He was on a cot, surrounded by many other cots filled with people. A lady in the cot beside him appeared to have a mangled arm. Louis could not tell if she was dead or merely unconscious. When he tried to sit up, the room started to spin around him, and he collapsed back to his cot and drifted off again.

When Louis next awoke, he was still sweating and was desperately thirsty. He noticed an older woman standing beside one of the other cots. When he tried to ask her for water in both French and Arabic, she seemed not to understand. She came to him, placed a hand on his forehead, and spoke to him in a language he could not comprehend. Louis soon gave up trying to get water and drifted off again.

Louis vaguely recalled drifting in and out of consciousness several more times. His recollections of when he was conscious were not clear. It was all a jumble of aches, fever, and thirst. When he finally came fully awake, he was still on a cot in what he thought was the same room, but there were far fewer people than before. He tried to sit up, but as soon as his head raised just a little, the room started to spin, and he felt he did not have the energy to rise. He lowered his head and closed his eyes, waiting for the room to stop spinning.

Sir Louis felt someone lay a hand on his brow, and then something cool and wet was placed on his forehead. It was one of the most welcome sensations Louis had ever experienced. Then, to add to the comfort, water trickled into his mouth. He slowly opened his eyes and saw a hand just above his face. The hand held a rag soaked in water, which was slowly squeezed so the water ran into his mouth. He heard a voice speaking softly and slowly; he did not understand the language, but the tone had a calming effect. As his eyes gradually focused on the face of the speaker, he could see that it was a young woman. She was the most beautiful thing he had ever seen. He tried to ask her where he was, but his throat was too dry, even with the few drops of water she was guiding to his mouth. The woman placed a gentle hand on his shoulder and said something in the same soothing tone. Louis closed his eyes and fell quickly into a restful sleep.

The next time Louis opened his eyes, he was suddenly aware that he was starving. He didn't try to rise immediately; he just lay there calmly, taking in his surroundings. Louis was now in a smaller room, and only a few other people were in there with him. He cleared his throat a bit; it was still rough and dry. A man stepped into his view. He looked down at Louis and said something in that same language the beautiful woman had spoken. The man turned and said something louder, as if he were talking to someone else, then walked out of Louis's sight line.

After a moment, he was about to try to speak to ask for some food when the beautiful woman came and sat beside him. She held a wooden bowl in her hand that gave off an aroma that caused Louis' stomach to growl in hunger. The woman laughed softly and talked soothingly to him as she spooned him small amounts of the warm broth.

It was another day before Louis could sit up, and a couple more before he could stand and walk around on unsteady legs. During that time, he learned that the woman nursing him back to health was named Irina Popova, and she spoke only Rus. Louis had picked up a few words from talking to her but was trying to learn more. While recovering his strength, a man who spoke French came in to talk to Louis. Irina had found the man, so they could find out who Louis was.

The man said, "My name is Povel, and your name is Louis?"

Louis said, "Yes, I am a knight bound to the King of Scotland."

The man asked Louis, "What are you doing in Muscovy?"

Louis explained to the man how he had come here with Dudel and was supposed to help plan a tournament for the prince, but had fallen sick on his way to meet with the prince's advisors. Povel asked, "You need not worry about meeting with the prince's advisors regarding a tournament. When this illness struck the city, Prince Yury, his advisors, and soldiers all left Muscovy for some battle. Do you have a place to stay here in the city?"

Louis said, "I think so. From what I have gleaned from Irina, I have been here for over a week. I assume my friend, Dudel, is still in the city getting his trade center established. Do you think you can get word to him for me?"

Povel said, "I will see what I can do. The city is in some disarray, but I will try to locate your friend, assuming he is still alive. You still need to rest. This illness seems to hit this city every few years, but it is usually not this bad. Many people have died, and those who survive are recovering slowly."

CHAPTER FORTY-THREE

At first, Sir William could not believe what he was seeing. Leif had gone with Captain Gregory, Cinead, and the other sailors on the ship. What was he doing here? Were the others from the ship nearby? Before he had time to discover the answer to his questions, it was clear that they must first attend to the wounded men. Ten of the men were dead, including Master Acel. The wolves had shown themselves to be able hunters. They had gone for either the throat or the groin, and their teeth had proven to be fierce weapons. Five more men were severely injured and needed immediate care. Luckily, the bitter cold slowed and often stopped the blood flow from many of their wounds.

A couple of the men went about dispatching the wolves that were still alive but too injured to leave when the rest of the pack had departed. They counted twenty-two dead wolves and noted several blood trails leading away. Once they got the wounded taken care of, Sir William suggested they scout the area around them as best they could. They needed to find a place to build a fire and set up a more established camp while they tended to the wounded. They soon discovered a spot just west of the ridge they were on.

The campsite had several large boulders surrounded by trees. They cleared the snow from between the boulders with some work and soon had a roaring fire. They butchered several wolves, and the smell of roast meat heartened all the men. Soon they were all sitting around the warm fire, and although the sun was still hidden by clouds, William could tell it was close to noon.

William told the group, "I believe the wounded and a few others should remain here. Tomorrow morning, I will take four men and press on to the Mi'kmaq village; it must be close by now. Once we arrive, we can return with help. The wounded are in no state to travel. Those who remain here will have plenty of meat from the wolves we killed, and there is an abundance of firewood nearby. I believe we have hurt the wolf pack enough that they will not bother us again. Leif said he got a good count of the wolves before they attacked us. He feels there are fewer than ten wolves remaining, and some of those are injured.

"For the remainder of today, we need to decide what to do with our dead and collect a cache of firewood for those who remain behind.

Does anyone have an idea of what to do with our dead? We cannot dig in this frozen ground, but I do not want to leave them exposed to wild animals."

Leif suggested, "We can move the bodies away from the site of the attack because the blood at that site will surely attract scavengers. Then we dig a grave as deep as we can in the snow. We can lay the bodies in there. Maybe later, before the thaw is complete, we can return and bury the bodies properly."

No one had a better idea, so even though Sir William did not completely like that option, it was really the only choice. They all got about the work. Two men stayed with the wounded and tended to them while the others collected wood and moved the bodies. One of the injured had passed away by the time the grave was prepared for the dead. His body was added to those in the frozen pit, and the snow was piled on top of the eleven corpses.

It was a somber group that sat around the fire that night. Counting Leif, there were fifteen men left alive, four of whom had serious injuries. Sir William said, "Before we try and get some sleep, I have asked Leif to tell all of us what happened with the ship and the men who sailed her. I am sure you all have already heard that Leif is the only survivor of that group, but I would like more details than what he has been able to briefly tell us while we all worked."

CHAPTER FORTY-FOUR

The exhausted but well-fed Templars sat around the fire as Leif began to tell them about his journey. Leif stood and said, "I wish the tale I am about to tell you is one that would lift our spirits, but that is not the story I have been asked to relay. When our ship left all those weeks ago, we sailed south, remaining in sight of land. The wind was at our stern, and we made good speed. On the fifth day out, we noticed a pair of large islands. Captain Gregory wanted a closer look, and we sailed around them but found no good place to go ashore. We considered turning back north at that point, but Captain Gregory wanted to continue since the weather was holding fair. We left the islands and pushed a little further south. Later that same day, we encountered a small natural harbor, and the captain decided to take the ship in and take soundings to map the depth of the harbor. He sent a few of us ashore for fresh water and to scout out the area.

"Six of us went ashore, including Cinead and me. We stayed with the other four until we discovered a freshwater lake. The four sailors then started the task of filling casks with water and taking them back to the longboat. Meanwhile, Cinead and I scouted around the area. It became apparent to the two of us that there was a lot of wildlife there. We found signs of beaver, deer, bear, and other game. We each killed a deer in no time and carried them back to the long boat. When the six of us returned to the ship in the long boat, Cinead and I recommended to Captain Gregory that the two of us should be allowed to return to shore and hunt and trap for two to three days. We felt certain we could harvest enough game to help fill the larders back at camp. The captain agreed and said that he would return on the third morning and that we should be ready to be picked up at first light.

"Cinead and I were rowed back to shore and immediately started hunting and setting snares. By that evening, we had killed two more deer, snared several rabbits, and even killed a moose. We were delighted as we sat around the campfire. Cinead kept talking about the bear signs we saw. He wanted to get that bear, which the tracks indicated was a huge animal. Cinead wanted it not only for the meat but also to make a great coat out of it. The next morning, we checked the traps and discovered seven beavers, a few muskrats, and many rabbits. We also ran across fresh bear tracks that followed a small river into the foothills. Cinead was impatient to get started following the tracks. We decided I would take the animals we trapped back to the camp while he followed the bear signs. As soon as I could, I would catch up to him, and we would kill the bear.

"After processing and hanging all the animals we had harvested, I returned to the tracks and began following them. I only walked about three hundred yards before I saw Cinead. He was crawling toward me and was covered in blood. I ran to where he lay on the ground, still dragging himself forward. I had to force him to stop and let me examine his wounds, which were many and severe. He was missing three fingers on his left hand, one eye was gouged out, his legs appeared useless, and a bone protruded several inches from his right thigh. He had lacerations all over, and many were very deep. He did not know it was me at first. He tried to push me away and continue his crawling. Finally, he stopped being combative and seemed to regain his sense of where he was and what was happening. He began to tell me about his fight with the bear. He used many words I didn't understand, but I am sure they were his colorful way of swearing.

"He had come upon the bear while it splashed in the river, looking for fish. He approached the bear from downwind and was able to sneak within about 40 feet from the bear. The bear didn't notice him as he crouched along the bank, so he decided to shoot the bear rather than wait for me. He waited for a clear shot at the bear's heart and lungs. He said his arrow hit true, and if it had been a regular bear, it would have been a death blow, but the great beast turned while he nocked another arrow. The bear saw him and charged. He released his second arrow into the bear's center mass and drew his sword. Cinead said the bear moved so quickly and struck him so hard that his sword flew out of his hands before he could use it. He said the great brown beast rolled him around, bit him, dragged him, and even seemed to try to crush the life out of him by pushing on him with its great weight. Cinead was finally able to draw his long knife, and he began to stab the bear until his blade broke off in the bear's body. Cinead said that after a few long minutes of this struggle, the bear suddenly seemed to become calm. It moved off a few paces and acted confused, then turned back to him and let out a great roar. Cinead believed this was the end of his life as he could do nothing to protect himself any longer. As the beast started returning to Cinead, it stopped, swayed a bit, and then slumped to the ground. The bear lay there huffing breaths for several minutes before it finally died.

"He knew his condition and was fully aware that the bear had also killed him. He made me swear to take the bear meat back to the ship and make a coat of the bear fur. I tended to Cinead's wounds as best I could while he told this story, but the damage to his body was too great, and he soon died. I brought his body back to the beach and covered him with rocks to keep the animals away. I planned that we would have a proper burial once the ship returned. Then I spent the rest of the day skinning and quartering the bear. Then I packed it all back to the beach. I found Cinead's sword and brought it back to his grave, placing it on top of the rocks covering his body. I spent that evening scraping the hide of the bear and preparing tanning solution from the bear's brain.

"I worked on the coat all the next day, waiting for the ship. By nightfall, I had the bear coat stretched and drying. I had prepared the meat from all the animals we had taken as best I could. Once the ship arrived, we could store the meat in salt or dry it. The wind grew stronger and colder that night, and then it started snowing.

"I waited for the ship for two more days, and when it still hadn't arrived, I put on the bear coat and started walking south along the beach. It was snowing off and on, and the temperature had dropped significantly. Later that day, I began to encounter wreckage on the beach. The next morning, I saw the long boat, which had been dragged up on the beach and turned upside down. As I got closer, I could hear a man's voice calling weakly and hoarsely. I discovered one of the sailors lying under the overturned longboat. His name was Joel, and he was nearly frozen and weak from hunger. I covered him in the great bear coat. I then built a fire and gave him some of the meat I had brought. We spent the rest of that day camped under the longboat. While he ate and regained his strength, he told me what had happened to the ship and the rest of the crew.

"Joel said they had just left the small harbor where they had dropped Cinead and me off. They had not traveled far down the coast when they hit something just under the water's surface. They soon discovered the ship had struck a rocky peak just out of sight under the surface of the water, and it held her fast. The waves and current began pushing the stuck vessel around, ripping the bottom of the ship apart. He said they struggled most of the day attempting to free the ship, but eventually, the captain decided to abandon her. So, they put nine men in the longboat to row for shore. They would leave five men on the beach, and the other four would row back and get the rest of the crew. The surf was massive, and they lost control of the longboat. It flipped over, still far from shore. Joel was the only one who made it to the beach. The longboat, being tossed by the waves, eventually came to shore. He knew there was no way he could manage the longboat by himself, but he felt he should try. Before Joel could right the longboat, he heard the awful crack of snapping timbers, and the ship shifted off the rock that had caught her. He watched as the ship, once free of the rock, rolled on its side and quickly disappeared below the waves.

"Joel searched the beach for survivors, but not even a body washed ashore. Joel had no provisions. He had found mildly brackish water but had eaten nothing since the ship had hit the rock. Joel dragged the longboat as far up the beach as he could and camped beneath it. He considered walking north along the coast, but he felt he was already too weak to attempt the trek with no provisions, so he just waited. I have no idea what he imagined he was waiting for. I believe his spirit was broken, and he had given up.

"The morning after I found Joel, we started back to where Cinead and I had been left. It took longer than it should have, as Joel slowed us down. He regularly complained that he needed to rest and eat. I soon learned Joel seemed to look for things to complain about. We arrived at the harbor site the following afternoon after leaving the place where Joel was shipwrecked. I piled more rocks over Cinead's body and spent three days smoking and preserving as much of the meat as we felt we could carry, and I made another warm coat from the deer skins for Joel.

"Once we were prepared, we started to walk back to the Templar camp. It was snowing intermittently the entire time, and the temperature continually dropped. Joel grew listless about a week into our trip, and I had to force him to eat and walk. One morning, he refused to get up. He told me just to leave him there and go on alone. I made a switch from a thin tree branch and hit him with it until he got up and started to move. We made very little distance that day, as I constantly had to force Joel to move. I built a big fire when we stopped for the night, and Joel instantly fell asleep. I lay awake for a long time, deciding what I should do. I couldn't drag Joel; we needed to move faster than we had been, but I didn't think Joel would improve in the coming days.

"When I awoke in the early morning, I found Joel was gone. I followed his tracks through the knee-deep snow. I came across his deer skin coat first. As the trail continued, I found the rest of his clothing. I discovered Joel a little further on. He was naked and curled in a ball, frozen to death. I was so angry at him that I refused to bury his body.

"The rest of my journey took some time; I really don't know how long. I stayed along the coast as much as possible, so I had fewer snow drifts to plow through. When I had to travel around rocky protrusions that went out to the sea, forcing me to move inland, it was long days of pushing through the snow. I started to think I had somehow walked past the campsite. Then I saw, ahead to the north, a large column of smoke rising in the air. It took me two days to reach the area where the smoke was rising. I discovered the Templar longhouse burned to the ground. From there, I followed the trail you had made. I saw the wolves circling you in the night, and, well, you know the rest."

CHAPTER FORTY-FIVE

Alfred continued to have conversations with Father Thomas/Dion daily, but Alfred kept the topics mundane. He knew Father Thomas was annoyed by their chats, and Alfred took some delight in that fact. Alfred knew from the start that the priest was probably up to no good. Cardinal Soprano only called on Alfred when there was the potential for violence. When Alfred began to work for the Cardinal, he made Alfred swear not to kill anyone except in self-defense or in defense of an innocent. Alfred wondered if he could justify killing the priest to defend innocent Templars. Would the Cardinal see it that way? Probably not. Alfred knew time was running out. He had to decide what he was going to do soon.

Once they reached France, Alfred noticed Father Thomas speaking to local priests whenever he could. He was certain he was trying to contact Brother Jaye. He had to stop Thomas before the Inquisition was involved.

Aware that the party Alfred and Thomas traveled with should arrive at Troyes in a couple of days, he knew he had little time. Once in the city, he would be unable to keep tabs on the Priest openly and easily. He could take the Priest as a prisoner, try to transport him back to Avignon, and let the Cardinals decide what to do with him. But that would become a difficult trip unless he kept Thomas bound, gagged, and hidden, perhaps in a hay wagon? No, Alfred realized that would never work. There were too many miles and too many possibilities for something to go wrong. He couldn't appeal to any of the Church leadership in Troyes; Alfred had no idea where they stood regarding the situation with the Templars.

It seemed to Alfred that everyone was afraid of King Philip IV. In Alfred's opinion, the Pope was not much better. Alfred could tell Pope Clement V had no backbone. Cardinal Soprano had tried to make Alfred understand that the Pope was in a precarious situation with King Philip. As Alfred saw it, Pope Clement was too afraid to stand up for what he believed was right. Wasn't that the opposite of what he should do as the mouthpiece of God?

Alfred decided that he would have to risk it. He resolved to watch the priest as closely as possible and wait for word from Cardinal Soprano.

He would just have to hope that Father Thomas/Dion had trouble locating Brother Jaye.

Two days later, the caravan of merchants, Father Thomas, and Alfred rode into Troyes. As they rode into the town, Alfred was again at the priest's side. Alfred said, "Well, Father Dion, traveling with you has been a pleasure, but I must take my leave. Perhaps we will meet again, Father."

Thomas paid no attention as the chubby monk trotted away on his donkey. Father Thomas rode to the Cathedrale Saint-Pierre and Saint-Paul, where he hoped to find information about Brother Jaye. As Thomas rode toward the Cathedrale, a man, also on horseback, cut him off. Just as Father Thomas was about to reprimand the rider, he noticed two more men step out and block the way behind him. The man on the horse in front of Thomas took hold of the reins for Thomas' horse and said, "Have no fear, Father Thomas. We were sent to find and bring you to the man you seek."

Thomas's fear did not decrease as the man led Thomas down the road. Thomas knew from the start that he could not know how Brother Jaye would feel about his return. They had not parted well. Thomas hoped Brother Jaye would not hold any of what happened against him. Yet with men like Brother Jaye, one never knew.

Thomas was taken to a small, isolated cottage outside the city walls. The ground around the home contained a small stable and several pigs in a pen. The man who led Thomas' horse dismounted, told Father Thomas he would take care of his horse, and indicated that he should enter the house. As Thomas went inside, he could initially see very little. A few embers glowed in the fireplace, providing little heat or light. The rest of the room was mostly in shadows. Thomas looked around the dark room. He noted a chair in the center of the room, but no other furniture that he could see.

Then a familiar voice from the darkness said, "Father Thomas, it is so good to see you. I heard you have been looking for me."

Father Thomas turned toward the voice and said, "Brother Jaye. Yes, I have news that I think you will find very interesting."

Brother Jaye said, "Oh, I am sure we have many interesting things to share. Much has happened since the last time we spoke."

Thomas felt as though someone had poured ice water down his back. He tried to think of what to say, but suddenly his mouth was dry, and neither his brain nor his tongue would work properly. Finally, he said, "How did you know I was looking for you?"

Brother Jaye said, "How could I not know? As your party rode through France toward Troyes, you seemed to ask everyone about my whereabouts. I am not as important as I once was, but I still have some reputation left to my name. By the way, did you know the monk who traveled with you was no monk?"

Thomas squeaked out, "Brother Alfred?"

Jaye said, "Yes, although that was not really his name. Oddly, I never could discover his true name. He was a man sent to keep track of you. I feared he might kill you before we could get together, which would have been a shame. You need no longer worry about him. He has by now befallen a grave misfortune."

Thomas's mind swam in a sea of murky water. He had the distinct feeling that something terrible was about to befall him. He knew he had to make Brother Jaye listen to him. Finally, he blurted out, "Brother Jaye, you must listen to me. A large number of Templars are hiding in the Swiss Confederacy, and they were sent there by Pope Clement V himself."

Brother Jaye said, "I see, and why do you think I would care?"

Thomas didn't understand and said, "What?! Why wouldn't you care? Several of the Templars had previously confessed, so they are relapsed heretics. Worse, some of those Templars were the ten who challenged King Philip at His own castle in full view of the populace of Paris. Pope Clement knows of all this and has decided to help these Templars escape justice. You must get word to Guillaume de Norgaret and the King."

Brother Jaye was quiet for a moment, and Father Thomas was hopeful that he had finally understood. Brother Jaye turned, slowly walked to the fireplace, took the poker from a hook, and stirred the fire so the embers rekindled a small, cheerless flame. With his back still turned toward Thomas, he said, "I can see you do not understand the current situation. Let me educate you. To begin with, no one except Guillaume de Norgaret really cared about the Templars. The only reason King Philip IV went along with de Norgaret's plan was to get the property and treasure the Templars had in their trust. You may not have been aware,

174

but the Crown was broke. The King even had to borrow money from the Templars shortly before the arrests to cover expenses. Running an empire is very costly.

"Did you really think anyone cared anything about the Templar's guilt? Guillaume de Norgaret devised this scheme and used it against the Jews, from whom the Crown had also borrowed large sums of money. It was revised and reused against other smaller groups and individuals who, in some way, were a problem to the King. It worked so well that they decided to use the same ploy against the Templars. That operation against the Jews was carried out in 1306, just one year before the arrest of the Templars. Expelling all the Jews from France had great positive financial results for France, and no one cared about a bunch of Jews. So, Guillaume, who incidentally has always hated the Templars, convinced the King to do the same thing with the Knights Templar.

"At first, the King was against the idea. Then Guillaume showed King Philip how much land and how many businesses the Templars owned and controlled in France. The crown received no taxes from those lands and businesses since they were technically part of the Church. Then Guillaume showed King Philip how much the Crown owed the Templars for the loans the King had borrowed from them. When the king saw this, he went into a rage, feeling that the Templars controlled far too much of France.

"The King was still worried the Templars were too popular to arrest. Then there was the fact that the members of the Templar Order were technically not his subjects but answerable only to the Pope. The matter got very complicated at this point. There was manipulation of the Holy See and possibly the murder of some high officials within the Church. Eventually, Guillaume and King Philip felt they had everything ready. They planned the raid expertly and captured most of the Templars on that first day. They even used the Templars' belief that the Pope would extricate them from the arrest to get them to surrender peacefully.

"After the arrests, the Crown could not locate any of the treasure they had been certain the Templars had. Yet the lands and businesses the Templars owned, which the Crown took control of, amounted to far more than they had previously thought. Add to that the eradication of the loans the King had borrowed from the Templars, and everything seemed to have worked out.

"The problem that arose was what to do with all the Templars? The Pope was vacillating, and so was the population of France. The other Monarchs did not agree with King Philip until we started getting confessions. Even then, the support was only half-hearted at best. There were trials, but they only made things worse. Eventually, the King decided to wait, hoping that interest in the Templars would eventually fade away.

"The King hoped everyone would just forget and move on with their lives. They slowly released many Templars who confessed to minor crimes from the prisons. Some joined the Hospitallers, and others joined various monasteries as brother monks. Some simply died in the dungeons, but many remain. They are the biggest worry for the King. Those who remain are among the most notable members, including Grand Master Jacques de Molay. The Grand Master was originally convinced to confess to crimes, but he later recanted. Since then, he has held steady to the Templar's innocence. The King could have him killed as a relapsed heretic. But they fear there would always be doubt regarding the Templars' guilt without the Grand Master's confession. So, it was decided to continue to pressure him to confess or to wait for the people of France to forget about the Grand Master.

"So, given all that, why do you think King Philip would desire to have more Templars arrested? It would only stir up public awareness again. No, the King does not want to know about any Templars anywhere."

Thomas had known some of this but not all of it. Father Thomas said, "What about Pope Clement V? Wouldn't the king be interested to know that he is protecting Templars?"

Brother Jaye said, "You are slow to understand. The King would be pleased if the Pope could rescue all the Templars and relocate them from France. As long as the Pope does nothing to take back the Templar properties that the King has seized. King Philip doesn't care that the King and Queen of Portugal actively protect the Templars in their country or that England does nothing to the members of the Order there except slap them on the wrist. He just desires to move on to other matters."

There was silence in the small cottage. The only sound was the cracking and popping from the fireplace. Then Brother Jaye turned to fully face Father Thomas and said, "Before we move on to other matters, there is one more thing you and I need to discuss. After my return from the meeting that you and I had with the Pope, Guillaume de Norgaret tossed me aside for having failed to convince the Pope of the Templars' guilt. After what I just told you, you might wonder, why would Guillaume care that I failed? The winds of politics blow every which way. I failed, and at that time, convincing the Pope was still important. Even now, Guillaume still views me as incompetent. You must remember that although the King did not hate the Templars, Guillaume hates them passionately.

"Due to my failure, I am only allowed to work on matters of low importance for the Inquisition. You, my dear Father Thomas, are a matter of very low importance."

Just then, two members of the Inquisition who had been in another room of the house joined Brother Jaye and Father Thomas. One took Thomas by the arms, seated him on the chair in the middle of the room, and bound his arms behind him. The other carried a small table with torture instruments and placed it beside the chair. Brother Jaye said, "Now, Father Thomas, I understand that you have broken the vows you took when you became a member of the Poor Fellow-Soldiers of Christ and of the Temple of Solomon."

One of the assistants tied a gag around Father Thomas' mouth as Brother Jaye continued, "You will have no need to speak, Father Thomas. This is not about determining your guilt. We are quite aware of that. This is only about me having a little fun before we feed what is left of you to the pigs in the pen outside. Perhaps we will let you watch as they eat the smaller pieces I cut from you."

CHAPTER FORTY-SIX

Louis was helping Dudel's men unload another caravan of goods he had brought up to Muscovy. Dudel was checking every item off as it was taken into his warehouse. As Louis walked past Dudel carrying a large bolt of some heavy material, Dudel said, "Louis, my friend, my men can do this work. You are still recovering from your illness. Please don't overdo it."

Louis said, "Nonsense, I feel fine, and work only strengthens me."

Dudel said, "You are a stubborn man. Have you decided if you will travel to Ankara with me when I return?"

After Louis set the bundle down, he said, "I have decided. Once we are done unloading these supplies, I would like to speak to you about my decision and seek your counsel."

Dudel said, "We are nearly done. I will get Jacob to complete the inventory, and we can talk now in the back office."

The two men settled into a couple of chairs. Louis began, "I have decided that I will recommend to King Robert the Bruce that there should not be another crusade. I have considered everything you told me and what I have witnessed since arriving in Outremer. I see no reason why a crusade is necessary. The Christians I have met don't appear to be suppressed from worship. The Church of the Holy Sepulcher in Jerusalem operates with no interference, and the priests are well cared for and safe. I believe that another crusade will only bring death and destruction.

"But I have decided not to return with you to Ankara. I was ordered to seek out Prester John, so I must continue my search. I personally do not feel I will locate this figure. I believe that this mysterious person was probably one of the Khans, who is long dead. I have been led to understand that some Khans have occasionally embraced Christianity. Even if I were to find a Christian Khan, I doubt he would prove to be a good ally. Considering all this, I still have an obligation to complete my search and report my findings to the King."

Dudel said, "I understand and applaud your commitment to your word, but I have two pieces of advice. First, this land is dangerous, be careful and be certain of who you befriend. Second, do not waste too much of your life on fruitless searching. Find a woman, have children, make a home."

After Louis saw Dudel off the following morning, he walked to the hospital to spend time with Irina and help her with the sick. It appeared that the illness was nearing the end of its cycle as there were fewer patients each day. As he walked toward the hospital, Louis kept thinking about Dudel's admonition that he should start a family. He found himself thinking of Irina and smiling. As Sir Louis stepped around a corner that led to the courtyard that fronted the makeshift hospital, he almost walked into a large man. Louis excused himself and then realized he knew this man; it was Kirill.

Kirill said, "Ah...Sir knight. We supposed you had left the city, not wanting to face our warriors in a tournament."

Uncertain how to take the comment, Louis replied, "I am certain the competition would have been fierce, but that is not why I missed my appointment. I was unable to attend the meeting with Prince Yury to plan the tournament due to illness, which led to a collapse. I only recovered a few days ago."

Kirill asked, "Was it a weak constitution that caused you to succumb to the illness, or was it fear?"

Louis was beginning to think he had somehow offended this man, but could not figure out how. Louis tilted his head slightly at Kirill and said, "I do not know how I have offended you, sir, but I will not simply stand here and be insulted. Let us speak plainly and resolve this issue one way or another."

With obvious anger, Kirill said, "After you left your meeting with Prince Yury, I told the prince that I would challenge and defeat you in single combat during the tourney. The prince said that he would like to see that. We don't have knights here in Rus like you Latins have. Here we have Bogatyrs, skilled warriors who have performed great feats of arms.

"Prince Yury said that if I could defeat you, or better still, kill you, during the tournament, he was sure I would become a Bogatyr to the people. But you never returned, and Prince Yury blamed me for having introduced you to him. He was certain you were making fun of him by saying you would organize a tournament and then ignoring his order that you return the next day. He ordered me to find you and forcibly bring you to him. I searched the city and spoke to several of your little friend's servants; they had no idea what became of you. Prince Yury said that I did not deserve to be the head of his guard if I could not even keep track of one man. He made me a part of the wall guard. So, I had to remain here in Muscovy while the rest of the army went off to seek glory."

Louis said, "I am sorry that I grew ill and destroyed your opportunity to kill me."

Kirill's mouth twisted into an evil grin as he slowly pulled the strangely shaped axe he carried on his back. He then said, "Perhaps I can achieve some acclaim here and now."

Louis was not armed or armored in any way. On the other hand, Kirill had on a quilted gambeson that covered his arms, torso, and legs almost to his knees. Over that, he wore sleeveless chain mail with a wide leather belt around his waist. The axe Kirill carried had a handle about five feet long. The blade was about two feet long and came to a wicked point that extended at least six inches beyond the top of the axe handle.

Louis said, "You have me at somewhat of a disadvantage. I am neither armed nor armored."

Kirill reached his left hand slightly behind him and drew out a dagger with a twelve-inch blade. He tossed the knife at Louis's feet and said, "I hear you Latin knights are the greatest warriors in the world. That should be enough of a weapon for you to use against a simple peasant soldier like me."

Louis looked down at the knife at his feet and said, "Kirill, perhaps we could have a drink and discuss this. I have no desire to fight you. I am here today to see if there is anything I can do to aid the sick in your city. If you are committed to fighting me, we can arrange a trial of arms when I fully recover from my illness."

Kirill laughed, saying, "I will not give you another opportunity to run from me. Pick up that knife and fight me."

Louis noticed that several people had begun to appear and were watching this interaction. Realizing that he had no choice, he reached for the blade. As Louis's hand closed on the handle, Kirill lunged forward, driving the axe's point into Louis's left thigh. The wound was painful and felt deep, and as Kirill withdrew the blade, Louis felt his muscles begin to falter. Kirill raised the axe over his head as he prepared to swing it in a long arch that would strike off Louis' head.

Louis saw all this happen, and his years of training took over. He rolled forward and came up in a crouch to the left of Kirill just as the axe head tore above and past him. Louis drove the blade of the knife up into

Kirill's side, but the tip stopped abruptly as it connected with the chainmail rings. Louis stood as quickly as he could with his injured leg and attempted to get a hand on the axe handle. Louis missed his grab as Kirill instinctively stepped back to keep the distance between himself and Louis.

Louis knew he needed to close the gap between himself and Kirill if he had any chance of surviving this encounter. He had to get inside the range of that long axe where his knife could be effective. Since Kirill's torso was well armored against a blade, he would have to strike at the head or neck.

The two men circled each other slowly. Louis noticed his left leg was bleeding profusely, and he had trouble putting his full weight on it. Suddenly, very quick for such a big man, Kirill lunged forward with the point of the axe aimed at Louis' chest. Louis sidestepped in time and raised his left arm, allowing the axe to pass under his left armpit. He quickly tried to lower his arm and pinch the blade between his arm and body while trying to grasp the haft with his hands. He couldn't grip the wooden handle well because of the knife in his right hand. Kirill also started to step back, using his weight and the large muscles in his arms to free the weapon.

As the blade pinched between Louis' arm and body was pulled free by Kirill, it cut a furrow just above his left elbow. More importantly, as the haft pulled out of Louis' right hand, the knife tumbled out of his grasp. The knife landed with a clatter on the stone floor between Louis and Kirill.

Louis looked down at the knife, trying to judge if he could recover it before Kirill brought the axe down on his back or head. He knew that he should have been able to hold onto the axe handle. Louis was obviously slower and weaker due to his recent illness and his present loss of blood. He was now bleeding heavily from two locations and was unarmed. He had to think of some way to end this fight quickly, or he would have no chance. If the contest continued, Kirill could wait for blood loss to take its toll and then attack when Louis could no longer defend himself effectively.

Louis stepped to the side and almost slipped on his own blood. Kirill moved like a cat about to pounce, waiting for Louis to reach for the knife. Louis quickly devised a plan. He decided to make a faint for the knife. As Kirill lowered the tip of his weapon, Louis would pivot to the side and grab the axe handle with both hands. Sir Louis would then use the momentum of the spin to swing Kirill off balance, thereby taking control of the axe.

Louis stepped to the right and reached his hand toward the knife. While his outstretched right hand was still about a foot from the knife handle, he shifted to his left, starting to spin around. In a flash, Louis wondered how he had supposed this would work. His injured left leg could not support the weight or rotation required to make such a maneuver. He ended up on his knees with his back to Kirill. Before Louis could think of regaining his feet, he felt a sharp pain as the axe blade plunged into his back.

Kirill pulled the axe free and was about to swing it up and over so that the long edge of the blade came down on Louis' shoulder. Before he started the downward stroke, Louis collapsed face down, obviously dead or dying. Kirill stopped the swing and brought the butt end of the haft down onto the stone floor. Without a word, the big Rus soldier picked up the knife he had loaned to Sir Louis, turned, and walked away.

Irina, who had appeared in the crowd just as the killing blow was struck, ran to Louis's side, knelt on the blood-soaked stone, and rolled Louis over on his back. Louis looked up, his brain only half recognizing Irina as she wept. As her warm tears fell on his face, Louis thought, "Why did I think that would work? I should have known better." Sir Louis died, his eyes losing all focus, and he stared up at nothing as Irina continued to cry.

CHAPTER FORTY-SEVEN

Sir William selected the four men who would travel with him to the Mi'kmaq village. The four included Leif, who, even after his long solo trip, was in better shape to travel than many of the others in their party. He also included Sir Justin and two other men who were not injured and seemed to have a better ability for plowing through the snow than the rest. The five men left early the next morning, just before sunrise.

As it turned out, they were closer to the village than any of them had known. It was a bit past midday when they first smelled smoke, and just a couple of hours later, they caught sight of the village. They arrived just before sunset. The men were ushered into the log house, where a central fire was always maintained. They all gathered as close to the fire as possible and were given a hot drink that seemed to taste a bit of ginger and something sweet. Sir William explained what had happened at the camp to Father Lull, Nattesg'g, Derrick, and several of the Mi'kmaq. Once William finished his tale, he had Leif tell the story of his journey.

The next day, Sir William led Nattesg'g, Derrick, and six other Mi'kmaq men to where the other Templars were waiting. They brought four travois to bring back the injured. As it turned out, they only needed two. Two of the injured men had succumbed to their injuries and had been buried with the other dead.

They stayed the night there and left for the Mi'kmaq camp the following morning. They used the other two travois to haul the butchered wolf meat back to the camp. They all noticed that the days had grown less frigid since the night of the wolf attack, and in spots where the sun shone for a while, the snow had begun to melt. As they walked through the beaten-down path of snow, Nattesg'g said to Sir William, "Perhaps the long winter is drawing to a close."

William was too exhausted to feel any hope by the approach of spring. These last few months had been the worst of his life. His command had dwindled from nine ships and a few hundred people to a small band of refugees at the mercy of the Mi'kmaq. It seemed that all the losses had been caused by the weather, either storms at sea or the bitter winter on land. He should have listened to Nattesg'g and built the camp closer inland. Or maybe they should have stayed in Norway. He had thought they were prepared for anything. Yet, in less than six months, his expedition to a new land where he could resurrect the Order of the Knights Templar in freedom and safety from the monarchs of Europe had failed. The remnant of his command would be lucky to survive another winter in this inhospitable place.

He wished he could feel grateful for the apparent safety of his remaining men. Instead, he felt only defeat and failure. He thought back to when Grand Master Jacques de Molay had given him command of the small band of men in Paris to deliver a crate to Rennes-le-Chateau. It seemed like things had continually drifted out of control from that point on. What had happened to his original command? Sergeant Bertrand had died on the road; Sir Henry de Creon and his squire Odo had returned to Paris only to be arrested and disappear. Father Thomas was apparently a traitor to the Order. After being made a knight, his squire abandoned him. Sir Louis de Champagne decided not to remain with the Templars. Instead, he had journeyed to the Holy Land under the orders of the King of Scotland.

Nothing had gone as planned. Sir William's desire to serve God and the Church was in turmoil. The Church had abandoned him. Although the Templars in his group still held to their belief in God, the rituals that had been pillars of strength in their daily lives had slowly faded in importance as their break with the Church grew wider. What were they if they were not part of the one true Church? Could they reconcile with the Church? Was the Holy Father on the Templars' side, or did the Pope now stand against them? He had no answer to any of these questions, and he didn't know how to get them in this faraway land. William felt on the verge of walking off into the winter wilderness and letting the freezing weather take him.

Shortly after getting all the survivors to the Mi'kmaq camp and settling into the long house, Willaim walked off alone to the edge of the camp. Derrick appeared at Sir William's shoulder, saying, "Mary would like to see you. She is in our wigwam with the baby."

Since arriving in the camp, Sir William had not seen Mary or the baby. William silently followed Derrick to the wigwam. Even though the sun was shining and the temperature had noticeably risen, William felt like a dark cloud was hanging over him. As he entered the wigwam, he felt the warmth from the fire and sensed the joy that seemed to fill the tent. He slowly felt something akin to a promise fulfilled well up within him. Something about being there and seeing Mary, Derrick, and the baby triggered a feeling of newness. Mary sat on a fur pallet with another fur over her shoulders, and in her arms, she held their baby boy, who cooed softly.

At the sight of them, Sir William couldn't help but smile as a wave of hope engulfed him. Perhaps he needed to look at everything from a new perspective. He was in a new land, and almost everything from his old life was gone. Maybe he should try to find his own answers and not blindly follow what those he had trusted previously thought had his best interest at heart. Perhaps he could recover by embracing the new and not relying on the old.

Mary said, "Sir William de Sevrey, I would like to introduce you to the newest member of your command. We have not decided on a name yet. Derrick was thinking of Cinead, and I am thinking of either Bertrand or Gregory. What do you think?"

Sir William leaned in to gaze at the baby and said, "I think this child, born in this new land, should not be burdened with the memory of where we came from. I loved those men and wish to honor them, but not by encumbering this child with a name linked to a past. This child should have a new name that speaks of a new dawn, not of days past. I think my war as a Templar is complete. Now we must start a new life here in this new land among our new friends."

CHAPTER FORTY-EIGHT

Cardinal Soprano had known Alfred for many years and had employed his talents on several occasions. The man was very good at gathering information and tailing individuals without them noticing him. Cardinal Soprano knew that, at times, the man seemed less committed to God than he was to his craft, which concerned the Cardinal. The Cardinal had spoken with Alfred about his beliefs and priorities several times. Alfred had assured the Cardinal he devoutly believed in God and the Holy Church. Still, he felt there were times when evil needed to be dealt with directly. Alfred believed the Church needed a man like him, someone who would step outside standard practices to keep the Church safe.

During one conversation, the Cardinal told Alfred, "You cannot use evil means and achieve a holy outcome."

Alfred replied, "I believe what I do is far less contrary to the teachings of Christ than what the Holy Inquisition does or the practice of some monks who travel around selling indulgences."

Cardinal Soprano had received word from Alfred only three times since Father Thomas had left Lucerne. The first message said Father Thomas had strayed from his path to Engelberg, Italy, and was now traveling west. Alfred's note also said that Thomas seemed to have a large sum of money for someone who was supposed to be penniless. Alfred explained that he had to purchase a donkey to continue tailing the priest since Thomas had bought a horse.

The second time the Cardinal received word from Alfred was from Bern. The message said Father Thomas was joining a group of merchants traveling to Troyes. Alfred added that he would try to tag along with the group, posing as a monk. He hoped this would allow him to talk with Thomas and verify exactly what the priest was up to. Alfred felt certain that Thomas was attempting to betray the Templars in Lucerne. Alfred also included in the note that he needed to know how far he should go to stop the priest.

The last message said they were in France. Alfred explained that Father Thomas was attempting to contact Brother Jaye of the Holy Inquisition. Alfred was more emphatic that something needed to be done about the priest soon.

Cardinal Soprano had held out hope that Father Thomas was sincere about having changed, but over the last few months, he saw the dishonesty and fear growing in the man. The Cardinal knew he had taken a risk by letting Thomas go on the pilgrimage, but he believed he had to give him a chance. Now, it was all too clear Thomas planned to betray the Templars again.

Cardinal Soprano would not give Alfred the order to kill Father Thomas. Cardinal Soprano sent word to trusted men in Troyes that Alfred would soon arrive with Father Thomas. He wanted them to make contact with Alfred, and together they should take Father Thomas into custody under Cardinal Soprano's authority. They were then supposed to take Thomas to Avignon and turn him over to the College of Cardinals.

Several weeks later, Cardinal Soprano received word from his men in Troyes. The message stated that before they could act, Father Thomas was taken by some men of the Inquisition under the command of Brother Jaye. They believe that Thomas had been killed. They had uncovered information indicating Brother Jaye and his men had tortured and killed a man who met Father Thomas' description. But they could not verify the story. They did, however, know that Alfred had been killed. Alfred's body had been found strangled in an unsavory part of Troyes just hours after he had entered the city.

Cardinal Soprano was certain that Father Thomas was dead. He knew Brother Jaye was an evil man and that he had hated Father Thomas. The Cardinal was only slightly concerned about what Thomas may have told Brother Jaye. Soprano believed King Philip probably wouldn't care one bit about some Templars in the Swiss Confederacy. Even if he did, the Crown could not afford to send his men here to do anything about it. These Templars would not give up like they had in 1307. Besides, King Philip had bigger issues to deal with.

Cardinal Soprano believed the problem of Father Thomas was resolved, although not in the way he had hoped. He would say a mass for Alfred and beseech God to forgive the man his faults. The Cardinal decided it was time for him to return to Avignon and resume his responsibilities there. Things were well in hand in Lucerne, and his presence was no longer needed.

The Cardinal met with Sir Henry, Sir Gilbert, and Sir Garrard the day after he had received word from his agents in Troyes. After the preliminary updates on the status of things in the compound had been completed, Cardinal Soprano said, "I have received word about Father Thomas that I would like to share. It appears that Sir Henry's concern about the untrustworthiness of the Father was well-founded. The father was trying to contact members of the Inquisition in France. I also believe he intended to seek out Guillaume de Norgaret."

Sir Henry interrupted, "I knew I should have stopped that creature from leaving here."

Cardinal Soprano continued, "Be that as it may, I did have the father watched after he left here. I am certain he has done nothing that will cause us any problems. One of the men he attempted to meet with had an even bigger issue with the priest than you, Sir Henry. This man took Father Thomas captive and dispatched him in a most unsavory manner."

With anger, Sir Henry said, "Good riddance."

Sir Garrard asked, "How can you be certain that Thomas did not reveal our location?"

Cardinal Soprano said, "Oh, he may have, but I don't think anyone will care even if the knowledge were to become public. I am certain we are very safe here, my friends, safe enough that I believe as soon as we complete the church here, I will return to Avignon. I believe you, gentlemen, have things well in hand, and the community of Lucerne is grateful for your presence here."

Sir Henry said, "Your Eminence, we will be sorry to see you go. You have been a great source of guidance to us here. Our financial situation, encompassing businesses, property management, and banking operations, has become self-sufficient. I wonder what the Holy Father wants us to do next?"

Cardinal Soprano said, "Continue as you have. I would not neglect the training of your soldiers. The confederacy here is still young and may need your help. Additionally, the Holy Father may request your aid in the future. There is also talk of another crusade to the Holy Land, although I doubt it will occur. I think I would focus on building a life for yourselves here."

Sir Gilbert asked, "Will you send us any more Templar refugees?"

Cardinal Soprano said, "I cannot say, but I do not think so."

Sir Henry asked, "Your Eminence, what about our Order? The Grand Master is still a prisoner of King Philip. Are we just going to ignore all that has been done to us?"

Cardinal Soprano said, "No, we will not forget this grave injustice. I do not know what will happen to Grand Master Jacques de Molay; I fear he is beyond our reach. King Philip IV is not one to be intimidated, and the Pope has little influence over him, as much as I hate to admit that. I think that, for the time being, you will need to stay out of events in France. The bravery, honor, and devotion of the Knights Templar will not be forgotten. Your Order was started to protect those who could not defend themselves as they traveled to the Holy Land. Maybe it is time to reevaluate your area of protection.

"The world may no longer need monastic, warrior knights to protect pilgrims who travel to Outremer, but there are still people who need to be protected. The world is changing. As a result of the Crusades, we have learned much about science as we have rediscovered many Greek and Roman texts. Maybe you will need to become a new order of knights. I will speak to the Pope about this and send word to you.

"All these new ideas will create change, making people uncomfortable. Many in power will want to handle change by crushing any opposition to what they believe serves them best. You have seen firsthand that a lie can destroy honorable intentions and a noble cause. If you cast enough dirt and bring enough doubt, it doesn't matter what the truth is. Ideas have great power, regardless of whether they are true or false. You Templars are so well known as a group that it was easy for the King of France and his men to convince the populace to believe the lies. The more you denied the accusations, the more the people believed in the falsehoods.

You are not the first group this has happened to. The Cathers and the Jews have both suffered similar attacks. And that is only over the last few years and only in France. Perhaps the world needs an Order of knights who help the unjustly accused who are too weak to protect themselves."

Sir Henry said, "That may all be true, but I don't think we are suited to become such a group. We are an Order of warriors; we train with swords and shield, not with talk and deception in dark corners."

Cardinal Soprano said, "Do you not also loan money, invest in businesses? In the past, your Order operated a worldwide operation. You learned to send information secretly to other members of your Order across many miles. You are educated men who have had to work with many leaders worldwide. In Outremer, you were respected not only for your feats of arms but also for your honor."

Sir Henry said, "Perhaps what you say is true, but none of us here were really involved with any of that side of things. We are simple soldiers."

Cardinal Soprano said, "You are more than that. Look at what you three have built here. Not just the buildings, but the trust of this community. I believe you will still need a military arm to protect yourself and others, as some people only respond to the force of arms. But financial management has great power behind it, maybe more than swords. Controlling purse strings can make you a valued advisor to powerful men. It can provide you with great influence while keeping you out of sight from prying eyes and wagging tongues.

"If you were to have financial operations in many countries worldwide. If your establishments were known to be honest and secure. If your advice was seen as sound. Well, there is no telling what type of influence you might have in many countries."

Sir Gilbert said, "This all sounds deceptive. I know people think that because we have closed meetings and keep secrets, we are a clandestine organization, but we are not. Those methods were developed because we are a military organization and did not want our enemy to know what we were up to."

Cardinal Soprano said, "Yes, but don't forget Templars also used codes to transfer money throughout Europe and the Holy Land. Your Order did this so well that only those in your Order knew where assets were located. Even the King of France has been unable to find any of the treasure and money that your bankers have hidden. I am not saying you become world influencers overnight. I suggest you start here. You slowly expand your influence to aid the Swiss Confederacy. Hopefully, the Papacy will return to Italy and get out from under the French Crown. If that happens, the Holy Father may need the help of a well-trained military order. Suppose that the same military order could also help by providing information from around the world? In that case, I'm sure they would be seen as very useful indeed. What better way to clear the name of the Templars than by becoming the guardians of truth? Perhaps it is time to rebuild the Templars.   Time to examine what you have become and cast off the fetters that hold you down. Rediscover and cling to the strong foundation in the heart of Hugh de Payens when he founded the Order with his eight other brothers and nothing but their honor, courage, and faith."

Sir Henry was silent momentarily, and then he said, "We will think about what you have said. Thank you for your advice, Your Eminence. My brothers and I will consider all your recommendations. If we are to become a new order of knights like you recommend, we will need to discuss such things in private."

Cardinal Soprano smiled and said, "I will take my leave then."

After the Cardinal left, Sir Henry asked his brothers, "What do you think?"

Epilog

Grand Master of the Knights Templar Jacques de Molay was in his sixties when he was arrested on October 13, 1307. He was the twenty-third Grand Master. After being tortured by men trained to cause maximum pain without killing the individual, Jacques did confess to crimes. These crimes were the standard spin of the time that would cause the populace of the Christian world to be shocked and horrified. They included denying Christ, spitting on the cross, idolatry, and homosexual acts.

There were court trials, but King Philip IV of France and his minion Guillaume de Nogaret ensured that convictions were fixed before the hearings began. The first trial started just six days after the arrest. It primarily consisted of 138 prisoners who had been tortured, confessing to various crimes, such as spitting on the cross. In 1308, a second trial was convened. In this trial, 54 Templars admitted to similar crimes before Pope Clement V. When asked if they were tortured, the Templars said they had been tortured and threatened and had a diet restricted to bread and water and other harsh treatments. Still, they claimed their confessions were freely given.

In 1310, three Templars, who had legal training and were still prisoners of the King of France, said they lied when they confessed and now wanted to defend the Order. Before a new trial could start, King Philip had at least 50 Templars burned at the stake. When the proceedings were supposed to begin, the Pope discovered there was no one to testify on the Templars' behalf. The three Templars who had asked to be tried again could not be found. The Pope was told that one had somehow escaped the King's imprisonment, and no one could locate the other two.

On March 22, 1312, Pope Clement V issued Papal bull Vox in Excelso, officially suppressing The Poor Knights of Christ and of the Temple of Solomon (the Knights Templar).

In 1314, after seven years in prison, Grand Master Jacques de Molay and other leaders of the Templars again recanted their confessions. They stated they were only guilty of betraying the Knights Templar by confessing to the original charges. The men were tortured once more in an attempt to induce them to confess again. When they refused, they were convicted of being relapsed heretics and condemned to be burned at the stake.

March 18, 1314, Jacques de Moley and the other "relapsed heretics" were taken to Ile des Juifs, a small island, and burned at the stake. It is said that in the last minutes before he died, Grand Master Jacques de Moley called upon Christ to prove the innocence of the Templars by bringing God's judgment on their prosecutors. Some claimed the Grand Master cried out that King Philip IV and Pope Clement V stand with him before God in one year.

Thirty-three days later, Pope Clement V died of an unspecified disease. Within seven months, King Philip IV of France died of a stroke while out hunting. Over the next few years, King Philip's family line, the Capetian dynasty, which had been on the verge of controlling all the major European countries, disappeared as each monarch died childless. History remembers the Capetian house as "The Accursed Kings."

www.ingramcontent.com/pod-product-compliance
Lightning Source LLC
Chambersburg PA
CBHW051511170626
46811CB00002B/761

* 9 7 8 1 7 3 3 6 9 9 0 2 0 *